CAMOUFLAGE

"An extremely intelligent thriller . . . Haldeman's adept plotting, strong pacing, and sense of grim stoicism have won him wide acclaim . . . His prose is laconic, compact, seemingly offhand but quite precise . . . Like the grammar of cinema, it is a mode that looks natural and even easy but requires exacting skill."   —*The Washington Post*

"Sometimes grim, always interesting, *Camouflage* is written with all of Haldeman's characteristic toughness, care, and clarity."   —*The San Diego Union-Tribune*

"Haldeman trips through history wearing alien goggles but his message is all about human nature."
    —*Entertainment Weekly*

"Haldeman handles this complicated scheme effortlessly, and the ending is satisfying."   —*The New York Times*

"A classic tale of aliens with a smooth, simple brilliance that is a joy to read."   —*The Denver Post*

"Joe Haldeman has quietly become one of the most important science fiction writers of our time . . . Fresh and original . . . [Haldeman] is a skillful storyteller worth your time . . . *Camouflage* is an addictive read, one of the strangest love stories around. If you haven't discovered the appeal of Haldeman's unique brand of science fiction, it's time you did."   —*Rocky Mountain News*

"There's a vapid movie about aliens and predators that, for millennia, have used Earth as a proving ground. Better to use your imagination and read Haldeman's book."
    —*The Kansas City Star*

"Award-winning SF veteran Haldeman proves as engaging a storyteller as ever, especially given this book's irresistible premise and page-turning action."   —*Booklist*

GUARDIAN

Chosen by Locus as one of the year's Recommended Reads

"Eminently likable."   —*The New York Times*

"A series of brilliantly told adventures . . . Frontier Alaska is described with vivid and loving detail. Haldeman is a magnificent writer and the details and characters are superb. Reaching a place where the science fiction experience passes close to mysticism, *Guardian* doesn't try to fit into any of the conventional science fiction pigeonholes."
—*The Denver Post*

"An amazingly fine historical novel . . . Haldeman is a marvelous storyteller."   —*Rocky Mountain News*

"Joe Haldeman is an excellent writer . . . He does wonderful work."   —*The San Diego Union-Tribune*

"An elegant parable of many worlds and multiple possibilities . . . the tale of a courageous woman whose life spans most of a century and whose hopes and dreams cross the barrier between worlds."   —*Library Journal*

"Haldeman is a skilled stylist. He writes thoughtful books, rich with characterization. But who knew he could so completely get into the head of a woman born in 1858? That this master of science fiction, who has made the interior of spaceships and the far reaches of space so believable, could also so readily bring to life the world of the Midwest and Alaska in the latter part of the nineteenth century? Trust me, he does. Haldeman conveys the voice of the character perfectly, so much so that you never really think about who's actually writing the book: a male professor at MIT and Vietnam vet. He also does a wonderful job describing this lost time, from train travel and railroad strikes to steamboats and life in the rough mining towns that provided the launching bases for prospectors on their way to the gold fields. Highly recommended."
—Charles de Lint

Ace Books by Joe Haldeman

FOREVER PEACE
FOREVER FREE
THE COMING
GUARDIAN
CAMOUFLAGE
OLD TWENTIETH
A SEPARATE WAR AND OTHER STORIES

OLD TWENTIETH

JOE HALDEMAN

ACE BOOKS, NEW YORK

THE BERKLEY PUBLISHING GROUP
Published by the Penguin Group
Penguin Group (USA) Inc.
375 Hudson Street, New York, New York 10014, USA
Penguin Group (Canada), 90 Eglinton Avenue East, Suite 700, Toronto, Ontario M4P 2Y3, Canada
(a division of Pearson Penguin Canada Inc.)
Penguin Books Ltd., 80 Strand, London WC2R 0RL, England
Penguin Group Ireland, 25 St. Stephen's Green, Dublin 2, Ireland (a division of Penguin Books Ltd.)
Penguin Group (Australia), 250 Camberwell Road, Camberwell, Victoria 3124, Australia
(a division of Pearson Australia Group Pty. Ltd.)
Penguin Books India Pvt. Ltd., 11 Community Centre, Panchsheel Park, New Delhi—110 017, India
Penguin Group (NZ), Cnr. Airborne and Rosedale Roads, Albany, Auckland 1310, New Zealand
(a division of Pearson New Zealand Ltd.)
Penguin Books (South Africa) (Pty.) Ltd., 24 Sturdee Avenue, Rosebank, Johannesburg 2196, South
Africa

Penguin Books Ltd., Registered Offices: 80 Strand, London WC2R 0RL, England

This is a work of fiction. Names, characters, places, and incidents either are the product of the author's imagination or are used fictitiously, and any resemblance to actual persons, living or dead, business establishments, events, or locales is entirely coincidental. The publisher does not have any control over and does not assume any responsibility for author or third-party websites or their content.

OLD TWENTIETH

An Ace Book / published by arrangement with the author

PRINTING HISTORY
Ace hardcover edition / August 2005
Ace mass-market edition / August 2006

Copyright © 2005 by Joe Haldeman.
Cover art by Fred Gambino.
Cover design by Rita Frangie.
Interior text design by Kristin del Rosario.

ISBN 0-441-01343-0

ACE
Ace Books are published by The Berkley Publishing Group,
a division of Penguin Group (USA) Inc.,
375 Hudson Street, New York, New York 10014.
ACE and the "A" design are trademarks belonging to Penguin Group (USA) Inc.

PRINTED IN THE UNITED STATES OF AMERICA

10   9   8   7   6   5   4   3

For Gay and Rusty and Judith:
Travelers in an antique van

Warm thanks to the Eastern Frontier Foundation, for the quiet and beautiful Norton Island residency, where *Old Twentieth* turned its final corner.

This book was inspired by *The End of the Twentieth Century and the End of the Modern Age* by John Lukacs (Ticknor & Fields, New York, 1993).

CONTENTS

1915

The smell of death is always with you, like a rotten oily stain in the back of your mouth. Rum won't burn it out and a cheap cigar won't cover it. An unwelcome condiment with every mouthful of rations.

It had never been worse than today. Thousands of dead baking and rotting under the Gallipoli sun, and me on the burial detail.

Three days ago, the Turks had gathered what they thought was an overwhelming force and attacked us around three in the morning, quietly, which was unusual—normally they'd be screaming Allah this and Allah that, bugles blaring.

But we had been warned and were ready for them, and it was a pigeon shoot. For most of the Anzac line, they had one to two hundred yards to cover between our trenches and theirs. Very few of them made it even close enough to throw a bomb, although some few did get close enough to find out what an Aussie can do with a bayonet in his hand and nothing at his back but a cliff that falls to the sea.

So No Man's Land became a charnel field in which hundreds of wounded men whispered or groaned or shouted for help, and none came. To give aid would be suicide. Snipers on both sides had clear shots at every square inch of blasted ground, and the best of them could hit any square inch they wanted.

But the Turks as well as we knew that we were separated by a cauldron of pestilence no less than misery. If those corpses were not burned or buried soon, we would all be in danger of infection. So there was a temporary access of common sense, as sometimes can happen in any war, even this absurd one: their generals met ours under a white flag and agreed on a nine-hour truce to bury the dead and retrieve such wounded as had survived. We traded artillery and rifle fire all night, but soon after dawn it sputtered out.

At six-thirty, we chosen few (most of us, including me, chosen because of insubordination) set out to do our grisly duty. It was cold, and the rain poured like a waterfall, but we were glad for both, for temporarily mitigating the smell.

We eyed our opposite numbers, the Turks on burial detail, with suspicion at first, but as time went by we came to regard one another with something approaching camaraderie, just a gang of men forced into nine hours of the most repulsive and distressing sort of hard labor. We used pick mattocks to loosen the rocky soil and dug three long communal graves, one for Anzac and one for the first few thousand Turkish bodies, and one for the rest of the Turks and the large number of both who couldn't be identified.

By ten the rain had stopped and the sun was glaring down. The bodies were in ghastly shape, many of them paralyzed in a posture of running, bayonet-fixed rifles at port arms or thrust out in attack, as if some magic spell had frozen them in midaction. Most of them were in a state of rigor mortis, and it took two or even three of us to drag a body to the lip of the trench and tip it in. It's odd how much heavier dead men are than live; any one of us could have carried any one of them to safety during a fight. It's as if when the vital spark departs, it takes with it some physical lightness, like helium or hydrogen gas, that in life keeps us separate from the ground, the earth, until it's time for us to join it.

I was working the middle trench, arguably the worst, since it was mostly unidentifiable fragments, and you didn't even have the respite of carrying weapons and iden- tification discs back to where the sentries stood guard. The man on the other side whispered, "Tommy! Tommy!" I al- most told him I was no bloody pom, but then was mes- merized by the sight of the pint of whiskey he was holding out. He pointed to the unbroken seal and pantomimed smoking.

There were only three or four fags left in my packet, probably fewer than he would want. Without looking in it, I scaled it to him across the narrow valley of death.

He snatched it handily and peered inside, scowling, but then shrugged and smiled and gently tossed the bottle over.

I cracked the seal and held the bottle up to him in toast. "Here's to your bad aim tomorrow."

He smiled and nodded, I supposed not understanding, and as I took a sip, with an addict's haste he lit one of the cigarettes in a cloud of sulfur. He inhaled deeply, and let the smoke roll seductively out of his nostrils, eyes closed, thoughtful. Then he stared down at our handiwork. "Bloody fucking show," he said slowly, and I wished I knew the same in Turkish. A little hoarse from the whiskey, I whispered, *"Selamunalekum,"* which I was told meant *Peace to you* in Turkish. He bowed slightly, perhaps with irony, fingertips touching, and we both went back about our business.

If you had to fight someone, the Turks were not bad. They were fierce but not cruel, unlike the Germans in whose service they were offering their lives. If it weren't for the bloody Boche we could all throw down our arms and go home.

By three-thirty we had all of the corpses and pieces of corpses in the ground, and dirt and rocks mounded up over them. Presumably they were at peace. I've never made up my mind about that. We stood smoking, and I shared around the last of the bottle with three of my mates.

There was a miscalculation that fortunately did not prove fatal. The Turks' watches were eight minutes faster than ours. Someone who spoke Turkish saw them lining up to leave and got it sorted out.

At a few minutes till four, a single shot rang out. Everyone fell silent as it echoed. We stared at the Turks, and they at us, in a moment of shared terror: tens of thousands of rifles, loaded and cocked, looking down at us from both sides. There could have been a minute of crossfire that added several hundred to the ones we had just planted. But the silence lengthened, and we went back to the business of gathering and leaving.

I clambered back up the slope with a bundle of Enfields tied together with three blood-soaked belts, and was safe in a deep trench when the firing started again. I started toward my post, but realized the armorer was less than a hundred yards down the trench, so I turned and hurried in that direction, to drop off the rifles and get back.

It's true that you don't hear the one that hits you. The closest Turkish artillery battery would often shoot at a very high angle, double or triple charge of powder, in hopes of dropping a round directly into a trench. That evidently happened to me.

I'm suddenly airborne, floating rather than flying, through sudden ringing quiet, and before I hit the ground I have a sense of how badly I've been wounded.

I slam against a parapet and slide to the bottom of the trench. Pain so great it's like numbness, like ice. I roll over to look down the trench and see my leg there, shredded, beside the still-intact bundle of rifles. My other leg is only hanging on by a scrap of flesh, splintered bone sticking out of raw meat. In between, nothing but gore, my manhood carried off in the blast.

My face feels as if someone had hit it hard with a shovel. I reach up with my right hand, missing two fingers and the thumb, and touch soft bloody pulp where my nose used to be. All my front teeth and upper jaw have been blown off. My lower jaw makes a grinding noise when I move it.

In the rush of pain, a silent cymbal crash from head to toe, there is something like peace. This won't last long. It's all up for me. I'll know all the answers soon enough.

Bruce has appeared out of nowhere. He must have been nearby; the round landed just yards from our post. But there's not a mark on him. He's taken his belt and mine and is making two tourniquets.

I try to tell him no, it's a waste of bloody time, just let me be. But I can't make words, just grunting vowels and jaw grind.

"It'll be all right, Jake," he says. "You can't die here."

I demonstrably am, I want to tell him.

A number of people have gathered around. I vaguely

hear the clatter of intense rifle fire. Another shell whines in and impacts not far away. A Sten chatters briefly.

Bruce holds out his hands and someone pours a panniken of water over them, rinsing away my blood. "Something to show you."

He wipes his hands dry on his tunic and pulls out a small packet wrapped in brown paper. He slips off the twine, and I see that it's a stack of tinted postal cards.

What the hell, Bruce? I would say if I could.

"Take heed, now," he says, and displays one after another. The Eiffel Tower. The Taj Mahal. The Washington Monument. Times Square. They start to fade and I turn my head sideways so as not to vomit blood on the pictures.

Bruce crabs around in the dirt and holds my head up so I can focus on the images. They're a blur, now, though— and out of the blur a woman's face appears.

Diane? Why would I think of Diane?

"Look, Jacob," her face says to me. "You have to get hold of yourself. Just look at the goddamned pictures."

My tongue explores the ridge of shattered bone where my teeth used to be. I wish I could tell her to go away.

"You can't die here," Bruce repeats. He holds the pictures out, fanned like a poker hand. "Where would you most like to go?"

Big Ben. It must be cool in London, this time of year.

O N E

WINE AND TIME

My family has a tradition, going back to the nineteenth century, that whenever a child was born (only a male child, originally), the father would buy a case of promising wine of that year's vintage. The first bottle would be opened on the child's birthday, eighteen years later. The other eleven bottles he or she would open to commemorate important occasions, and if any remained when he or she died, it would be passed on to the next generation.

Father's grandfather was the luckiest of our line, born in 1945. His father presciently bought a case of Château Mouton-Rothschild, the "Victory Vintage" celebrating the end of World War II. It was two dollars a bottle, and became the wine of the century.

His luck wouldn't last, though. He went off to war himself, a professional soldier in an unprofessional conflict, and didn't live to see his only son, my grandfather.

Of the ten precious bottles Grandfather inherited, along

with a case of some forgotten 1973 vintage, four were passed on to my father. He left me one of them.

I would carry it to the stars.

My father died in what they now call the Immortality War, or just the War—a worldwide class struggle precipitated by the Becker-Cendrek Process, which at the time seemed to have made obsolete the idea of death by natural causes. A few months after you take the BCP pill, your body becomes a self-repairing machine.

There's a limit to its repairing ability, of course. After my father was captured by the enemy fundies, he was tied to a pole, drenched in gasoline, and set afire, and stopped being immortal a few years after he began. Most of us suffered similar fates if we were caught, and the War became increasingly vicious on both sides.

It ended quietly with Lot 92, a biological agent that was never given, nor ever needed, a dramatic name. It killed 7 billion people in a month, leaving the world safe for 200 million immortals.

Most of the enemy died in their sleep. At the time, I felt that that was too good for them. I resented the backbreaking and disgusting labor of finding their bodies and hauling them out for disposal, at first burying them, then consigning them to huge pyres.

The people who killed my father had sent my mother and me a cube of his death. So it didn't greatly bother me, at sixteen, to warm my hands in the heat of their flames.

That was more than two hundred years ago, and now I feel sadness rather than anger. The first BCP pills were incredibly expensive; my father had sold two of the 1945 Mouton-Rothschild bottles, each worth as much as a millionaire's mansion, to give the three of us the ambiguous gift of provisionally eternal life. Not one person in a thousand could then afford the treatment. War was inevitable, and so was its ferocity, and so, I think, was its outcome.

There have been countless scenarios about how the War could have been averted, most of them involving secrecy. The cost of the BCP decreased by a factor of ten after a year and a half; when the War was no-holds-barred *on*, BCP cost less than a hundredth of its original price. That was still out of reach to anybody not wealthy, but the trend was obvious, and if the world were rational, people would have patiently waited for the price to come down another factor of ten, of a hundred.

But the world was even less rational then than now, and it became common knowledge, among the ignorant, that the pill cost only pennies to manufacture—so the obscenely rich were becoming even richer, withholding life from ordinary people. Populist politicians and fundamentalist religious leaders made that a *cause célèbre*, and they had access to all the tools of the science that were not called "mind control" only because, as advertising, it sold products for industry and policies for government.

The paradox is that if there actually had been a conspiracy among the rich, and they had agreed to keep BCP secret, war might have been averted. Keep the stuff underground until the per-unit cost came down to where most people could afford it. But the price couldn't come down until a lot of people bought it at the obscenely high rate, financing the company's research and development and production facilities. So it was heavily advertised and propagandized, until there wasn't one person on the planet who didn't know that millionaires and movie stars and grafting politicians could all buy a pill that gave them life everlasting.

It was only a small step from there to "they're withholding it from us," and another small step to "let's go get it." Even though when war broke out, there wasn't enough to treat one person in a thousand.

It ended with Lot 92, which sought out everyone who wasn't immortal and stopped their hearts within minutes.

The world of 2047—the year the War started—seems faraway and quaint, now, but it actually was a bewilderingly complex set of interlocking systems, and after the War, 97 percent of the people who had run it were gone. The 3 percent who were left comprised most of the world's leaders, certainly its financial leaders, but it was light on the rank and file who did daily administration and maintenance, and nobody was left alive who did small-engine repair or lawn care or waited on tables. They were the more or less invisible lubricant that had kept daily life running smoothly. Without them, the world ground to a halt.

The extremity of our situation was hidden at first by sheer magnitude—production and supply were largely automated, and the system was set up to serve thirty times as many people as existed. There were food and drink in plenty, and of course shelter was no problem, the planet one large ghost town.

There was no produce, with no truckers and few farmers, but there was a cornucopia of frozen and dehydrated food. Then the power went out, here and there and almost everywhere, and the frozen food spoiled. People who would never call themselves looters ransacked stores and institutions for packaged food to make it through the winter.

There was little violence, most of us sick of it from the War, and a lot of sharing, once it was obvious that there was enough food to go around for several years, if it was distributed rationally. In most regions, co-ops grew together to centralize food supplies, and they formed the nucleus for local governments.

Some areas, where the people had been mostly Christian or Moslem or Hindu fundies, had such a sparse and scattered population that they became deserted, people moving naturally to be with other people. A few large cities, like New York, London, and Tokyo, attracted enough people with technical know-how that they were able to cobble together a simulacrum of what had been normal life—at least to the extent of fairly reliable running water and electricity, and communication lines reopened all around the world.

People knew the clock was ticking. They could only live for a few years as scavengers on the corpse of the old world. They rolled up their sleeves and started to rebuild.

Immortality certainly helped that. They weren't building a new world for their children and some abstract posterity. They were cleaning up the mess so they could live in comfort in the coming centuries and millennia.

I was not much help at first. I was sixteen at the end of the War, with almost no formal education, having been seven when the world fell apart.

My mother and I walked about three hundred miles, to New York, trying to find me a school. We must have been a sight, me pulling a kid's little red wagon full of food and ammunition, my mother carrying a backpack and a shotgun. I had a pistol and a rifle, and was alternately excited and scared at the prospect of using them, but as it turned out, we had no trouble with humans. Several times we had to shoot dogs, who roamed in feral packs, and once a bear, in upstate New York.

That was close. My mother emptied the shotgun at it, seven buckshot shells just pissing it off, before I killed it with a lucky shot through the eye.

Before that, we had sort of enjoyed strolling through the countryside. We decided to move faster.

Central Park was rank and wild. People lived there, but kept their distance. Three uniformed police officers were waiting for us when we emerged onto Eighth Avenue; they nervously told us we had to surrender our weapons, or turn around and go back to where we came from. That raised my mother's libertarian hackles and didn't set well with my teenaged hormones, but you could see the sense of it. New York was an actual city, with nearly a million people. There had to be law and order.

They gave us information in exchange for our guns, and we spent a couple of days standing in lines, becoming citizens of the brave new world. We got a two-bedroom apartment in the Bronx, and my mother, given a choice of several jobs, went into hospital administration—immortals didn't get sick, but they still broke bones and had babies—and I was put in the tenth grade and given an early-morning job as a garbage collector. I sort of wished we'd stayed in Maine.

There weren't many children right after the War. A lot of people had to live with the memory of watching their families die, having bought immortality for themselves first, figuring there was plenty of time for the kids.

The kids got Lot 92 instead.

The population of New York doubled and redoubled over the next few years. It was the only large city in the east that had survived the War largely intact. Boston, Philadelphia, and Washington were burned-out, blasted ruins, so if you wanted big-city life you drifted to New York.

Of course, a lot of the people who came were predators in search of prey. In 2059, the entire City Council was murdered during a meeting, and a group of armed thugs who styled themselves the Mob tried to take over the city. It was like a gruesome comedy; they thought they had control of the police force, but really had only infiltrated the top. The volunteer beat cops spread through the neighborhoods giving back all the weapons they had confiscated. Mother and I got ours, but never had to use them. Mob rule was over in less than a day, the bodies of fifteen ex-mobsters hanging from a makeshift gibbet at the end of Wall Street, and a new volunteer Council was sitting a week later.

We were allowed to decide whether to keep our guns. We kept the shotgun and handed the other two back for the City's use.

All the rest of that summer I would go down with the other kids and monitor the progress of decay on the Wall Street bodies. By fall, there were only partial skeletons with a few sun-bleached rags of clothing. One day they disappeared, replaced by a plaque.

The next year I started college, which was no distinction. For years, every young person would go straight from high school to NYU, to provide something like meaningful employment for the thousands of professors who would otherwise be in the labor pool. I tried civil engineering but wound up fascinated by mathematics, and ten years later had a Ph.D. in Virtuality. Which would lead eventually to my taking the rarest bottle of wine in the world to another world.

Getting there was not straightforward.

T W O

THE BEGINNING OF HISTORY

Various forms of governance and anarchy were tried in the early years, and if you couldn't stand the way things were, you'd always be able to find the odd commune or charismatic leader with a flock. But by the third decade, most of the world had settled into some form of representative democracy, the countries linked to one another through a loose confederation initially called the World Order Institute.

Borders become less significant when individuals can be expected to outlive countries, and very little regional patriotism survived the dislocation of the War. The United States joined with Canada, Mexico, and the Caribbean to become the American Alliance, mainly to maximize their influence with the WOI. There were similar coalitions in Europe, Asia, and Africa; Anzac united most of the Pacific, including the ex-state Hawaii.

Everything was provisional except for freedom of travel

and the Rule of One Billion. Every state that joined the WOI had to agree to population control. Once the population of the world reached one billion, regions had to limit new births to strict replacement of individuals lost to traumatic death or pregnancy.

That would have been more difficult in the old days. But the Becker-Cendrek Process had to be turned off for conception and pregnancy, or the BCP nanozoans would attack the embryo as if it were an incipient cancer, while it was doubling to sixty-four cells. The transition process, to mortality coupled with fertility, was pretty grim, all those nanozoans exiting the body from whatever orifice was closest. So for the privilege of having a child, a woman had to go through a week of that, then gamble with the possibility of dying for most of a year. Most were content to leave reproduction to others, or have their offspring cultivated *ex utero*.

It was 91 (2138 o.s.) before the world's population actually worked its way back to one billion, and by that time almost every child was conceived *ex utero*. In the Alliance, like most of the world, couples who wanted children had to join a lottery and wait their turn.

Visibly pregnant women were so rare they were treated like an endangered species. For some women, and perhaps their unendangered men, that kind of attention made the risk worthwhile. None of the women with whom I've had long relationships has wanted the notoriety and danger, though I've fathered two children the safe way.

World population declined the first couple of decades because of the high suicide rate. Everyone alive had survived the most horrific event of human history, and the prospect of living forever with their memories was insupportable to about one in ten.

I'm not sure whether my own emotional situation was better or worse, for having been a child while it was all going on. Maybe better, because my mother was strong and protective. We also had the benefit of isolation; after my father was killed, we escaped to our cabin in the Maine woods and lived off the land, until Lot 92 made it safe to return to a nearly deserted Portland, to help gather and burn bodies for a week.

Our hermetic existence had made for a quirky education. There were no children's books in the cabin, but we had a wall of leather-bound antiques—twentieth-century science fiction and mystery novels and broken sets of the Harvard Classics and *Encyclopedia Britannica*. By the time I was fifteen, I knew everything in the world if it didn't begin with B or L.

This early immersion in the twentieth century would prove as important as any of my degrees in getting me a berth on the starship. I would be keeper of the time machine, and Old Twentieth was the most popular destination. The reconstructions are more accurate than for earlier periods, but it's more than that.

It was the last century when everyone's life was rounded with a death.

Romantics think that made life more vivid and meaningful, and most of the people eager to take a thousand-year ride into the unknown are romantics, or crazy in some other way.

T H R E E

ASPERA

Spaceflight was well into its second renais-
sance when the War stopped everything. The Chinese had
four people on Mars, overseeing the robotic construction
of a base along the lines of the lunar one. The Sino-
martians died sometime during the War, but the 138 lu-
narians at Water Hole dug in and survived. The base had
been designed on the assumption that they wouldn't be
able to count on support from Earth indefinitely. They
were all wealthy, and had BCP to spare. So they ignored
Earth and just kept digging into the crust, expanding, and
doing science.

The discovery of warm fusion in 22 (the year before I
got my Ph.D.) made space travel within the Solar System
relatively easy, and ultimately would make it fairly inex-
pensive. By 90, the WOI had ten ships buying lunar water
and going out as far as Titan with regularity.

The martian base was revived (the robot factories had

kept producing materials for a couple of years after their human overseers died), and research bases were established on Europa and Titan. The population of Water Hole passed a thousand, most of them immigrants who spent fortunes to live in a hole and listen to their bones weaken.

In retrospect, the element of hysteria is obvious. Almost everyone alive had lived through the holocaust of watching Earth consume itself, and we weren't a generation of optimists. If it happened again, it would be nice to be somewhere else.

The discovery, in 88, that Beta Hydrii was circled by at least one planet that had free oxygen and water fueled a growing desire to send a probe to another star.

After a lot of calculation and argument, Humanitas (the successor to the WOI) decided to mix fast and small with slow and large. The first phase would be a small probe— about the size of a thimble—that would be accelerated up to a large fraction of the speed of light and flash by Beta Hydrii going slightly slower, sending back data for a few minutes as it approached and passed the biosphere, the small shell of space around the star where water could be present as a liquid.

The ship that powered the thimble probe was as big as the old Atlas missiles that first sent men to the Moon— and, launched from orbit, it didn't even have to overcome Earth's gravity. It had seven successively smaller warm-fusion stages, the first six getting the thing up to half the speed of light, and the last one decelerating to $0.05c$, so the probe would have some time to search for planets and measure conditions on them.

And take photographs. Two of them showed a world eerily earthlike, even to the extent of having a relatively large moon. It had seas and clouds and ice caps and land areas both brown and green.

There were no large cities visible; no artificial lights on the dark side. Absorption spectra of the atmosphere showed a reasonable balance of oxygen with nitrogen, argon, and carbon dioxide. There was no measurable methane, which would long have been an indicator of human life on Earth. For millennia before we had radio and electric lights, we raised herds of ruminants placidly producing flatus.

The project caught the world's imagination—five worlds', actually—and the fact that it would cost more than the annual Gross World Product just added to its fascination. It would be an economic stimulant like a war, a hole to throw money into, without putting any lives at risk except for the lunatics who volunteered to be crew.

That was me and about a hundred million others.

What size crew would be practical for a thousand-year voyage? The Chinese on Mars had perished in a paroxysm of murder and suicide, demonstrating that too small a crew was a bad idea. They settled on a small-town model, about a thousand people. It was like the old generation-ship idea, where a thousand mortals would take off on a journey that their n-times-great-grandchildren would finish. But there would be few children on this one.

Redundancy was a driving factor in the design: you would be centuries away from spare parts. So they did the not-so-obvious, and split the one gigantic spaceship into five merely huge ones, which would travel together.

Four of the ships had identical overall design: each would have a crew of two hundred, but with life support adequate for twice that many. So if one broke down, or two, they were theoretically okay.

The fifth was a factory ship, *Manus*, jammed full of raw materials and carrying an orbit-to-surface shuttle. It didn't have active life support in the form of a large, closed ecology, like the other four; just spartan barracks and shop areas that could be warmed up as needed.

Each of the other four was self-sufficient in terms of basic life support, but each had a specialized function or two as well. Number 1 (*Sanitas*) was a hospital, nursery, and school, to take care of injuries and the occasional child. Number 2 (*Mentos*) was dedicated to scientific and other academic pursuits. Number 3 (*Ars*) was fine and applied arts. Number 4 *(Mek)* was engineering and entertainment. There were two ten-passenger shuttles rotating among the ships; people would be free to go from place to place, which ought to alleviate claustrophobia. There was also an emergency shuttle, which served as an ambulance.

Of course, people with a tendency toward claustrophobia wouldn't be asked to join the expedition. Those quick to anger and otherwise antisocial were also discouraged, but people change over time, and *Aspera*, as the five ships collectively would be called, was going to be a social crucible that would be observed with interest from Earth.

Each of the four inhabited ships carried a different biome. *Sanitas* and *Ars* were both subtropical, *Sanitas* resembling a Central American rain forest and *Ars* more Mediterranean. *Mentos* was cool and dry, like Scandinavia in the spring. *Mek* was northern California in the summer, cool to warm.

Their botanical and zoological populations were as diverse as was practical. We didn't bring aboard any king cobras or fire ants; we weren't playing Noah. But diversity means stability, which we figured would be true of the human population as well as the plant and animal ones. If you got tired of living in San Francisco, you could move to Greece or Sweden or Costa Rica.

The details of social and physical design would change over the eighty years it took to put the five small worlds together, but that basic arrangement held. Half the crew were chosen before a single part was orbited; we lived together at Chimbarazo, the research and development institute at the base of the mountain that would be Earth's spaceport. During the last twenty years, we'd spend more and more time at L4, the libration point between the Earth and the Moon, where the ships would be assembled and partially fueled from lunar resources.

Aspera's mission depended on what we would find at Beta Hydrii. We had to be autonomous, to a certain extent, since once we were there, we'd have to live with a forty-four-year lag between question and response between the ships and Earth.

We doubted we'd find advanced forms of life, since there was no sign detectable from Earth, but that might be parochial, anthropocentric. Life on Earth would be easily detected from that distance, but maybe other creatures could be so advanced they wouldn't make as much noise.

Whatever we found, there was the small matter of getting back—or staying, though it seemed wildly improbable that even an earthlike planet would be that hospitable. We could live in orbit around Beta almost indefinitely, recycling and using solar power techniques. That "almost indefinitely" becomes a slow death sentence when you think in terms of millennia. No recycling is 100 percent efficient. All space habitats leak.

We did have a partial solution to that, which seemed eldritch to me: two thousand doses of Nepenthe, which would slow your metabolism down to where you were hardly alive, and so needed little in terms of oxygen and water. There were also two thousand ampoules of its antidote, which so far as I knew didn't have a common name, just some latinate thing. I suppose the person who stayed awake to administer it could have the honor of naming it.

We could refill and go back the same way we had come, if we could find enough water in a convenient form. It would be an immense engineering challenge, and might take centuries if it was doable at all. Of course we knew that the planet had water, and also knew that the system had a giant planet like Jupiter, but the probe hadn't targeted it. It might even have a Europa-style satellite, a water-covered worldlet. What we couldn't tell from far away was whether the system's water had sufficient deuterium and tritium to make warm fusion possible.

A final alternative was rescue, although they might come up with a less dire word for it. Science marches on, and after centuries, Beta Hydrii might be no more challenging a target than the Moon is today. They might catch up with us on the way, or be waiting there when we arrived.

Otherwise, the five ships would orbit indefinitely. One by one, over centuries or millennia, life-support systems would fail and not be repairable. We would become somebody's mysterious artifact, in some unknowable future. Who were they? Where did they come from? Why did they do this?

Perhaps they were all a little crazy.

I had two jobs aboard *Mek*. I was the chief virtuality engineer, in charge of the time machine, which was basically a matter of updating and troubleshooting, and I also worked as a part-time chef at the restaurant during those days it was incarnated as El Bodegon. I'd studied cooking in both Paris and Barcelona. (It was a relief to be asked to do Spanish *cocina* rather than French *cuisine*. Spanish cooking was more amenable to improvisation. We could approximate French, but we couldn't bring along a few bushels of black truffles and four hundred kinds of cheese.)

Mek had the only actual restaurant aboard *Aspera* (as opposed to a mess or cafeteria), and it changed specialties on an irregular schedule. It could seat sixty people, and served two shifts, so anyone who wanted to could "eat out" once a week.

The time machine, full immersion virtual reality, was also a luxury, at least technically. They had been toys for the rich before the War. Afterward, it was as much a therapeutic tool as a form of recreation. Escape to another world, a simpler one, where your actions have no real consequences. After the session, consider what you did and why. It was similar to "talk therapy" in Old Twentieth psychotherapy, before psychopharmacology, and probably was no more useful than that old game in treating a specific, nameable mental illness. But it did make you feel better. More "centered," my mother would say.

Aboard *Aspera*, we suspected that it would have a more complex and important function, as a link to home as well as to the past. It could be addictive, we knew, and would have to be controlled and meticulously scheduled in advance.

People spent about twenty hours in the machine, per visit, but they perceived several days passing. The illusion normally begins aboard some conveyance—buggy, train, car, plane—among familiar companions, "template" characters that the user generates, based on past or present acquaintances. The template characters initially serve the machine, preparing the user for interacting with the time and place chosen. Soon they become part of the living dream that the user concocts on the machine's matrix, and usually disappear.

Most people soon forget that they're users, and live naturally in their illusory surround, which is as authentic as I and my assistants can make it. Some stay in that situation for the whole twenty hours, but most, after a couple of hours, go to someplace else in their chosen year.

The shift is conceptually no different from pushing a button beside the name of a place, but it's presented in a way consistent with the time and place being experienced: an album of photographs, a stack of stereopticon cards, a home video, a slide show. The list is presented, and the user desires to go to one of those places, and the machine resets its initial conditions for that user. (The other three or four people visiting that year may or may not be in the same place.)

I've done it more often than anyone else in the world, I think, and it's still a bit of a jolt—you're in the middle of a peace protest in the 1960s, and during a lunch break, a girl takes out her wallet and starts flipping through pictures, and suddenly you're in a helicopter in Vietnam, along with your template characters. You're confused, as if waking from a vivid dream, but the things they say and do facilitate your immersion in the new place.

Sometimes you meet the other users, especially if you want to. I schedule a year ahead of time, and people can reserve, say, 1945 together. The more you read up on an era, and think about it, the more complete and convincing the trip will be. Friends or lovers will prepare for a year together, and it's not surprising that each will imagine the other as a companion.

The time machine can service five users at once. I schedule four for each twenty-hour period, leaving a space for me or one of my assistants, or sometimes a last-minute switch. One or more of us ought to slip in and monitor the machine for an hour or so of every session, on the lookout for anachronisms or imprecise sensory input. There are no actual tastes or smells in the machine, of course; just electrical signals to the user's brain. A relatively small error can make a small flower's smell overpowering, or turn salt air into a fish-market funk. The users sometimes report anomalies, but more often they forget, only remembering some vague dissatisfaction.

Most of the crew went through the time machine a couple of times before the ships left L4 for the primary fueling at Europa. At the time, I thought that was about as busy as we would ever be, annoying everybody with extensive interviews about their experience inside. If anything had to be changed, it was best done within a stone's throw of Earth.

As it turned out, we came across nothing in orbit that we couldn't have fixed from a light-year out, tweaking databases and making individual adjustments. And although it was plenty of work for the four of us—twelve hours on, eight off, for more than a year—it was far from being our hardest time.

Because no one was hurt by the machine. At that time, everybody survived Old Twentieth.

A MEMORY

We all had one last trip to Earth before "first launch," leaving L4. I met my mother in Washington, and we took her flyer up to Maine.

We found the ruins of the cabin where we'd waited out the end of the world and landed less than a mile away. It was early April, and frost crunched under our feet as we silently walked up the hill to the old place.

There wasn't much left of the log house, old when we'd moved in. A bad snow load had collapsed the roof, and scavengers had long since gone through everything. But we weren't that interested in what we'd left inside.

The tree under which we'd buried the treasure chest was now huge, and besides the shovel I had to scrounge up a hoe and a pick mattock, to get through the roots to the metal box.

Valuable records and mementos; less valuable bricks of gold. The bottle of Mouton-Rothschild was going on 350 years old; it would be either ambrosia or vinegar. I offered *to open it on the spot and share it with her. She said no, with a smile.*

"I'm your mother, Jacob. I know what you have to do." She gave me a fierce hug. "Come back and tell me how good it was."

DEPARTURE TIME

The rest of my leave-taking from Earth was not so emotional. I did have to leave most of my belongings behind, giving them away or loaning them to friends or relatives for a couple of thousand years. There were a few things I would want returned if I came back, like the original Parendisi drawing from my flat in Paris and the small Rodin in the Tennessee cabin.

Otherwise, I gave my children first grabs on anything they wanted from either place. John-Michel took an armload of old books from the thousands that lined the walls in Tennessee. Tess wanted a medieval silver crucifix from the Paris flat, and she took ownership, or stewardship, of both places, though it was understood that she wouldn't have to take extraordinary measures to preserve them.

Both of them second-generation immortals, they had a sort of a "Dad's taking a long trip" attitude about it. They'd never known anyone who had died.

I was pretty certain I wouldn't be coming back. Part of that might be my connection with, obsession with, Old Twentieth, when everybody's life was a rainbow arc of accomplishments and failures, grounded in the peace of darkness at either end. Another part was simply practical. The trip was a quixotic leap into the unknown, with our main hope for return predicated on faith in the advance of science and engineering—the assumption that something as profound as relativity or warm fusion would come along and make interstellar travel an order of magnitude easier. It also presumed that people centuries in the future would care about our fate. I was not sure they'd even remember us.

Most people characterized *Aspera* as an expression of optimism, humans versus the mere universe. Many of us aboard had a darker vision, especially the ones born before BCP. We oldsters made up only 20 percent of the world's population, but comprised almost half of those aboard *Aspera*. Running away from the future, in a sense, with no confidence that there would be anyone left to come home to.

Getting to Europa to fuel up was more complex than the actual interstellar trip would be. We did carom shots around Earth, Venus, the Sun, and then Earth again, getting our speed up. It made for some interesting changes of scenery in the observation deck, which for a thousand years was going to show the same night sky, with one star directly overhead growing imperceptibly brighter year by year.

The three years we spent on that phase—waiting in line at the gas pump, to use a Twentieth expression—gave us our last chance to test all our systems and call back to Earth for replacement parts. Nothing essential broke, to our relief; we could have just taken on our four lakes of water and left for the stars. But every department had its list of things that would make life easier if there was room on the resupply ship Earth was sending to Europa. Anything that showed more wear than expected; anything for which improvements had been discovered while we were doing our dance around the inner Solar System.

Ars needed paint, for instance. An unexpected number of people took up oil painting, and in three years we used up 10 percent of our supplies. A lot of Ivory Black, which we might have predicted. (We didn't order any more canvas. Eventually people would have to decide which paintings they liked least and paint over them. We already had enough to put one bad painting on every wall.)

I tried unsuccessfully to get more guitar strings. As part of my personal ten-kilogram allowance, I'd brought my 1892 Martin guitar and two kilos of classical strings, mostly bass. The ten guitars we carried for general use were all steel-string, though, and we already had a thousand years' worth of replacements, since if they didn't break, you could clean them with ultrasound, let them relax, and reuse them.

The time machine was underused the first year or so. People were busy with extra duties and spent what spare time they had exploring the ships and getting to know the people who would be their friends and lovers—and rivals and enemies—over the oncoming centuries.

The machine staff and I spent a lot of time evaluating the various years, often all but one of us doing the same year at once, to compare notes, one always outside to bring us back in case of trouble. (Not that we really expected trouble. The early virtual experience simulators had sometimes been dangerous, precipitating heart attacks or strokes, but no immortal had ever been harmed by one.)

I modeled three of my template characters after my virtuality assistants: Bruce, who was also my main handball partner; Rebecca, who played flute in our chamber music ensemble; and Lowell, the only academic historian on the team. My other template character, Diane, was a simulation of my mother as a young woman. An unusual choice, but then our relationship was unusual: when I was a boy, seven to sixteen, she was literally the only human being I knew.

Perhaps I didn't want to leave her behind.

We spent a lot of time in that phase working on Wild Year, a deliberately strange Alice-in-Wonderland concoction that sampled various environments at random and generated its own logic without regard to historicity. It would not be for everybody; it was anything but comforting. Bruce and Alice and I loved it, but Lowell wouldn't even try it. It was a kind of apostasy, I suppose, to his worship of the past. He had an incurable case of *jamais vu*, nostalgia for a time you never experienced.

One reason Wild Year was unsettling was that you kept remembering who and where you actually were, sitting in a dark booth with wires and tubes hooked up to you. It was sudden and complete, but momentary—an instant of whole-body déjà vu that was one strangeness among many, while your virtual self shifted times and places and tried to deal with absurd anachronisms. I remember being a Chinese peasant on the Long March, and the man toiling alongside me turned out to be Elvis Presley, who picked up a thing like a balalaika off the muddy trail and began crooning "Love Me Tender." Under his peasant rags he had on a U.S. Army dress uniform. The political officer executed him on the spot, and when I tried to stop it, I was back in the machine for an eyeblink, and then in a poolside cocktail party in Los Angeles, talking to Clark Gable, holding a martini instead of a rifle while the grime and cold of China faded, replaced by California sun.

You often did run into famous actors during Wild Year, possibly because you were somewhat aware of playing a part yourself. In normal years, that's suppressed, although you have a hint of it during transitions.

The day we left Europa, I took a ten-year marriage contract with Kate Larsen, who had done enough time travel to try Wild Year, and although she sort of enjoyed the absurdity of it, she said once was enough. She had a taste for quiet years, and would never have visited 1943 or 1968, for instance, if she had a choice.

I sort of liked them, but then I liked every year for different reasons.

FIVE

MEMORY TRICKS

Kate and I got to know each other at open studio, which met over in *Ars* every Saturday morning. I went to keep up my drawing skills; there's no subject more challenging than the human body. It's also a socially acceptable excuse for staring at women.

We had both worked with paper and ink back on Earth, materials reserved for experts now, and were initially clumsy with the lightbox. We got together once or twice a week to practice, using each other as models, and one thing led to another.

She also lived and worked in *Mek*, a sanitation engineer, so moving in together was simple. I traded my room with the man living next to her, and we opened the door between them. It took two trips with a handcart to move all my things, the ten kilograms from Earth plus the clothing I'd chosen and a few racks of data cubes. We moved on Tuesday, which was linen day in *Mek*, saving a trip.

Kate couldn't be the one to move because she was painting a mural on one wall of her room, with acrylics she'd brought from Earth. It was a beautiful and intricate semi-abstract, faceless human forms—some of which I recognized from the studio, one of them me—tangled together in a sphere, about two-thirds completed. She also had holos of her parents and two matching Chinese scrolls, gold leaf and watercolor.

I had a painting my father had done of the cabin in Maine, and the cover of *Life* magazine for August 27, 1945, celebrating VJ Day, the end of World War II. In an unoccupied corner of the room I leaned my walking stick from childhood, ornate with over two hundred years of increasingly delicate carving. Maybe there would be hiking on the new planet.

There was no one place aboard *Mek* where all two hundred of us could see outside. The sternward dome might hold forty people, packed in like weightless sardines, and a like number could look out of each of the four windows, where the sky rolled by as the ship rotated, once each two minutes.

Kate and I went to the window nearest our place, Ninety, and looked down at the familiar sight. Jupiter rolled by, with its constantly changing crazy-quilt clouds, then the cracked ivory billiard ball of Europa and the welding-arc glare of the tiny Sun. Io was near, a reddish brown fingernail crescent. The other four ships slid by in their fixed positions, *Manus* and *Mentos* a kilometer away, *Sanitas* and *Ars* about twice that, four points on the pentagon we would try to maintain all the way up to a fiftieth the speed of light.

There had been an assembly down at the park, an exchange of speeches between our six leaders and various officials on Earth, the Moon, and Mars, more or less coordinated on the big screen. (The Earth and Moon were on the other side of the Sun, and so had an extra eighteen-minute delay, as well as a slightly degraded picture from solar interference.)

"Well, that wasn't too excruciating," Kate said, as we stared down.

"At least it ended on time." They let us go ten minutes before launch time, so everybody who wanted to could get to a window. The one at Zero, the park where assemblies were held, was too crowded. I checked the watch tattooed on the inside of my wrist. "Two minutes."

"We should feel something."

"Maybe a little bump," I said. "A hundredth of a gee."

She laughed. "God, you're more of an engineer than *I* am. You know, emotion? Feel something?" I hugged her waist and laughed back. "Okay, okay, joke. I'm still getting used to that."

A bright little chain of water ferries went by. "Never saw all eight of those together before. Going to call your folks?"

"Once we're under way. I wrote them when I did the mail this morning."

I'd talked with my mother for a few hours after midnight. Nothing resembling conversation, of course, with the time lag. She was talking from the balcony of their beach place in California. I watched a spectacular sunset while we reminisced and speculated about the future. She pottered around with plants during the long pauses; I worked on an abstract montage that incorporated the sunset colors and garden greens with the icy

black of space. I was getting comfortable with the
lightbox.

She approved of the mission but had no desire to join us.
There was no way she could have brought her life along;
most of the week she was out in the field, working to restore the huge Yosemite Park, which had burned out of
control at the end of the War and grown back rank and
chaotic. Working from old pictures, they were force-
growing large trees to match the original ecosystem and
landscape. Weekends, she was involved in a drama group
working with some incomprehensible twenty-first-century
French plays.

"I don't know," I said. "I guess I feel more impatience
than anything else. Get this show on the road."

"I want to see Jupiter close up," Kate said, "but you
know, that's the big problem. When do we actually
leave?" We'd slowly draw away from Europa's grasp,
then fall in toward Jupiter, for a last gravitational assist
before crawling out to the stars. But it wasn't exactly like
casting off and watching the land behind you sink beneath
the horizon.

"Leaving L4 was the big separation for me." Before that,
you could return to Earth on one of the manned shuttles
(most of them had been robot dumbos), though only four
people took advantage of the possibility during the years of
loading.

"In that sense, I think it was leaving Earth," she said. "I
never saw returning as an option."

"There," someone on the opposite side of the window
said. A pale blue nimbus appeared at the stern of each ship
and snapped into focus as a reverse teardrop of flame. Not
a novelty, of course, since we had seen it every time we
looked outside on the way here from Earth.

But it was different. We held each other a little closer for a couple of minutes, and then, without discussing it, headed back to the apartment.

To some people sex was a futile and time-consuming anachronism, with reproduction completely out of the picture; some even went so far as to be modified so that desire dried up and left their hands free for other things. Kate agreed with me that that was bizarre and unnatural.

(My friend Alex, who's been sexless for fifty years, argues that everything else about us is unnatural, so why not go all the way? But even he needs love, or at least companionship; he's been married twice since he opted out, once to a man who was still sexed. I never asked how they handled that, but they both kept the contract for ten years.)

The second day out, we threw a wedding party. Kate and I each drew two weeks of alcohol allotment—four bottles of wine and one of fuel, lime-flavored—and since I was a cook I was able to concoct a few trays of savories and pastries, and diverted a few bunches of grapes and ten apples from the kitchen.

We held the party in the half-gee meeting room that overlooked the orchard, only a little crowded for the thirty-some who came. There were the traditional ribald jokes and songs, fueled by the extra alcohol some of the guests brought—hoarding nondrinkers found themselves invited to a lot of parties.

Kate's daughter came, of course; they were one of only eleven parent/child combinations aboard *Aspera*. There was almost no family resemblance other than a vague similarity in nose and chin and frame. Kate, like me, had fixed her appearance around "age" forty; her daughter Jenn was a nubile blond bombshell, though well over eighty. "So people can tell us apart," she said. Her mother thought it went a little deeper than that. Jenn had never married, and went through men pretty fast. She *acted* twenty with them, which was probably intriguing at first.

I played a few pieces with the string quartet, but people wanted something more lively; nobody does gavottes anymore. There were enough willing people, twenty-one, to try some matrix dancing. I was content to watch. Kate did it for about ten minutes, but then signaled for a replacement and gratefully broke from the formation, panting, and put her clothes back on.

I loved her mercurial spirit. She didn't dance often, or well, but she threw herself into it when the time was right. A case of opposites attracting, perhaps; nobody would ever call me impulsive.

She had a serious side, too, though, and could focus intently on work or study. I began teaching her guitar back at L4, and she would practice on the steel-string so hard and long that for weeks it drew blood on the fingertips of her left hand. I offered to loan her my Martin, with its easier action, but she said no; the pain wasn't great and it helped her determination.

We slouched arm in arm on the couch for awhile, watching the dancers, and then Bruce and Renée joined us with a dangerous-looking pitcher of fuel that was boiling with white fumes. Edison Doyle, the *Mek* Coordinator, had brought up a block of dry ice, and the pitcher had a small piece foaming at the bottom. Since fuel is about 80 percent alcohol, the dry ice cooled it to below the freezing point of water, and so it went down very easily, your throat anesthetized. One sip was plenty for me.

Bruce and I have been close for almost a century, since

Chimbarazo; my main template character in the time machine is based on him, and his on me. We're both virtuality engineers. We've pulled each other out of trouble in dozens of different places and years.

"You saved my butt last week," I told him, "in 1915. Gallipoli; I was an Aussie infantryman."

"Sounds rough. I've never been there, though Ypres and Paschendale were no picnic. I suppose the desert's worse than the forest?"

"Bad enough. Too much sun to share with thousands of bodies."

"So how'd I save your butt?"

"Oh, I got blown up by a shell. Wounded past caring. You showed up with postcards, and I went on to London. Otherwise, I wouldn't have lasted another minute. Would've been pulled and recalibrated."

"That's always a pain."

"London was exciting. The city itself hadn't been attacked, but it was cranking up to a total-war footing. There was a big thing about women working on the trams."

He nodded. "I did 1916 there once, when the Zeppelins were attacking. It was pretty tense."

"I guess that started about a month after I was there."

"The last day in May 1915." He poured himself another glass of fuming fuel, but I declined.

Kate and Renée stood up with a change in music, a quick dance tune. Kate tugged on my arm. "Would you boys stop talking shop and give us some exercise?"

The festivities went on well past midnight. That room was popular for parties because it wasn't near any residences. Edison Doyle showed that his leadership qualities included an impressive capacity for fuel. I took it pretty easy because I was going to be in the time machine all the next day, tracking down reported anachronisms; Kate had a little more than she was accustomed to. She got home without help, but I spent that honeymoon night learning about the variety and volume of snores a small woman can produce.

1918

I shivered with fever, wrapped up in a scratchy woolen blanket, in a trolley car that rattled and rocked and bounced. It was autumn, wet leaves on untended lawns, everything gray and chill.

"You're awake," Bruce said. He was dressed in a gray suit, yellow spats and gloves, bowler hat. "It's 1918, North Philadelphia."

"Where is everybody?" My voice quavered and my teeth wanted to chatter.

"Indoors, afraid of the flu," Diane said. "Before it runs its course, it will kill three times as many as the war." She was standing in the aisle, holding on to a hanging leather strap. Large shapeless black velvet hat framing her pale features. White frilly blouse and long, pleated khaki skirt. Not long, I realized, compared to 1914. Sensible shoes.

I had a coughing fit, strangling. Bruce handed me a handkerchief, into which I spat a mouthful of blood-streaked foam. "People who contract the rapid strain," he said, "like you, die in two to four days after the first symptoms appear. So we're not spending a lot of time here."

The trolley driver, motorman, turned around in his seat. It was Lowell, with dark skin and slightly Negroid features. "A lot went on this year, Jake, all things considered. Max Planck won the Nobel for quantum theory, though because of the war, they couldn't award it till 1919. The Dada movement started—"

Something clicked. "No, it didn't," I said. "Nineteen-eighteen was the manifesto, Tristan Tzara, but the movement actually started in 1916. Cabaret Voltaire in Zurich." I coughed again, folded over the handkerchief and used it. "What do we tell users in 1916?"

"We're still building the arts module for 1916," Bruce said. "Not many people use that year."

Massey dinged a bell twice, and the streetcar squealed and shuddered its way to a stop. I immediately recognized the three-story Victorian home, tan with new purple and dark red trim, the paint still bright. The home from which I conducted a successful veterinary practice. *Had* conducted. I would probably die here, and soon.

Two women had heard the bell and were hurrying down the walk. My wife Nell and nurse Hortense. Hortense, a large tall Teutonic woman, was wearing a gauze mask. Bruce and Diane helped me up and guided me down the steps into their care.

Something I just said. About art. It was important.

"Nell," I said, "I'm contagious. You stay away."

"But I can't—"

"He's right, Miz Brewer. You let me," Hortense said with her "Dutch" accent. We never referred to Germany.

She put her strong arm around my shoulder and wrapped the blanket tighter. "Let's get you inside."

My three friends watched from the trolley, Bruce looking unconcerned for some reason. I felt light-headed. Where did I know them from?

A Negro butler held the door open. "John," I said, and he nodded, keeping his distance, looking as if he'd seen a ghost. Probably very near the truth. Nell gave him a sharp look, and he flinched.

Straight down the hall and into the parlor, where a bright fire was crackling. Warm with a slight smell of pine smoke laced with carbolic acid.

The fussy prettiness of the room—busy floral wallpaper, Persian rug, frilled lamps—was overcome by the stark sterility of the sickroom conversion. A hospital bed, all starched white and cranks and gleaming metal. Rolling enameled table with a basin and folded white cloths, a stack of disposable paper cloths beside them. Two buckets.

Hortense guided me toward the bed. "Miz Brewer, would you have Johnny bring the water off'n the stove? And a pail of fresh water?"

She seemed uncertain how to respond to orders from a "servant." Hortense normally lived on the clinic side of the house and rarely ventured here. "Of course," she said, and left in a rustle of crinolines.

Hortense eased me into a sitting position and knelt to unlace my boots. "Your *frau* is strong-willed, Jacob. You should speak to her about not wearing a mask."

"I already know the answer. If God wants to take her, a mask will not stop Him." I patted her arm. "It won't stop a filterable virus, either."

"That's but a theory." John came in with a steaming cast-iron kettle and a bucket of water. "Thank you, Johnny. Close the door on your way out."

She watched, and when the door clicked shut she began to undress me, unbuttoning the shirt gently, peeling off the sweat-slick celluloid collar.

The last time she had done this, I wasn't sick.

"*Liebe*," she whispered. "Be strong."

"If only it were a matter of will," I said, and stifled a cough. "You ought to say, 'Be lucky.' "

"I will give you luck. Here." I lifted myself enough so that she could pull off my trousers, and then again, for the long johns. "I'll give you a little bath, and dry you, and leave you to rest."

She half filled the basin with hot water, then added a ladle of water laced with carbolic acid. That's where the smell had come from.

"Can you lie on your stomach?" I did, with her helping by raising up my legs. With a large soft sponge, she stroked me from shoulders on down, then patted me dry with a rough towel. "Over?" With some effort and assistance, I rolled over onto my back.

"You know . . ." she whispered, daubing at my chest.

"*What is this?*" my wife said from the door.

"A bath, ma'am." She looked up evenly. "Why did you think I needed hot water?"

"It's . . . it's unseemly." With her left hand she flapped Hortense away. "Let me finish that."

"I'm a nurse—"

"Yes, and I'm a mother. I've given baths." Not often, I thought. She brought over a steaming mug, and thrust it toward me. "Hot milk and oil of cinnamon. Dr. Wesley recommended it."

The smell, in combination with old sweat and carbolic

acid, was revolting. I choked back a sip and put it on the table. "Put on a mask, Nell, if you're going to—"

"Oh, all right." She produced a triangle of gauze and tied it behind her neck. "I will call if I need you, Hortense."

She left without saying anything, and Nell began scrubbing me as if I were a floor. She handed me the sponge for the delicate bits, which Hortense would not have done, and I saw she was crying.

I had a sudden impulse to confess my infidelities—Hortense was by no means the only one—so that she would not be so sorry to see me go, but resisted it. She probably knew.

"Reverend Byrd is coming by this afternoon," she said in a quavering voice.

"Is there a message he'd like me to take to his Boss?"

"Jacob! Don't blaspheme!" she said with real fear. "And you're going to be all right."

"I know I am," I lied. "This is the low point. I'll be much better tomorrow." I proved that by coughing up a handful of bloody foam, for which I grabbed some of the paper cloths. I dropped the sodden mess on the floor, missing the bucket. "May I dry myself? I'm getting a chill."

She rubbed my chest down roughly with the towel and let me finish, then covered me with a cold, starched sheet and a woolen blanket. "Would you like some music?"

"Oh, I don't think so, no." The parlor had a brand-new Brunswick floor-model phonograph with garish phony Chinese lacquer and a motor almost as loud as the music. "Perhaps I could just rest?"

"Of course," she said with palpable relief, and whispered away, closing the curtains on her way out.

I watched the flickering yellow light from the fire refracting through the chandelier, dancing reds and blues and greens on the stucco ceiling. A leaden kind of peace settled over my body. Was death this simple?

As if in answer, I was seized by a racking coughing fit, and reaching for the papers, I tipped over the mug of spiced milk. It hit the Persian carpet with a thud and didn't break.

There was a silver bell on the table, but I didn't ring for help. Perhaps the milk would leave a stain to remember me by.

I dropped my shoulders back onto the damp sheets, gasping with the slight effort. I remembered a summer vacation in New Mexico, running with my cousin until we fell in the dust, laughing, unable to draw enough air, at nine thousand feet, to continue. This was like that, not enough oxygen. But it was because my lungs were turning to liquid. The air was going in, but there weren't enough viable alveoli to take advantage of it.

In another day or two I would no longer have the strength to clear my lungs. I would drown in the fluid of their dissolution. Unless heart failure spared me that fate.

So I should relish these moments of calm. You only have this experience once. Dying, going back to earth.

I dozed, I don't know for how long. The rattle of the door woke me. My hands and feet were blocks of unresponsive ice. I began to cough and couldn't get my hand up in time to intercept it; I felt the warm foam flowing over my chin. Then Hortense was over me, blocking the gruesome sight, mopping up the mess.

"How are we feeling, Jacob?" It was Reverend Byrd, aptly named, with his squawking voice and egretlike build, long legs and short torso. He had seen the blood before Hortense got in the way; his face was chalk.

"Unwell, Reverend." I raised a palm with some effort. "Don't come any closer without a mask."

He stood awkwardly in the middle distance, both hands clutching a Bible. "Do you want one?" Hortense asked. His head bobbed.

She covered his mouth and nose with the triangle and tied it in back. He looked incongruous, a nervous bandit with a Bible. Nell, standing at the door, put on her mask as well.

The Bible had a half dozen scraps of paper serving as placeholders. He looked down at it and opened it at one, and stepped toward me. "I came to offer you some comfort."

"You could try."

He looked around. "Could we have a few moments alone?" My two women reluctantly left the scene.

He edged closer, but kept the table between us. "Jacob . . . have you accepted Jesus Christ as your personal Lord and Savior?"

I hesitated. "Actually, no. It would be a little late in the game to start lying about that. Wouldn't it?"

He cleared his throat. "This is a difficult time for you."

"No, I mean it literally. How often have you seen me in church? I was never even baptized."

He set the Bible down and reached for a glass of water. "I can do that."

"Don't be ridiculous." I started coughing, but was prepared for it, with paper Hortense had pressed into my hand.

"What harm could it do?"

It took me a few moments to catch my breath. "What good? Is that going to fool God into thinking I'm something I'm not?"

"God gave us these rituals for a reason. We don't have to understand the reason." He paused. "You have to be born before you can die."

"Watch me."

"What?"

"I believe I can die without your help, or God's."

"This is *serious*, Jacob. It's no time for word games."

"It's more serious for me than it is for you," I said quietly. "Though I suppose you'll be needing the practice."

"Well . . ."

"Your loving God wasn't content with the carnage overseas. He had to send this blight around the rest of the world."

"One might be punishment for the other," he said sharply. "Men started that war, not God."

"You can't know that!" He flinched at my vehemence. "Anyhow, if He knows everything that's going to happen, why does He punish us when it happens? You've never heard that one before, I'll wager."

"You're fevered. The disease is affecting your mind."

I coughed into the paper. "Answer that one for me and I'll agree to be baptized."

He picked up the Bible and held it to his chest. "Without free will, moral choice would be meaningless."

"I see. I chose to contract influenza, and now I'm being punished for that choice. Like the boys who choose to cower in the trenches while other boys toss bombs at them."

"I'm not doing you any good, Jacob. I'll come back later, when you're more—"

" 'Ask for me tomorrow, and you shall find me a grave man.' "

"Yes, of course," he said, backing away. "Tomorrow." He eased through the door and clicked it shut loudly behind him.

Where did that "grave man" thing come from, I wondered. It sounded like Shakespeare. I hate Shakespeare.

Hortense came in, looking over her shoulder. "You

naughty thing," she said. "What did you say to scare the Reverend so?"

"Raving, I think. I should be more considerate of him; he's just doing what he's paid to do."

"Maybe you gave him something for his next sermon." She bent to pick up the fallen mug. "Should I refill this, or ask Miz Brewer to?"

"No, don't. The cough is bad enough without it." On cue, I began coughing. This was the most severe yet. Hortense held out a large cloth. The amount of foam and blood was disturbing.

She dropped it in a pail out of sight, and I fell back heavily. Out of the corner of my eye, I saw her take something out of her apron pocket.

"What's that?"

She set a small booklet next to my left hand. "Just something to distract you, when you feel like it. Take you away from here."

"I think I'd rather rest for awhile."

"You do that, Jacob." She turned off the electrical light beside me. "Don't forget it's there, though. You can reach the lamp?"

"Sure." I demonstrated, pulling the chain twice.

She patted my arm. "See you in your dreams."

In fact, I couldn't sleep, though I was glad to be alone. The fire had burned down to embers, and everything was a soft reddish orange twilight. My eyes pursued fantastic shapes through the random patterns of the stucco ceiling, animals turning into human faces, or inhuman, which then became part of maps or buildings.

I hadn't coughed in awhile, I realized, but my breath was alarmingly fast and shallow. Heartbeat loud and insistent in my ears. I almost rang the bell, to bring Nell or Hortense to play the blasted gramophone, just to drown out the sound of my heart.

Instead I turned on the lamp and picked up the booklet that Hortense had left. *Vacationlands*, it said, in slightly fusty Victorian capitals, in an arc over a sun setting into the sea, or rising.

I flipped through it. Oddly, about half the pages were torn out. London was there, but not Paris. Tahiti but not Hawaii. There didn't seem to be any logical pattern.

Spain, now that was interesting. With no warning, I coughed explosively, spattering blood, and there was a sudden spike of pain in my chest. I couldn't breathe. My back arched in reflex, and I couldn't reach the bell, and a dark red cloud enveloped everything. It smelled like hot metal. The pain doubled and redoubled, and the red deepened to black.

I was sitting at a small table in bright sunshine, on a broad pedestrian avenue that was almost deserted. In front of me, a stack of cages filled with bright birds, on top of cages with rabbits. The birds were finches, constantly flurrying and chirping.

Were the rabbits pets or food? Where was I?

Bruce came up from behind me with two small cups of coffee. *"Bienvenido a Barcelona,"* he said, welcome to Barcelona.

"¿Cómo estás?" I said, the words somehow coming out in Spanish. "What's going on? Where is everybody?"

"It's the flu," he said in Spanish, picking up his coffee. "People are avoiding crowds." He gestured down the avenue. "This is the Ramblas, which ought to be bustling this time of day."

"Of course. The Spanish Flu, they called it."

"Which was unfair. It's raging all over Europe. But since

Spain's not in the war, her press isn't controlled, censored by the government. It became the Spanish Flu by default."

We were both dressed in white linen suits, straw hats, a couple of dandies. "I remember . . . I've had the flu, really bad. I think I remember . . ."

"Dying of it, *verdad*. But do you really remember it? Really?"

I thought, and shook my head slowly. "It's like, like a cinematograph. Truly realistic. But like it happened to someone else." Straining to concentrate. "It *is* a machine, like a cinematograph, but much more powerful. The screen is your brain. It runs inside your brain."

"That's right. Most people don't know that. You can forget it now."

"And we're not really in Barcelona. We're *inside* the machine, and it's inside a ship. A ship that's a world!"

"You can forget that now. Drink your coffee."

"It's not really coffee."

"Drink it. And forget."

I sipped the coffee. It was roasted almost to the point of being burnt, very sweet and also bitter, and licorice-flavored. The gall and the licorice were absinthe. "Forget? Forget what?"

"Bebemos para olvidar." We drink to forget.

I looked into the oily surface of the coffee. The birds suddenly quieted. "A lot to forget, this terrible year."

"They say the influenza has peaked. The Germans are on the brink of surrender. A new day is coming."

I held up my cup. *"Al nuevo día."* His cup clinked against mine, and I drank off the rest of the potent brew.

There was a light touch on my shoulder, and Kate leaned down to kiss me, firmly, with her eyes open. *"Mi marido,"* she said. "My husband."

She sat down across from us, still staring. She was wearing a spectacular black-and-red dress, shimmering frill of glass beads.

We were newly wed, but the wedding hadn't been here. Back home. "I'm . . . so glad to see you." Inane thing to say. "I'd forgotten . . ."

"I was in London. It was grim." I nodded, trying to articulate a memory.

"Not grim here," Bruce said. "Shall we go see some Gaudí?"

"Always," I said. "The first thing to do in Barcelona."

"Picnic lunch at Parc Güell," Bruce said. "Then go see whether they've finished Sagrada Familia."

"Fast work if they have." Bruce laughed, but I had an instant flash of false memory. Seeing the cathedral finished, as a small child.

"Jacob?" Kate put a hand on my knee. "Is something wrong?"

I shook my head and laughed. "Absinthe for breakfast. Let's go."

As we strolled up toward the top of the Ramblas, more people began to appear. Perhaps church had just let out. I wasn't sure what day of the week it was.

I put my arm around Kate's waist, and she bumped me with her hip, an affectionate gesture that said "Not here." That's right; we weren't at home. If we were at home, we wouldn't exactly be sightseeing.

Time enough for that, though, later. The Ramblas was beautiful, trees in bloom, songbirds everywhere. We stood and listened to a gypsy couple—performers dressed like gypsies, perhaps—doing rapid-fire flamenco. The guitarist was very accomplished, high position work crisp with blinding speed, and the dancer was appropriately haughty and sensuous, her arms and hands moving in graceful curves while her high heels beat out a complex rhythm on a round board that had once been painted red. Her dress was a tight soft glove from breasts to hips, brocade of crimson and gold, and a swirling tease below. She sang in a tongue that was not Spanish, and sometimes not even language, trills and shouts.

When they finished, Bruce dropped a few coins in the man's hat, and we continued to the top. There was an open carriage waiting, a kind of landau. We got aboard, men first, and I helped Kate with a touch on her bare elbow that was electrical.

The driver seemed vaguely familiar, a dark man with a big friendly face. He smiled broadly when Bruce said we wanted to take the scenic route to Parc Güell. "Every route is scenic in Barcelona." Indeed it was pleasant, though I was distracted by sitting so close to Kate.

At the entrance to the Parc Güell there was a little house that sold souvenirs and food and drinks. Bruce chose a bottle of red wine and got some cheese and cold crisp toast and ripe tomatoes. The vendor opened the bottle and drove the cork back in. I carried the food in a mesh bag; Bruce carried the wine and three tumblers.

Kate saw an orchid, purple and bright red, that she had to have, and the man said just take it, no charge. She slid it into her hair right under her small hat, and it perfectly matched the colors of her dress.

The path up to the picnic area was like walking on some exotic foreign planet, winding uphill through grottos of stone. Gaudí had designed it with natural caves as inspiration, but these were no plain stalactites and -mites. They twisted in tortuous fantastic ways. There were disturbing stone mushrooms and toadstools that looked as poisonous as the real ones.

It was all slightly uphill, and we gained perhaps a hundred meters of altitude when the path opened up into a large flat area, the Gran Plaça Circular, that overlooked Barcelona and the sea. There was a fantastic undulating bench along a low stone barrier on the cliff edge, decorated with mosaics of glistening ceramic chips.

"The longest bench in the world," Bruce said. "One hundred fifty-two meters." He spread a large white silk handkerchief and produced from somewhere a small bottle of olive oil and a paper of salt crystals. "Do your stuff, Maestro."

No parsley or basil, but you could make *pan com tomat* without them if you had to. I opened a sharp clasp knife and cut the tomatoes in half, squeezed the pulp of each half onto pieces of toast, drizzled olive oil, and sprinkled salt. Meanwhile, Bruce uncorked the wine and poured.

Kate and I took glasses. "You didn't give yourself an inch," she said.

"I won't be staying." He gestured with a nod. "Business downtown." We clicked glasses and sipped. He picked up a piece of toast and took a bite. *"Muy sabroso. Buenos días."* He turned and walked back the way we had come, munching on the toast.

"He always knows when to disappear," I said.

"I have friends like that," Kate said. "Being there for you, but knowing when to leave. How long have you known Bruce?"

I thought about that. "Forever."

We finished off the *pan com tomat*, and I carved the cheese into slices. It was a dry tangy manchego, the best I'd had in years.

"You lived here before, you said?"

"Long time ago . . . about a year, off and on, learning to cook in the Spanish style." Funny, I couldn't remember the name of the school, but I could walk straight there. "That was after a year at Cordon Bleu in Paris."

"Which would you rather cook?"

"Oh, Spanish. Everyone's an expert in French. 'That's not the way they do it at Le Canard.' Which is a lie."

She pinched my leg. "You're bad."

It was a postcard day, harmless puffy clouds drifting in a cobalt sky. We had a light pleasant breeze, but down on the water the sailboats were leaning dramatically into the wind.

We finished the food and most of the wine, sitting hip to hip, watching the city and the water.

She cleaned up and put the trash in an ornate wire receptacle. I put the cork in the bottle. "See what's at the top?" We'd only come about halfway up the hill.

It was a pleasant walk along a winding stone path, through dense forest, mixed pine and deciduous. The still air was all pine scent and flowers.

Children were playing on the rocks at the top of the hill, laughing and yelling. "That's not Spanish," I said. "Catalán." *They're still allowed to speak it*, came a thought from nowhere.

We came to a particularly dense part of the grove, and Kate took my hand and pulled. "They can't see us from here," she whispered. I let her lead me down a slight incline, almost slipping on the pine needles. She kissed me with some force and ran her fingers roughly through my hair.

She dragged me down behind a bush. "Kate! Someone will—"

"So what?" she said, and started unbuttoning my shirt. "This is a place to play."

I looked around while she busied herself and decided that it would indeed be hard for anyone to see us. She had

my shirt open and was smothering my chest with kisses
while she fumbled with my belt.

I wasn't sure what to do with her garments, but it turned
out to be simple; she delicately hiked up the skirt and
didn't have anything on underneath. She held on to me like
a kind of saddle horn and managed to mount me, an erotic
but silly sight, completely composed, even to the flower
and small hat, from the waist up. She embraced me and we
thrashed around as quietly as possible. The coupling was
brief but intense for both of us.

Panting, she buttoned me back up. "You see? There's a
time and a place for everything."

We lay for awhile, looking up through the branches at
the calm sky, not needing to talk. Then we brushed each
other off and continued up the path.

There were benches near the top where you could sit and
watch the children play. We laughed along with them, a little hysterical with our shared secret. The adults looked at
us with a mixture of expressions, perplexed or knowing.
We finished the wine by passing the bottle back and forth,
which may have shocked some of them.

"So," she said, "do you enjoy being married?"

"So far so good." I took her hand. "Actually, I can't
imagine living without you."

She paused, looking at me in a curious way. "Neither
can I, without you." She shook her head quickly and stood
up. "Let's go bother the children."

The very top of the hill was a pile of huge black boul-
ders, carefully arranged to look natural but also provide
stable pathways. The children were running around playing what looked like a form of hide-and-go-seek. We opted
for "king of the hill," picking our clumsy adult way up to
the top. The children giggled, and some of the adults

looked away. I suppose Kate was exposing a little too much ankle. They didn't know the half of it.

On the top of the pile, we were on the same level as the treetops of the copse where we had made love. I peered down with a little anxiety, wondering whether we might have provided a little premature sex education for the children, but the foliage was thick enough. In the other direction, the sea glittered, and the Old City looked magical behind a veil of haze.

"This is odd." She knelt and picked up a dusty booklet. "It's in English." She flipped through it and passed it to me.

Vacationlands. Touristy pictures of foreign sights. Some of the pages had been torn out. Maybe a schoolchild used them for some project, then threw it away.

I shook my head. "I could swear I've seen this before."

"Probably something like it." She was looking over my shoulder as I leafed through. "Ooh, Tahiti. Now *that* would be a place for a honeymoon."

"I wonder how the flu is there."

"I bet they don't even have it. It's an island."

I started to frame a logical response to that, but the picture was intriguing.

"Look! The girl isn't wearing anything up top!"

I had noticed. "Well, I suppose if you'd like to—"

The rocks around us lightened to pure white, and so did the sky, and we disappeared into it.

TROUBLE IN THE BIG CITY

Thursday's my service day. There were no emergencies, real or imagined, needing my help, so I went on down to the farms, as usual. I had to take an early shift, 0300 to noon, because I had to be at work for a couple of hours starting 1400.

My farm work is not exactly heavy labor. Because of my part-time job as a cook, I work in the herb gardens, which is not only pleasantly aromatic but also pleasantly distant from the goats and chickens.

It's bright in the farms, which bothers some people. I strip to shorts and soak in the light and heat, moving from tray to tray, breathing in the changing green and spicy smells.

More of my work is harvesting than anything else, which is as much instinct as method. I provide for three mess halls as well as the *Mek* restaurant; they'll get their boxes of refrigerated herbs-of-the-week on the evening shuttle. My notebook has their menus for the coming week, so I estimate how much of what they need for each meal and type it in, usually Wednesday night.

Last night I was up late at work, though, as well as up early. Three of us had done 1918 and were comparing notes, for Bruce to go in today and maybe tomorrow and work on some anachronisms. So I wasn't too scientific this morning. I scanned the menus for oddities and found only two. Otherwise, I eyeballed an average weekly amount of each herb and multiplied by three, putting them in large cold boxes, to be divided later. Some herbs I snipped into labeled envelopes; most of them I sent over still rooted. The kitchens would send back the pots of medium for recycling.

I made separate boxes for our restaurant, which was Arabic this week, and required some oddities like fresh cumin and a bushel of mint. Rashad cress and a kilogram of ginger.

It was pleasant work, as usual, requiring just enough judgment and manual dexterity to keep one's attention. In a way, I was rehearsing for next month's concert at the same time. I had the music program search for various versions of the pieces scheduled for that night's performance and play them at random. There was the inevitable twentieth-century piece, jazz, for which I'd have to use one of the steel-string guitars, amplified. That was going to take as much practice as all the others combined.

Kate and I took advantage of it being Thursday by having a picnic lunch. There are tables set up in various of the farms for that purpose—none by the goats, sensibly, but several in the herb section. I'd made chicken sandwiches and we walked around the various trays, picking a salad. " 'Do not bind the mouths of the kine that tread the grain,' " I quoted, and had to explain it. Cattle and the King James Bible were not everyday topics anymore.

She was glad to get out of her coveralls and soak up some tropical "sun." The noontime light from the four suns along the ship's central axis made it about as bright as dawn or dusk on Earth; plenty of photons for trees and grass and people.

We sat directly under one of the lights and enjoyed the thermos of cold tea she'd brought from work. "You'll have to fend for yourself tonight," she said. "I'm taking the one o'clock over to *Ars* and asked for a bunk."

"What's up?"

"Well, they don't know. A shortage of plasmids. What do you know about plasmid-mediated enzymatic bio-degradation?"

"It's for polymers," I said. "Shredded-up plastic and all."

"That's more than most people know. At the end of the cycle we should have all of our plasmids back. *Ars* is about half a percent down."

"That's serious." Considering we had about a thousand years to go.

"Yeah." She unrolled her sandwich and sprinkled a little salt. "It's only *Ars*; none of the other units has any short-fall. If I don't find anything obvious, and I won't, we'll do a radioisotope trace. The guys at *Sanitas* can send over a gram of iodine-something—"

"Probably 131. Eight-day half-life."

"Thanks, professor. We'll dope some plastic garbage with it and see where it shows up in the waste stream. The plasmids ought to stay in a closed loop. Any iodine shows up downstream, we can walk it back."

"I'd put aside four eggs to make us a soufflé." She didn't care for Arabic food, or maybe Ahmed's cooking.

"Guard them. We'll still be swimming in couscous when

I get back." She rubbed my leg with her toe under the table. "Appreciate it. You're still checking, what, 1916?"

"Nineteen-eighteen. Something peculiar about fine arts and maybe music. Bruce went in this morning to check."

"As an academic?"

"No, we don't have an art one for that era, not yet. Physical science, 'electrical arts,' various literatures. History, as always. So we sent him in as an art dealer."

"Earth in on it?"

"Oh yeah, Vienna. That's where the year was last updated. They'll be running the same template through; we'll compare notes." It wasn't just, or even primarily, their updating the fine arts database for the 'teens. The time machine evolves synergistically; something that had been added to 1968 could resonate a half century earlier.

Earth moved so much faster than we did in that regard, with a million times as many potential customers. We would update as often as possible for as long as possible. Other things had higher priority, of course, and the time machine data streams could suck up all the bandwidth for an hour at a time, just to update one year completely. It didn't happen often.

"Staying with anyone? Over in *Ars*."

"Jacob! I'm still a newlywed." We both laughed. Our contract didn't have anything about that, though some did. "What, you're . . . ?"

"The whole ballet troupe," I said, "boys as well as girls. We'll clean up afterward, though."

"See that you do. The last time, I found a tutu behind the couch."

She walked back to the office with me and we said good-bye. After she left it occurred to me that I might

worry. We treat the shuttle almost as casually as an elevator, or a kind of taxi without windows. Strap yourself in,
wait for the "clunk," unstrap and go through the door. But
it's a tiny spaceship jumping from one accelerating behe-
moth to another. What if it missed? After a minute, less
than a minute, it would simply be gone, as lost as if it had
disappeared. If nobody noticed it hadn't arrived.

No one else was in the office, so I keyed up emergency
procedures for the shuttle. Turns out that all five of *Aspera*'s propulsion systems would shut down instantly, if
the shuttle didn't arrive on time. One of the repair vehicles
would backtrack to it, following a radio beacon that had a
sealed, independently powered transmitter. Ferry it back to
Mek or *Sanitas*, depending on the nature of the problem.

Of course you have to ask "But what if . . . ?" If the
propulsion systems *didn't* shut down, it would be as if the
shuttle were accelerating away from us at a centimeter per
second squared. Not exactly rocketing away; a meter after
the first ten seconds. And someone would notice; someone
would be waiting. Or would they? A hundred seconds, a
hundred meters, and picking up speed. How long would it
take to turn everything around and go after them?

We did have a profile for turnaround, of course, since
we'd be doing it at the Spindown point. But it took almost
thirty minutes, minimum, by which time the shuttle would
be flying away at eighteen meters per second. I closed my
eyes and did the math. Speed up, slow down, match veloc-
ities; call it an hour and a half total. So nothing to worry
about. I resisted asking how much air the shuttle carried.

Then I shook my head. Silly. If there was a failure, they
wouldn't turn the whole damn thing around. They'd just
send the ambulance shuttle from *Sanitas*. It had plenty of
power to tow another shuttle back.

I punched up Bruce's profile; he was due to come out in twenty minutes. Rebecca and Lowell came in. She saw what was on the screen. "We're not late?"

"No, I was just checking. Go back and have a couple more desserts." Her appetite was legendary; she was built like a string bean.

"Don't encourage her," Lowell said. "It's pathetic, the way she stands by the recycler and whines."

She ignored him. "Check Vienna yet?"

"Just got here." I swiveled back to the board and entered two four-finger data chords. A clock counted down from one hour, eighteen minutes.

She checked her watch. "That's almost an hour after he gets out. Leave him wired up? Then go right back in to check?"

"See how he feels. No big rush, if he wants to rest."

Lowell looked at his watch. "Don't have forever. You've got 1929 at 1500."

As if I'd forget. "Yeah, but we can put Vienna's 1918 in the buffer for Bruce."

"We *can*," he said. It would complicate things. The buffer was like a limited one-person time machine. It was sort of like watching an old-time movie, except the people on the screen interact with you. Not realistic, but it was okay for checking data.

The problem was that Bruce would have to unhook from the main machine and then make the transition to the two-dimensional buffer. It would be easier if we could just keep him wired up while he debriefed, then put him back in the main machine, with the new Vienna database patched in. Send him back to wherever he'd found anomalies in the old version.

"Saw Kate, headed for the lift," Rebecca said. "What's up?"

"She's off to *Ars*. They have some plumbing problem. Marry a sanitary engineer and your life gets down to basics."

"Tell me about it." Her Avery was a nuclear engineer, obsessed with his warm-fusion research. "Like a blockage?"

"They wish. It's a recycling anomaly. 'The Case of the Missing Plasmids.' "

"That would be polymers?" Lowell said.

"Enzymatic biodegradation," I said, to beat him to it.

He nodded absently, staring at nothing. "What polymers do they use in *Ars* that the rest of us don't?"

"Well, they have that big sculpture class, 'Modeling the Figure.' That clay stuff has to be a polymer, but not much of it gets into the disposal stream. It doesn't dry. When the class is done, they just strip it off the wire frames and repack it for next time."

"Might have a catalytic function. Wouldn't take much."

"I'll mention it to her."

"You guys done talking dirty? Bruce is almost ready." She'd already put on her green gown. Lowell and I took ours off the hooks and pulled them on. It helps people reorient if you always look the same when they come out.

A blue LED counted down from twenty seconds. The lights dimmed. The time machine door, two meters square, slid open, and Bruce's chair rotated out. He was almost horizontal; he straightened up, blinking, shaking his head the way dogs used to do.

"Was ist los?" he said, and looked down at his nakedness. *"Wo sind meine* . . . where are my . . . clothes . . ." He looked at the three of us in turn. " 'Becca. Lowell. Jacob. Okay. Can I have a glass of water?" Rebecca had it ready.

He drank half of it and sat frowning, remembering. "The big reason we're getting anomalies is that the data from a good-sized collection, the Museum für angewandte Kunst,

Museum of Applied Art, was recorded prewar. The building was destroyed in the war, but most of the paintings and sculpture were saved and wound up in other collections. Austrian art since 1845, biggest collection in the world. So people see all this interesting stuff there, and then see it again, taking up a whole room in the Kunstmuseum.

"Somebody earthside really had their wires crossed. They edited the Kunstmuseum collection back to 1918—but left the old Museum für angewandte Kunst stuff in place. So it winds up in both places.

"That one's easy. I go back in edit mode and close the place down, the Applied Art Museum. Closed for remodeling, *geschossen für Umgestalten*. That's the main one. There are individual anachronisms here and there, but they wouldn't be obvious if you weren't looking for them. It's seeing the whole room that gave users the cognitive dissonance shock."

"You can do that in the buffer?" Lowell said.

"It's just signs. Half an hour."

"Good. We have to install 1929."

"Hope it's the cat's pajamas." He unplugged himself and rolled slowly out of the chair, groaning. "When's my shift?" He accepted a robe from Rebecca.

"Not till 0300," I said. "Live it up."

He studied me. "You look beat, Jake."

"Took service day eight hours early. Just going in for three hours, catch up when I get out."

He got an energy bar from the fridge and poured a glass of orange juice. "Wait . . . '29 so soon? We just did it."

"Yeah," Lowell said, "and two people came out with blinding headaches."

"Both of them just came from New York," I said. "I'm gonna go in and check it out."

"What about the users scheduled for '61?"

"Three of them didn't mind switching to '29," Rebecca said. "We opened a '61 in October for the other two, and found volunteers to replace them here."

He nodded. "I'd rather do '29 any day. Maybe not New York City. Businessmen plummeting to the sidewalk."

"They didn't really do that," she said.

He laughed. "I know; I've been there. Ask people in '32, though. They'll swear they saw it."

"Like everyone in England in 1912 saw the *Titanic* depart. That must have been one crowded dock."

"You were Hitler this time, Jake," Bruce said between bites.

"What?"

"Good old Adolf Schicklgrüber, war veteran and starving artist. My primary guide."

"Where the hell did *that* come from?"

"I don't know. You must have done something really bad."

"Hitler wasn't in Austria in 1918," Lowell said. "He was in Munich, being political. *Deutsche Arbeitpartei*."

"I know, and he didn't call himself Schicklgrüber, either. You look funny with that big moustache."

"You resent my leadership qualities," I said with a German accent. "Your subconscious is rebelling. Would you like me to *fix* it for you?"

"Oh yes, please, whip it into shape. You *are* a better painter, if it's any consolation."

"Yeah, after a couple of centuries' fiddling with it, I ought to be." The clock gave a five-minute *click* warning. "Briefing," I said, and waved good-bye as I stepped into the adjacent room.

Five naked people sitting there. I said hello and undressed while I talked.

They were all pretty experienced users. I told them about the headaches and advised them to steer clear of New York City when the pictures came up. They should remember that subconsciously.

If only one person had come out with a headache, we wouldn't be worried. Two people who'd shared the same data space, though, that was a cause for concern. We talked to the other three who'd gone to 1929 and the only other one who'd been to New York City said she'd felt "achy" and nauseated when she came out.

We treated it seriously because headaches were sometimes the first symptom of an update conflict. It could have been from the 1918 one that had the screwed-up Viennese art museums—it might have had a New York City edit that resonated up to 1929; the years weren't neat little separate packages.

I was going in to troll for trouble. Just walk around on the lookout for anomalies. Sensory paradoxes, cognitive dissonance, things that seemed paradoxical or illogical in a larger context.

We kept all the updates in separate storage, of course; if I did find problems that couldn't be fixed with DO NOT ENTER signs, we could close down both 1929 and New York City temporarily and go find the bug in the update.

I told the five what I was doing while we plugged in. They all already knew that we were going to pull them at the ten-hour mark for a quick checkup.

"Want a volunteer to check the New York scene out with you?" Alyx Kaplan. I glanced at her data.

"You've been to 1929 three times," I said. "New York?"

She nodded, grinning. "Frantic, man. Plus Chicago and New Orleans. The music." She was a great dancer, I knew; all-around athlete.

"If you want to take the chance, sure. Check out the music scene and compare it to what you remember from previous times; could be useful. No refunds if you get a headache, though."

"Start out in Harlem?"

"Sure. I'll be in observer mode, though. You might not want to stay with me." In observer mode you were never unaware of being in virtual reality, and you could come back anytime. I would have a small black box with a red button in my pocket. When I pushed the button I would be brought back.

"We'll see how it works out."

Once you get all the tubes stuck in and the sensory contacts in place, you can go anytime. I was the fastest, no surprise, and hit the START button first.

My eyes started to dim as the chair rolled toward its slot. Everything went black with blue sparkles.

1929

Trickle of music, a band tuning up. Pungent tobacco with a grace note of marijuana. My fingers were doing something unfamiliar. I could start to see.

I was rolling a cigarette, something I was obviously skilled at.

Alyx sat across from me, about twenty-five now and gorgeous in a shimmering bias-cut dark green sheath, neat short hair under a lavender cloche. Her eyes were half-closed and her lips were moving slightly; she was seeing her template characters, being eased into 1929.

Her beautiful eyes opened, the right blue and the left green. She was the most dramatic chimera I'd ever known. "Roll me one, too, baby?"

Every now and then you think about the actual age of people. My twinge of desire for her was dampened by knowing that she was actually older than my mother.

I licked the length of the paper and smoothed it into a

tight cylinder, and handed it to her. "Don't believe in the germ theory?"

"I'll burn 'em off. Thanks." Ronson lighter, diamond cuff links, the same tux as 1918: Bruce. Diane on his arm, also dressed late flapper, red and tight.

"You dig jazz, Bruce?"

"Once in a dirty while." Quietly: "You say 'dig' in 1929?"

"Here you do." We were in the Cotton Club, most of the clientele hip and dressed to the nines. I pinched flakes of golden tobacco onto the creased paper. Part of my brain, a couple of hundred years in the future and a couple of billion miles away, noted that most white people didn't say "dig" until the midthirties.

I lit a wooden match, and the sulfur sting was not unpleasant, along with the harsh rasp of cigarette smoke. My whole body relaxed, still alert.

A waitress in a short tight outfit brought our drinks, martinis. Alyx held hers up. I clicked it and we both drank. The gin was flowery.

"I mean, are we going to see Louis?"

The drink tent on the table said it was August 2. "Not here, sweetheart, not tonight. He's downtown, in *Hot Chocolate.*"

"I thought it was the Great White Way."

"Times change." This month, Armstrong would release a "double whammy" record from that show—"Ain't Misbehavin' " and the mild but groundbreaking protest "[Why Am I So] Black and Blue," which would make the top ten in September. Billie Holiday's brutal "Strange Fruit" was still ten years in the future. Martin Luther King, almost forty years away.

Here in the middle of Harlem, possibly the most prosperous Negro neighborhood in America, there were no black faces on this side of the bandstand, except for staff. I was on the lookout for anachronisms, but that wasn't one.

Alyx crushed out her cigarette and snapped her fingers at a passing cigarette girl. "Luckies." She looked at me apologetically. "Sorry, sweetheart. Too strong for a girl."

"No accounting for tastes," I said, and gave the Negro girl a quarter. "Keep it."

Alyx had the why-can't-I-remember-half-of-this? look. Bruce and Diane sat down quickly. "Thanks for calling," he said. "Who's your new beau?"

I stuck out my hand. "Jake Brewer." We were saved from elaboration with a big chord from the orchestra, and all turned that way. A black man in white tie and tails stood behind the big microphone.

"The Cotton Club is once again proud to be graced by the presence of . . . Duke Ellington and his Jungle Band!" The Duke gave a downbeat on the last word and the band jumped into "Tiger Rag." The crowd applauded and whistled.

We stayed through the midnight show, and when I helped Alyx into the cab, she was totally integrated, if partially inebriated. She gave the cabbie the address of the new Gorham Hotel on Sixth Avenue.

She obviously wanted me to invite myself up, but I produced a wedding ring and regretfully declined. Gave her a kiss on the cheek and handed her to the doorman, and asked the cabbie to take me to Grand Central.

There was a fair crowd milling around at two-thirty, waiting for trains back to Westchester or Long Island. About half of them were subdued and half still partying.

All prop characters; no one but me from the time machine, which was not unusual. You can't tell them apart

when you're a user yourself, but in observer mode they
have an unmistakable aura. I stood under the Clock and
surveyed the place and people for a bit. Nothing seemed
out of line.

I went into a men's room stall and did an observer mind
trick, keeping the location constant but moving the time
forward. When I went back out the place was as crowded
as, well, Grand Central Station. I joined the mob flowing
upstairs and found myself hustling along Forty-second
Street, going to work or shopping along with everybody
else, this warm Saturday morning.

I checked people's clothes for anachronisms, the models
of cars and cabs that crawled down the street, the mer-
chandise in the windows. Nothing obviously out of line. I
walked up to Broadway and then all the way down to the
Village, and then back up Fifth Avenue. I was almost to the
park, imaginary sun beating down, when it finally hit me.

The smell—or, rather, the *absence* of smell.

There was car and truck exhaust to spare, sometimes
choking on crosstown streets, and if you passed a flower
shop or deli, the machine would generate roses or garlic.
But there was nothing underneath it.

A whole data substrate was missing: the constant slight
odor of rotting garbage, a hint of sewage, the ground-in
dusty smell of centuries of dirt. Eau de Gotham.

You probably wouldn't notice it if you weren't trained
for it. I might have missed it (or rather, *not* missed it) if I
hadn't been in observer mode.

That was probably what had caused the headaches—not
causing them, the way eyestrain or an overload of noise
would, but rather indicative of some sensory input problem
that also knocked out the olfactory baseline.

I got a bag of peanuts and sat on a bench in the park, trying for a few minutes not to think, just absorb sensation. One peanut for me, one for the pigeons, one for the squirrel, one for me . . . flavor and texture were right, and the other senses seemed in order. Quiet scraping shuffle of the pigeons' feet, the squirrel scolding, the hardness of the bench under and behind me. Central Park was subdued under the dusty heat, proper for the month and time of day, crowds watching the miniature boats race in the pond.

When the peanuts were gone I walked back downtown. The sidewalks were bustling with Saturday shoppers. The feeling of prosperity wouldn't last much longer; the seeds of Black Tuesday were long sown, and the crash was only a couple of months away.

Other seeds were sown, too. I stopped in front of Scribner's Bookstore and looked at the best-sellers in the window. Churchill's last volume of *The World Crisis: 1918–1928*, with its bitter prophetic ending: "It is in these circumstances that we entered upon that period of Exhaustion that has been described as Peace." Erich Maria Remarque's pacifist classic *All Quiet on the Western Front*. I remembered Bruce kidding me about Hitler before I got in the machine. Did Remarque know that Hitler was one of his fellow soldiers in the front line at Paschendale? Not at the time, almost certainly, but he would know later.

Four years from now, the author of *Mein Kampf*, not in the window, will take power and sentence Remarque to death, a traitor to the German cause. But his trenchmate will be safe over here, still doing the famous-author cocktail-party circuit. Hitler will arrest his sister as a substitute symbol and have her decapitated with an axe.

I drew my face close to the window and could smell the glass warming in the sun, the slight tickle of dust. But nothing underneath. The base level of traffic sound was low, too, but that was just the weekend.

Was the lack of background smell enough to trigger headache? I had never heard of anything like that, and the literature search hadn't made me suspect anything. The two victims' medical records had shown nothing unusual in common; nothing linked to the time machine or any other experiences with virtuality.

In observer mode you can stop time for a minute or two. It's an effort, the mental equivalent of lifting and carrying. I didn't much like the sensation, but it was obviously time to try it. Look for a visual equivalent to the lack of background smell.

I walked down Fifth Avenue toward Forty-second Street, a nice busy corner, full of data, where I'd come up onto street level a couple of hours before. Some people rushing, others strolling; tourists and window-shoppers chatting. Sharp tang of ozone as the trolley crackled and clanged by.

I concentrated my effort. Light and color dimmed slightly, as if the sun had gone behind a cloud. Pedestrians stopped in mid-step; a child who was hopping off the curb was frozen in midair.

Careful not to bump into anyone or anything, which I recalled would accumulate deferred pain that would come back all at once, I crept toward the closest couple, an attractive middle-aged woman in business attire and her companion, a large florid man with a cigar clenched in his scowl. Sweat-stained seersucker suit a size too tight.

There was pain between them. It crackled like static electricity. Where was it coming from?

In this mode I had a pure kind of objectivity—these two people were mathematical constructs that my team or its predecessors had generated to reflect our perceptions of that year, before the crash.

No one on that street was insignificant; everyone was equally real. That was the essence of virtuality. No bit players. Everyone was an element of a fractal that added up to the whole, contained the whole.

I studied the man and allowed time to slowly squeeze through him. With glacial slowness he pulled the cigar from his lips, leaving a shred of tobacco on an incisor, which his tongue moved forward so he could blow it away with a puff that was like a kiss in reverse. He held the cigar out, regarding the ash, and took a slow breath in order to blow on it.

The woman took in all of this with an unconscious familiarity that was part patience and part contempt. She hated his cigars but loved him. In her time and place, she kept both feelings to herself.

As they stepped off the curb to cross the street, she brushed him with her hip, a small physical reminder, and he raised his right hand, the one without the cigar, to touch her shoulder.

He was a gangster. He owned a speakeasy and did loan-sharking and had a part interest in a Harlem whorehouse. That was just "business," though. I'd encountered him in 1929 before, and knew that he didn't really consider himself a criminal. He hadn't had this cloud of pain and sadness before, though.

The life stories of people you meet in the time machine aren't scripted. Initial conditions are set up, and things happen, more or less as in real life. A year like 1929, that gets a lot of traffic, becomes more complex than less popular ones. The characters grow, but they don't grow through time, like actual people. They grow "in place," so to speak, in the process of living through the same day thousands of times.

Maybe the gangster was growing a conscience. Maybe his girlfriend was giving him some well-deserved grief.

Could that be related to the clients' headaches? To the olfactory deficit?

There just might be a connection. The time machine's information storage is dynamic and complex, but not infinite. Maybe as the characters grow more complicated, the machine reallocates memory from the sensory surround to the people. The physical situation is supposed to have first priority—if the world isn't believable, the characters' actions aren't significant—but the machine decides how to partition things.

Have to look into that. Time to leave. I took the box out of my pocket and pushed the red button.

A MEMORY

Night class at NYU every Wednesday after dinner, trying to stay awake for "Philosophies of Social and Religious Morality."

The professor is entertaining enough; it's just the time and the subject matter that make it hard to stay awake this fly-buzzing summer evening.

He uses an old-fashioned blackboard. The dry chalk dust in the air tickles Jacob's nose, and he stays awake by repressing the urge to sneeze.

Dr. Schaumann is one of the few normals left. He hid out during the war in a temple high in Tibet. Lot 92 never got to that altitude.

It had taken him seven years to make his way back to this university, which in 2045 had given him the sabbatical that saved his life. When he returned, he was offered the Becker-Cendrek Process, but declined. It was contrary to

*his worldview as a Buddhist. But he would teach for food
and shelter.*

*He is physically remarkable for a man in his seventies.
He can put one hand on a table and lean forward, his body
weight balanced on his elbow, until he is parallel to the
floor. All the time talking with no strain in his voice.*

*"Birth and death are both illusions," he says, balanced
like a compass needle. "Your essence simply exists. When
conditions are right for birth, you are born, and you go
through life. When conditions are right for you to die, you
do. But it's all illusion. Your essence is unchanged by those
mundane trivialities."*

*At eighteen, Jacob thinks the professor's crazy. A couple
of hundred years later, he would not be so sure.*

SEVEN

MEMENTO MORI

The street dimmed out, and I was lying in the dark on a soft couch, communing with tubes and wires. I slid the catheter out carefully and was stripping off electrodes as the lights came on.

The couch slid out to its prep position, and I sat up, blinking away dizziness. Rebecca handed me a glass of water, and I drank it. "Find anything?"

"Think so. The olfactory substrate isn't coming through at all. If you'd never been to New York, you probably wouldn't notice it. But it doesn't smell that clean even on a Sunday morning after a spring rain. Not in 1929."

She nodded and took the glass away. "I'm going to go observe 1930. If the substrate's gone there . . ."

"Then we're in real trouble," I said. "But nobody's reported headaches from 1930?"

"Nobody's been there in months."

"Okay. We'll compare notes when you come back out."

"Like hell." She handed me my clothes. "You're going to sleep for at least eight hours. You were beat when you went in." She looked at the wall clock. "Meet you after lunch tomorrow—1400 here."

"Yes, doctor." I did feel fatigued, the rush of observer mode washing away. I fumbled zipping up the suit.

"Kate left a message. She'll be in on the next shuttle, but has a face meeting with public health right after. Home before dinner."

"Good." I was famished, as usual after observer mode, but just made myself a cheese sandwich to last me till then. I ate it while I walked home, detouring down through the farms to snag a handful of grapes. At home, I poured a glass of wine, but couldn't stay awake long enough to finish it.

Woke up to the smell of Kate fixing dinner, heating pasta she'd picked up at the mess. "Just as soon not go out to eat," she said. "I've been social all day."

I checked the pot. "What, no couscous?"

"I brought it from the *Ars* mess. They owe us a million calories." It was a good-looking pasta primavera. I'd picked the herbs for it this morning.

"You solve the polymer mystery?"

"Partway. We nailed down the source, but the loss vector isn't obvious. How did 1918 go?"

"Pretty routine, artifacts being in two places at once because of sloppy coordination. Rebecca fixed it in the buffer while I did 1929, New York City." I told her about the clients' headaches and the olfactory deficit while she doled out the pasta and a salad.

Smell is different from the other senses in the way the information is processed. The earliest mammals, the little ratty things that coexisted with the dinosaurs, stayed out of the way by only coming out at night, and so sight was less useful to them than smell. They developed a little gray matter, the neopallium, to deal with the elusive and ambiguous information that smells provide. After about a hundred million years, the neopallium evolved into the human cerebral cortex, without losing its preference for smell. So smells, whether dramatic as garlic or subliminal, like eau de New York City, go straight to the limbic system. Every other kind of sensory input is slowed down and evaluated in the thalamus.

But not everybody smells the same thing in a given situation. The genetic machinery for perceiving smells has evidently worn out as humans evolved, but the loss is not expressed the same way in every individual. There are about a thousand olfactory receptor genes in the human genome, but the nose knows only about four hundred receptor proteins. The other six hundred are "pseudogenes"—they're passed on like genes but are just place markers, having lost their ability to function.

What affects virtuality, normally, is that some of those pseudogenes are throwbacks, and continue to function in some individuals, and so we all have a slightly different setup. If somebody comes out of the time machine with some idiosyncratic complaint, like "the ocean smelled like rotten bananas," the first thing we do is genotype for active pseudogenes.

But it doesn't work the other way. Everybody has the receptor proteins for things like sewage and exhaust, the main components of the New York City substrate. So this is sort of a reversal of the usual problem.

I checked my watch. "They'll be coming out of '29 in about ninety minutes. I ought to be there for the debriefing."

"Knock yourself out. Did they say that in 1929?"

"Not till the fifties. You want to do something tonight?"

"Sit and read. Unless you have something in mind."

"Sounds like the cat's pajamas to me. Or the bee's knees. The clam's garters."

"Nobody ever said that."

"Trust me. The frog's ankles, the elephant's arches."

"Any animal's anything?"

"Within reason."

"Like garters on an invertebrate. Reasonable."

I put on some Sibelius while she served, and we ate on the small balcony overlooking the reservoir, "the lake," and the rice paddies. Six kayakers were engaged in a noisy race.

"That looks like fun," she said. "Wonder how far ahead you have to schedule one."

"Reserve one for me, too. We can go bother the crayfish." They lived in the rice paddies; big ones you could almost catch with your bare hands, though if you caught one you might regret it.

"Yeah, but I need some exercise now. Think I'll go down with you and stop off at the gym."

"As you say, knock yourself out. Think I'll go back to bed after the debriefing."

She gave me a look. "I'll be waiting?"

"Sure." I wasn't much in the mood, but she could still change that, newlyweds that we were.

The phone buzzed, and I picked it up. "Jake." Silence. "Hello?"

It was Rebecca, her voice cracking. "Jake. You have to come down. We pulled 1929."

I looked at my wrist and stood up. "An hour early?"

"Somebody died. A client died." I knocked over a chair, running for the door.

EIGHT

LEAVE THIS TROUBLED WORLD
BEHIND

No one on the whole project had died since
Earth, the explosion at Chimbarazo. No one, doctors included, had seen a dead person who hadn't first been trau-
matically injured in almost two hundred years.

My heart was hammering and I was panting when I
slowed to a walk and stopped at the time machine door. I
hesitated, then touched the panel and stepped through as it
sighed open.

Rebecca and Bruce were standing over the couch where
Alyx lay, still hooked up, naked, dead. Her skin was pale
and waxy, grayish. Lips pale. Her open eyes were dull, dry-
ing, flattening out of round.

The last time I'd seen her, she'd tried to drag me up to her
hotel room, drunk and giggling. That wasn't really her, physically, of course. But I remembered the soft skin of her cheek
when I kissed her good night—the smell of perfume mingled
with tobacco and gin. Her blue and green chimera eyes.

I was almost certainly the last person to kiss her.

"The people from *Sanitas* will be here in a few minutes," Bruce said. "They told us not to move her."

"Yeah." I gingerly picked up her wrist. Her arm was cool and heavy, her fingernails pale. "How long has she been dead?"

"The machine stopped getting feedback about an hour and a half ago. It treated it as a data drop problem and went into an automatic checking algorithm." He touched her arm with a finger, pressing lightly. "Do you . . . did you know her?"

"Only virtually. We went on a date at the Cotton Club last night. You were there." As one of her template characters.

"Did anything seem odd?" Rebecca asked, almost in a whisper.

I thought for a moment. "No . . . she was having a good time. Drank too much. Tried to seduce me."

"God. You might've—"

The door slid open and two men and two women came in with a wheeled gurney. They were wearing green tunics like the ones we put on for clients. They introduced themselves, and we stepped aside for them to examine the body.

One of the men started weeping. He knew her well, he said, but ground the tears away with his fists and turned to the job at hand. One woman stood apart with a small camera while they tentatively moved her limbs around and looked in her mouth, nose, and ears with a light. "Blood in her left ear," the other man said, his voice shaking. Of course he knew her, too, if she lived in *Sanitas*.

The other woman slid a thermometer probe into her, wincing. "Just a degree below normal, one-point-five." She put a hand gently on her abdomen. "Skin somewhat cold."

She looked up at Rebecca. "We have to take the body for

autopsy, probably the sooner the better. One of you should come along to be a witness."

"That would be me," I said, and no one protested. I couldn't take my eyes off her face.

They gingerly removed the electrodes and catheter and clumsily picked her body up by the arms and legs. I could see her back was darkening, as blood pooled there. They put the body on the gurney and covered it with a sheet.

I followed them out into the corridor and called Kate and told her what had happened. "Don't know how long I'll be over there. Probably be at least a day." She suggested I stay with her daughter, and said she'd call and warn her.

That was a good idea. I was starting to feel a little shaky.

"Hard to believe she's gone," the first man said hoarsely. "Best link I had with the old days."

"Before the war," the one named Dolores said. "I wonder if that's a factor."

The corridor was lined with curious people, of course. Word got around fast. It was about two hundred meters to the lift, and we must have passed nearly a hundred people.

Rebecca and Bruce had followed along, and while we were waiting for the lift to the airlock, she squeezed my shoulder and gave me a quiet kiss on the cheek.

It was the passenger lift, and would have been a little crowded with six people even if they were all alive and vertical. We squeezed in around the gurney and held on as the lift whined up toward the ship's axis. I tensed my stomach against the feeling of falling as gravity diminished.

There was a bin of sticky-soled gecko sandals on the lift door. I slipped a large pair over my shoes and floated out when the door opened, pushing down to get my feet on the carpet. They folded up the gurney's temporarily useless wheels and pushed it floating toward the airlock door.

It was a double lock, for safety. The first door opened into a chamber even smaller than the lift, burnished shiny metal. It always smelled of metal and lubricant. I left the sandals at the door and kicked up to the top of the chamber to make room.

It's a good thing the body was strapped down; they had to stand it up for the door to close.

As soon as it closed, the outside door opened to an identical chamber. We repeated the pattern, and the door opened into the cramped ambulance shuttle. One of the men, Windsor, gestured for me to go first.

I grabbed a handhold and headed aft. There was no place to sit except for the pilot's chair, just restraining belts on the padded walls.

"Never been in this before."

"Consider yourself lucky," Dolores said. "Most of the people who ride in it have just had a bad accident." There was a permanent clamp for the gurney; it clicked into place next to an identical empty clamp.

There weren't any windows, just a viewscreen in front of the pilot. Windsor strapped himself in there. "Everybody right?" I murmured yes along with the other three. "Hold on."

The engine was loud, and it accelerated harder and longer than the passenger shuttle. "That's automatic," Windsor said. "No need to hurry this time."

In less than a minute, a pair of blips from the steering jets rotated us, and the acceleration repeated. Windsor held on to a joystick as we approached the airlock, but he didn't have to interfere. There was a last-minute stutter from the jets, and we touched the airlock with a quiet tap.

The airlock clamps shook us with a rapid push-pull, and a chime rang.

"There is no hurry," the door said, "but the regular shuttle will arrive in eighteen minutes. It will take four minutes after you clear for us to be ready for their approach."

"No problem," Windsor said. The door opened. "Jacob?"

"Okay." I unbuckled and gracelessly used the unfamiliar handholds to get into the airlock, which was of course identical to the one on *Mek*.

The first thing you always notice when you visit another ship is the smell. *Sanitas* is a little more warm and humid than *Mek*, and always has a hint of tropical plants in its air. Normally I like it; this time it seemed to have a tinge of decay.

None of the sticky sandals were my size, so I picked my way along the ceiling handholds to the lift, and then flipped so my feet were pointed "down."

Waiting by the lift for them to maneuver the gurney out, I felt sweat prickle on my forehead and back, though I knew *Sanitas* was only a couple of degrees warmer than home.

We took the lift down two levels, to .75g. I asked whether that was for the patients' comfort or the medics' convenience.

"I always assumed it was for the patients," Dolores said. "Since most of them have broken bones or sprains or strains."

"It might just be a case of 'why not?'; available space," Windsor said. "We don't need full gravity, except for the gym, and wouldn't benefit from quarter grav. So they stick us here." The door opened and we stepped out into a white world where the air was cool and dry, with a slight medicine smell.

"There might be an environmental isolation factor, too, but that's an anachronism. It's not as if someone's going to bring a plague aboard."

They pushed the gurney straight across the corridor and through a door marked SURGERY. "In this way," Dolores said, guiding me through swinging doors to the observation gallery.

There were twenty-five or thirty seats overlooking the operating theater, but they were all taken, with about a dozen people sitting or standing in the aisles and behind the front railing. I headed there, but Dolores asked a man in front to give me his seat, saying I was "the time machine guy." There was a little familiar murmur at that; almost all of them had met me as clients.

In all of the virtual times we visited, there were doctor and medic characters, and among them, the surgeons always had the most mystical power. They went inside you; they had life or death *mana* over your hidden essence. They ripped your body open and searched the entrails for signs.

Our surgeon was all glistening metal and cybernetic infallibility. It had human overseers, but that was only custom. The surgeon made decisions, and incisions, faster than any human could follow.

They first fed Alyx's body through a tunnel of sensors, and a large screen showed us what the machines were seeing, a recognizable cross-section view of a human body, from soles to crown. Then two big men in green moved the body to a metal table in front of the surgeon and stood off to the side to watch.

The surgeon's voice was uninflected but not deliberately mechanical, as the door's voice had been. "The apparent cause of death was a massive cerebral hemorrhage, shown in red on the screen." The screen showed a translucent diagram of a brain, with a red splotch the size of a baby's fist, slowly rotating through 360 degrees.

"The autopsy will begin in thirty seconds. Anyone upset by the sight of blood should leave." A man beside me tensed as if to stand, but didn't.

On Earth, by statute, the body of anyone who dies is dissected and completely analyzed, as an ongoing check on the efficiency of the Becker-Cendrek Process. No reason not to extend the policy into outer space.

An arm swung down and drew a white line across the tops of her breasts from shoulder to shoulder; after a moment blood welled out of it. From the middle of the cut (the xyphoid process, my memory said) it slashed down to the top of her pubic triangle.

Metal fingers opened the incision and a saw blade swung down twice to whine through ribs and cartilage; some of the blood spattered up to speckle the glass.

I would have sworn I could smell it through the glass. I've seen enough violent death in virtuality that my senses may be conditioned—and beneath that, perhaps more significant, the centuries-buried memories of the war. The unearthly smell as Mother and I walked into Portland.

A whisper of blades and then mechanical hands pulled free the lungs and heart with a wet sound, esophagus and trachea swinging free. It set the bloody mass on a metal table and two separate hands began sorting through it.

When my father studied for his M.D. degree, each four students shared one cadaver for study. He said the first thing they did was take off the face, so it was less like cutting up a person.

Alyx's beautiful face was as yet untouched, except for a few dots of blood. She had a placid, disinterested expression above the red ruin that gaped below.

The machine separated the large liver and pulled it out, and set it neatly next to the heart and lungs. Then it delicately plucked out the spleen, and then both kidneys together with the adrenals. Then four hands together held up the stomach and intestinal mass; as if in afterthought, a blade reached in and severed it at the end of the colon, and it all went onto a separate table, oozing pretty horribly. Behind me, I heard at least two people leaving in a rush.

Two hands and two blades quickly separated the bladder and internal reproductive organs; they joined the pile on the first table. Then it started to work on the head.

A blade made a deep slash from ear to ear over the top of her head, then with two hands it peeled the scalp down with a ripping sound. Her head thumped back on the table, face hidden by the scarlet flap and matted hair.

One metal hand braced the top of her head while a spinning saw blade whined delicately around the skull twice, tracing out the front quadrant. The hand pried off the wedge of skull and set it next to the head, where it spun once and clattered to the floor.

The machine was still for a few seconds, perhaps studying the brain *in situ*, and then two hands lifted it out, a quivering bloody pink-and-gray mass, and set it on the first table.

The surgeon wheeled itself over to where the specimens lay and began sorting through the mess. One by one, the organs were examined and samples snipped and stored. Then they were unceremoniously plopped back into the cooling body cavity. It took about ten minutes.

"There are no other obvious anomalies," it said. "Nothing that would indicate the subject's age is a factor." Two hands held together the lips of the huge wound while a third stapled it shut. "The brain will be studied in more detail, and then sectioned and preserved."

It lifted the flap of scalp covering the face and held her chin, moving it slightly back and forth. "Time of death was approximately two and a half hours ago?"

I supposed it was asking me. I looked at my wrist. "Yes, approximately." It seemed like minutes.

"Rigor mortis is beginning, consonant with a measured depletion of adenosine triphosphate in the specimens examined. This is evidence of violent exertion just prior to death. Normally the body would not be at this state until four to six hours after death."

One of the men in green spoke up. "Is that variable affected by the Becker-Cendrec Process?"

"No, but it isn't a completely reliable indicator, either, among immortals or in the records we have from earlier times. It is just an observation."

What could she have been struggling over, lying there in the darkness strapped to a couch?

"She didn't have much freedom of motion," I said. "At the time of death she was in total-immersion virtual reality."

"It may have been involuntary contractions in response to the stroke," the machine said. "It also happens in death by electrocution. I would suggest that the equipment be studied with that possibility in mind, although there were no burn marks on the skin. Virtual reality does involve the induction of electrical fields into the brain, but I have no record of anyone ever dying as a result of this."

"Neither have we." Of course not; the surgeon had access to all of our information. "The currents involved are very small."

"Nevertheless, it would be sensible to check the equipment." While it was talking, the machine was slicing away at Alyx's brain.

My phone buzzed, and I went out into the corridor to take it.

It was Kate. "How are you, Jake? That must have been awful."

"I don't know yet." I was still numb. "You watched it?"

"Everyone around here did." It's hard to read a face from the thumbnail picture, but I think she'd been crying, or maybe ill. "Do you think it was . . . could it have been the machine?"

"The surgeon suggested it. But no. How many millions of people have done it without having a stroke?"

"I know the math. But it's still scary."

"Yeah." I needed time to think it through. "Maybe we'll shut down the machine for awhile. Run tests. I haven't talked to anybody." That reminded me. "I don't know whether anyone's sent the word to Earth yet. We ought to report and get an opinion; they have a million time machines running."

A tall man dressed entirely in black came up to me. "Jacob, there's a meeting. Would you please come?"

I nodded at him. "I have a meeting, sweet. Call you when I know what's happening."

"Love you," she said, and clicked off.

I followed the black man to a spiral staircase, and we went down two floors to the one-gee level. I asked him what the meeting was about, which I suppose was an inane question. He answered with a shrug. "Dying in your machine."

The meeting room was a bright atrium full of real tropical flowers. There were four people sitting at a table big enough for eight or ten. One was the medic Desmond and one was Cleo Banister, the coordinator of *Sanitas*. The other two introduced themselves as Kiri and Mark, no title or function. They rarely used last names here.

Banister was a big woman who'd chosen an appearance around fifty, ten years older than mine. Before she even spoke, I'd resolved not to defer to her.

"Alyx was one of ours," she said, "but as far as we can tell, she never told anyone what she would want done with her body. If she died."

"Well, that's not odd," I said. "Have you done that? I haven't."

"I have now," she said, "after watching the . . . operation. I would want to be incinerated."

" 'Cremated,' they say," Mark said.

Banister nodded. "Of course I couldn't assume that Alyx would want the same thing."

Everybody was looking at me. I guess I was the outside authority; each of them knew how the others felt.

"I don't know of any established protocol." Banister shook her head in agreement. "Having the body burned, I don't know. I suppose it would take a lot of energy." An unwanted memory rushed back. "Body's mostly water. When we did it on Earth, after the war, it took a lot of gasoline and wood."

"We should bury her," Kiri said. "Return her to the soil."

"That was something we talked about in *Mek*," I said. "Have you seen the survey results?" They hadn't. "It's funny. A lot of people are phobic about that. Our people, anyhow. Her molecules would move into the food chain. It would be cannibalism. Involuntary and inescapable."

"That's ridiculous," Banister said. "Earth's soil is full of dead people. Nobody cares."

Kiri laughed. "We eat each other's shit, recycled. It's probably full of little bits of our bodies."

"I didn't say it was reasonable. But most of us voted for space."

"Just throw her out the airlock?" Kiri said.

"Throw 'it.' It's not a woman anymore," Mark said.

"That's wasting resources," Banister said. "If you cremated her and recycled the ashes, there would be no loss."

We'd talked about that aspect. "The mass of one human being is insignificant. If you want to return her to the biosphere, fine. But it's a philosophical rather than a practical matter. The body's mostly water and, among the five ships, we leak that much every few days."

Most of them wound up agreeing with the space position, though I became uncomfortable with it myself. It seemed so lonely. Granted there was nothing there that was actually Alyx, just some bones and spoiling meat; it felt inhumane to leave her behind, freezing solid in the interstellar cold.

You could do the equations, of course, and see that she wouldn't be standing still out there. We'd draw away from her, but she'd still be hurtling toward Beta Hydrii a thousand times faster than a rifle bullet. When we eventually flipped around to decelerate, her remains would fly toward us with increasing relative speed, and ultimately barrel past us, long after we'd reached our destination.

Whether or not spacing the body was a good idea, making it a public event definitely was not. Anyone should have been able to predict what would happen, definitely including me.

She had a sister in *Ars* who had elected not to come. It would have been good if her lover Francisco had also stayed away.

They sealed the remains in a white plastic bag and put it in the airlock. The air left in the lock puffed out when they opened the door, sending Alyx gently on her final journey. Two external lights were on, and if the bag had been an inert mass, it would have drifted slowly away as we accelerated.

It was full of room-temperature meat and organs, though. They outgassed, and the bag exploded. Then the naked body, slowly turning, itself swelled up and the staples popped out, leaving a trail of guts that bloated and froze solid in seconds.

Francisco started to wail, and although they sedated him, he was still sobbing uncontrollably when I left twenty minutes later.

It was not a sight that anyone would ever forget. Her tongue pushing out past her perfect teeth. Her beautiful mismatched eyes.

1933

Four years later, New York is a different planet. I'm in observer mode, and glad of it. It's not a year you would like to have been a part of.

We have more than a hundred times as many clients for 1929, for those months when the world was perfect and no one heard the gathering storm. In 1933, most of the world was hitting bottom. Mass starvation in Russia and the Ukraine, Hitler elected Chancellor and given dictatorial powers. Dachau, the first concentration camp, begins its work of extermination while all German books by Jews are thrown into bonfires. Thousands die in a Cuban revolt, a Japanese tsunami, a massacre in Iraq—Kurds killing Christians.

A couple of months ago, before Roosevelt was inaugurated, a lunatic stood up on a rickety chair and fired five shots at him, so close he could have hit him with a rock, but he missed. All five shots hit other people, including

Chicago's mayor Cernak, who eventually died. Some suspected that Cernak was the actual target, and it was a "Mob hit." But the assassin was put to death by electrocution five weeks later (a speed record that held for more than a hundred years) and after that there was nothing but speculation.

Roosevelt turned out to be such a linchpin of the twentieth century, as important in his own way as Hitler or Stalin . . . what would the world have been like if he'd died that day?

In spite of all the violence and poverty and insanity, there was a thread of optimism in America. At least you would finally be able to get a legal drink again, and millions of people would enlist in the NRA and have something like a job. The Chicago World's Fair was a celebration of "a century of progress." Wiley Post flew around the world in a week, and the Boeing 247, the first airliner, began service for those who could afford it. One Armstrong invented FM radio and another made a hit of the sunny "I've Got the World on a String."

I was standing at the just-completed Rockefeller Center, in the middle of a cheering crowd. A parade of a hundred thousand Jews and Jewish sympathizers, led by General John F. O'Ryan, was marching in defiance of Hitler.

They don't even know about Dachau yet. War is more than five years away. But the air is heavy with hate.

But no background smell. Whatever was wrong in 1929 was still wrong here.

There was no actual need to stay longer, since I'd found out what I needed to know, but I thought I'd walk around and look for other anomalies. It was a nice spring day, anyhow.

I walked up Forty-fifth Street toward Eighth Avenue,

the theater district. A lot of the small buildings would still be there, in the shadows of skyscrapers and slabs, when Mother and I would walk into town 125 years later.

The Empire State Building is finished; King Kong will climb it this year. The Chrysler and Woolworth Buildings. The architecture is charming, these few decades between skyscrapers and the geometrical blandness of Modernism and International Style.

There was an unmarked door at 269 West Forty-fifth. I knocked on it and a peephole opened. I said "Frankie," and a deep male voice answered "Johnnie," and the door swung open.

The place would still be in business in year 10, 2066 old style, though it will have been a legal steak house for most of that time. In 1933, until December, it was just one of New York's thirty-two thousand speakeasies. On December 5 the Noble Experiment would come to a close, having turned a nation of legal beer and wine drinkers into scofflaw hard-liquor boozers.

I followed the bouncer up a narrow winding staircase, with the black-and-white tiles that would still be there in my future, up to the bar, which smelled like new wood under the predominant smell of tobacco, spilled beer, and whiskey. There were a couple of dozen people chatting and drinking at small tables. I ordered a boilermaker—a beer and a shot of whiskey—and got a pack of "desert horses," Camels, from the cigarette girl. There was a radio playing tinny jazz. The combination of not-too-cool beer and cheap bourbon was pretty awful, which I didn't take to be an anomaly.

A young woman dropped herself on the other chair at

my table, looking around and then at me: "Bum a snipe, sport?"

I passed her the Camels and a small box of matches. She lit up, took a deep drag, and slumped back. "So. Jacob. Find anything?"

"Diane?"

"Bruce, actually." In observer mode you could look like anybody. "I see what you mean about the olfactory deficit," he said softly. "Anything else?"

"Nothing yet. I thought you were doing 1948."

"There and back, yeah. I just stayed hooked up and re-calibrated." He put his hands under his large breasts and looked down at them. "Wow. I wanted to come tell you before you outprocessed. The smell's back in 1948. Diane backed me up on it. But it's sure not here now."

"So what do you think?"

"I don't know. I guess for data's sake, you might want to go lateral." He pulled a set of postcards out of his purse. "Try Philadelphia, Bombay? I'll go with you, sniff around."

I riffled through the cards. "Miami?"

"You"—sudden bright sunshine—"got it."

We were on a crowded beach. Bruce was still a well-endowed woman, clamped in an unrevealing electric blue one-piece swimsuit. We were a generation away from bikinis. I had on long shorts and a T-shirt and a broad-billed hat.

I took a deep breath. "Maybe not the best choice. Nothing subtle here." The rotting-iodine smell of seaweed with an undertone of fish; coconut oil on sweating bodies. I steered us away from the sea, up toward the pastel Art Deco of this part of downtown.

"It ain't New York," I said.

Bruce stretched so hard his cartilage popped. "Like I'm complaining." The sky was a flat wash of cobalt blue; a biplane buzzed through it.

A couple of older women, passing, looked pointedly away. Bruce was underdressed for the street.

"They still have biplanes now," I said.

"See them over the beach till the end of the century," Bruce said. "They can cruise dead slow, towing a banner." He took a deep breath, impressive chest swelling. "I think it's here."

We weren't quite off the beach yet, on the sidewalk, but the smell was there, the city smell, not half as strong as New York, but the same components: sewage, garbage, petroleum products and their exhaust. "Yeah, I get it, too."

Bruce was still holding the postcards and flashed one. "Philadelphia?"

"Why not?" Suddenly it was gray and cool. I had on a trim seersucker suit and a straw boater, and Bruce, male again, wore classic dark blue flannel, double-breasted, with a tasteless orange tie. We were standing in front of the Liberty Bell.

One breath: "It's here, too." Bruce nodded.

A phone rang a few yards away, in a wooden booth. The door worked smoothly with a pleasant creak. It smelled of pine and shellac. "Hello?"

"Jacob, it's 'Becca. We have to pull you guys back for a meeting."

"All right. Give us ten seconds." I hung up. "Close your eyes, Bruce. Rebecca's pulling us back."

"What for?" He closed his eyes tightly.

"Didn't say. Some meeting." I squeezed mine shut, too.

Otherwise, in observer mode, everything runs together and gets painfully bright. At the end of a normal session, you quietly fall asleep and then wake up outside. Observers either push the button or just get yanked, and if you don't have warning, it can be an unpleasant surprise.

N I N E

MEETING OF MINDS

I felt the couch moving and opened my eyes, gently pulling out the catheter, then ripping off the electrodes with a couple of jerks.

Rebecca handed me a glass of water and had one in the other hand for Bruce. I drank greedily and took a couple of deep breaths.

"Seems to be just New York," I said, as Bruce rolled out. "At least not Miami and Philly. We ought to try the World's Fair in Chicago."

"Maybe tomorrow," she said. "We have updated visitors from Earth."

"Oh, shit." The telepresence carriers were AI and dumb as posts. It would be better just to live with the time lag, a few days, but Earth thought it was cool, it was George, it was the bee's fucking knees.

She handed me my greens and looked at the wall clock.

"We've got about twenty minutes. Not really time to go and change."

"I can live with greens if the toys from Earth can. This is about Alyx?"

"The death, yes. Of course Earth doesn't have the autopsy results yet."

"So this is just *Sanitas* with the telepresence modules?"

"Yeah. They're waiting in the comm room." She gave Bruce his water and repeated the scant information.

When we were both presentable, we went downstairs and walked across the pond to the comm center. We seemed to have a surplus of ducks. I considered fitting a French *confit* into my Spanish menu next week. The French cook, Maxine Chu, had tried that with the stock duck formula and given it up, so it was a challenge always in the back of my mind. That would be high on the list, if the current complications would allow me to do my other job.

(The protein sequencer could crank out a carload of ersatz duck meat from its data banks. Too old; imprecise data. I'd tasted it, and it was like dry chicken dark meat. To get the real flavor I'd have to supply them some actual fresh duck to analyze.)

The comm center stage was a corny holo box. They had it set up to look like a meadow with chairs. How was that better than a plain stage with chairs? The two telepresence modules were sitting there with the quiet patience most inanimate things have, an old-looking man and a young-looking woman. I didn't recognize the woman, but the man was Walter Cronkite from the 1960s, who reported on the American space program then. I'd talked with him, or it, a few times. He was usually the only one.

Of course neither of them was physically "there" any more than a template character in the time machine is. They were standard holo projections that were sent up weekly from Earth, semi-autonomous, like virtual robots carrying bundles of new data. People on Earth would eventually watch our conversation in a similar setup, about a week from now, with holo simulacra standing in for us. Probably not in a meadow.

There were three medical people from *Sanitas*, and their coordinator, Cleo Banister, sitting in a semicircle facing the modules. Bruce and I nodded hello and took the two empty chairs.

"I suppose we're all here now," the Cronkite clone said in his radio voice. "Thank you for joining us, Jacob and Bruce."

I couldn't suppress a yawn. "Okay. What's the score?" Oops, wrong century. "Why was this meeting convened?"

"The 'score' is zero to nothing," Cronkite said. "We're hoping to improve it."

"The autopsy results will be reviewed by dozens of specialists on Earth," the woman said, "and the virtuality records studied by nearly a hundred specialists. Meanwhile, we do have preliminary data that might be of use."

"Nothing quite like this has ever happened on Earth," Cronkite said. "Before immortality, we have records of eight people who died during virtual-reality experiences."

"We have those records, too," I had to say.

"They all seem straightforward enough," he plowed on. "Undiagnosed or misdiagnosed pre-existing conditions that should have disqualified the victims from VR. Diseases that contraindicated emotional stress, mostly heart problems."

"Except for two," I said.

"Those two are the interesting ones," the woman said. "Emotional stress. Deliberate emotional stress exacerbated by illegal drugs."

"That's what they said at the time," I agreed. "The people pumped themselves up and put themselves into such extreme situations that they died essentially of shock. That's not really possible anymore." I remembered my recent trauma in the trench in World War I. "Automatic asymptotes of physiological response to emotional experience. You could put yourself through a virtual meat grinder and survive to do something even more stupid."

"That's not relevant to Alyx's experience, either," Bruce said. "I was there as a template, along with Jacob. I looked at the record this morning in flatscreen. She was just getting drunk in a speakeasy and listening to the kind of music she loved."

I nodded. "She'd been to that time and place before. Maybe that's a factor."

"A lot of people have favorite targets," the woman said.

"This isn't Earth," I said.

She looked at me, slightly walleyed. "Please explain."

They were informed but not bright. "Earth's virtual-reality network is a thousand times larger and more complex than ours, and is updated every instant. The longer we travel, the more we diverge from it. So things could be true of our system that are not true of Earth's."

We can update discrete things like Bruce's Austrian museum, but they're like snapshots. The ship's communication and computing power couldn't keep track of a tenth of Earth's network, even if it did nothing else.

"It could also have to do with our smaller population," one of the doctors said. "With the same eight hundred people using the system over and over, we might be stressing it in ways the Earth system never would be stressed. What happens to a small system if a person does the same thing over and over?" he asked me.

"It's been done, especially by artists and historians. Of course people like me and Bruce do it pretty often, seeking out and repairing temporal anomalies. It doesn't seem to harm us."

"But you don't do it as patients, I mean clients. You're more or less in control of the illusion."

"When we go in like that, as observers, yes. But then we go in as regular users, too, to check the work. If too much time travel, especially to the same period and place, was dangerous, we'd be the first ones to be affected."

After a short silence, the female telepresence said, "We think the two who took drugs were suicides. Could Alyx have been?"

"That wasn't in the data we got," the senior medic, Martin, said. He was the one who had wept at seeing her corpse.

"It's not in the Earth data. Cronkite and I worked it out from the data and what we know of human nature."

Martin stared at her. "But you aren't human. You aren't even organic."

She stared back. "You don't have to be human to think. Or organic to be alive, in a sense." Technically true, but her saying it gave me a chill.

"There were traces of chemicals in their blood that at the time were used to control depression. Before the war," Cronkite said.

"I knew her," the senior medic said, something more than exasperation in his voice. "She was not depressed. She was not suicidal." He looked around. "God knows, we've all known suicides."

"Not in a long time," Cronkite said, and he was right. It was the leading cause of death for about twenty years after the war. But those of us who made it through that period seemed reconciled to the fact of continuing existence. Nowadays death was always accidental or, on Earth, brought on by disease during pregnancy.

Banister echoed my thoughts. "I don't know how long it's been since we've had a death that was not accidental."

"That's true," Cronkite said. "You don't know. 'There are no accidents,' an actual human said."

"Elie Wiesel." I remembered from my encyclopedic childhood. "But he was speaking from a theological point of view. Not medical."

"Our last death was back at Chimbarazo," Bruce said, "a fuel dump explosion. It was an accident."

"Unless the person who died caused it . . . on purpose. Was he the only one there?" Cronkite looked objective and wise.

"Of course he was," I said, wishing I could give his logic circuits a good shaking. "If other people had been there, they would have died, too."

"So it can't really be proven one way or the other. The historical record affirms that a person who kills himself or herself in such a catastrophic way will take pains to make sure no one else is hurt."

"Sometimes it's just the opposite." I wasn't going to let him get off that easily. "There were wars in the twentieth and twenty-first that were dominated by deliberately suicidal warriors."

"That's true, but not relevant to us. People were driven by different passions then."

Bruce shook his head. "I can't believe it. A Jesuitical robot."

"It is in our nature to ask and answer questions," the female said. Of course that was true; you didn't go through the trouble of making a simulated persona just to have tea with it and chat about the weather. Never a big topic inside a spaceship, anyhow.

"Suppose she was a suicide," Banister said. "How would you suggest a person go about committing suicide while she's strapped down in the dark, semiconscious, not even in control of her basic body functions?"

"She has control of her *mind*," the woman said.

"Not entirely. The machine's controlling her sensory input."

"Her will, then. She does have control of her will."

I wanted to ask what she could know about will, but Cronkite answered first: "That's all the two of us are, if you think about it. Take away our will, and there's nothing but raw data."

"That's just programming," Bruce said. "A set of instructions people gave you that determines how you respond to input."

"Forgive me for being Jesuitical. But how is your will different from that?"

. . .

T E N

TIMING

We made love and I lay awake in the darkness
for some time. I started to ease out of bed and she touched
my back. "You should try to get some sleep."

"Glass of wine," I said. Sometimes that worked.

"It's an idea." Dim lights came on when I opened the
bedroom door, and we padded over to the kitchenette table.
I asked for half-light, and that corner brightened.

There was half a bottle left. I gave us each a small glass.
Had to last another day.

"We're on the wrong expedition, you know." She closed
one eye and looked at me through the pale red liquid.
"Christopher Columbus gave each of his crew two and a
half liters of Spanish wine a day."

"Wow. No wonder they didn't make it to the Indies."

She smiled at that. "Is it Alyx? That horrible . . ."

"Alyx and other things. Those odd AIs from Earth."

"But you work with templates like them all day."

"Not quite like them. Ours have a degree of autonomy, but only within the terms of a detailed script. If you took a Parisienne from 1910 and dropped her in a Detroit ghetto fifty years later, she'd probably shut down in confusion."

"These were more general-purpose? I've seen the Cronkite one, but never met them."

"You won't meet the other; it was just here for the meeting, then disappeared. Data backup, maybe."

"You find their autonomy disturbing."

"Yeah, but it's more than just autonomy. Talking with them is almost like talking with people. They have originality, personality." I ran my finger around the edge of the glass, making a pure note. "I wrote to Jay Bee back at Chimbarazo; did you know him?"

"Of him. Cute Canadian AI researcher."

"Cute? How can you tell under all that hair? Anyhow, I asked him what's up, what's happened the past few years to make such a difference."

She went to the cooler and got out some tunoid and a package of rice crackers. "But you keep up with AI all the time, don't you?"

"Just as it applies to the time machine. Cronkite, and probably the new woman, present a new ball game every Monday. If they represent a new material technology, we might not be able to use it; can't wave a magic wand. If it's just technique . . . well, maybe." I shrugged.

"Maybe you don't want really smart robots stomping around inside your time machine." She spread some of the fishlike substance on a cracker. "Here, eat your lysine. It will help you sleep."

"Yes, doctor. Anyhow, it'll be awhile before Jay can answer. Saturday, at the earliest. We may be pretty busy." We were nearing the seven-hundred-day mark, when we'd stop accelerating and mate with the waiting fuel supplies.

"God, I hope it's not the wrong kind of busy. I can just see plumbing problems in all five ships."

"But it will make your life simpler, ultimately."

"Ultimately." She set her glass on the table and filled it almost to the rim. On Earth, or any planet, the fluid would go to the top and bulge out in a meniscus, because of surface tension. That would work in our artificial centripetal gravity, too, but with the ship's tiny acceleration the liquid dipped down about a millimeter away from the lip, in the direction of flight. She tapped the rim of the glass there. "*This,* I won't mind losing."

We'd talked about it before; over time, sediments pile up in a uniformly asymmetric way, causing uneven and constantly increasing stress. Most of the problems that were uninteresting, "shit details," were related to that. "But any change to the system, even for the better, is going to generate problems."

"Plus turning this beast around and chasing down the fuel," I said.

"Well. I'm not going to waste any time worrying about it." She drank off the small glass and stood up, leaning over to give me a kiss. "Thank you, Jake. Drink the rest if you want. I have to be up at seven."

I watched her walking away and felt like a pretty lucky man. The old joke about the perfect wife being a wealthy nymphomaniac whose old man owns a liquor store. Of course wealth has no meaning here, and everybody has the same liquor allowance. I still felt pretty lucky.

What was actually keeping me awake was how to word the referendum. Yes or no: should we discontinue the use

of the time machine until we can prove that it was not related to, was not a causal factor in, was not responsible for,
the death of Alyx Kaplan? In the absence of any unambiguous other cause, though, that could keep us shut down
indefinitely.

It would be a two-stage referendum—a preliminary vote,
the results of which would be published, broken down as to
gender, profession, and age (though that was becoming
moot). A week of discussion, then a binding vote.

Friday morning and evening, the day before mating with
the fuel tanks, I had interviews scheduled. The morning
one was a set piece, ten minutes on the news hour. The
evening was a call-in between 2100 and 2200.

"Time check, global," I whispered, and the full information appeared on the wall:

EARTH
MESSAGE

DATE	TIME	DELAY
2430405	01:32:22	06d 06h 25m

SPINDOWN WILL COMMENCE FOR *MANUS* 2430406
AT 1500.

The timing was lousy. Everybody distracted by Spindown.
But it would be irresponsible to put the referendum off.

We'd messaged everyone scheduled for the time machine in the next month about the possibility of danger. So
far, we'd only had two cancellations.

One for day after tomorrow. I'd take it.

1939

I rubbed my eyes and tried to focus. Rocking gently from side to side. Train-station smell, leather seat covers. We slid into the light and I recognized New York. Leaving Penn Station.

Bruce was sitting across from me. He was wearing a bottle-green blazer, snazzy, with a plain white cotton shirt, open collar, and linen pants, a jaunty straight pipe clenched in his teeth. The tobacco smelled like briar and cherry. "Waking up, sport?"

"I think . . . yeah. Penn Station. Where we headed?"

"It's 1939, and we're taking the ten-minute ride out to the World's Fair in Flushing Meadows.

" 'Building the world of tomorrow,' is what they called it. And in a literal way it is; it's set up to be the nucleus of creeping suburbanism. Robert Moses fought hard to have it built here, on the Corona Ash Dump that had been Fitzgerald's hell in *The Great Gatsby*, a generation earlier.

The nexus of the parkway system that would lead New Yorkers out onto Long Island. Of course that's not what the slogan was supposed to mean."

I looked around. "It's quiet. For a train."

Diane bumped his shoulder with a hip; he slid over and she sat down. "It's a special electric train that Penn RR put on—'ten minutes, ten cents'—so why buck the traffic and the parking?" She was all in blue, puff shoulders and a wide blue leather belt with a fancy medieval buckle, navy skirt to just below the knee. A touch of Chanel No. 5. Wavy marcelled hair to her shoulders. Bride of frankincense.

It was as if each detail clicked into existence when I thought about it. A strange feeling, a kind of clothing and grooming déjà vu. I looked down at my own rumpled-but-clean brown gabardine suit. The color was called "tobacco." Wide checked tie. Two-tone shoes, brown and black, that were a little tight.

Both of them had deep tans. I was white as a fish's belly. While I was staring at the backs of my hands, Bruce reached over and touched my finger, and I was suddenly as tan as he was.

"Zip-a-dee-doo-dah," he said.

It's not magic; we're all visitors here in some sense.
"We're . . . we're not in the war, the next war? Yet?"

"No. This is May. Britain will join the war in September. The United States will stay out of it for another couple of years. The Neutrality Act technically keeps them even from selling arms to the nations that will be their allies against Hitler."

"A lot happens this year," Diane said. "Today, May 22, Germany and Italy signed their pact. Japan has started fighting Russia in Manchuria. In March, Franco took over Spain, a sort of dress rehearsal for Nazi technology and tactics. Germany took Czechoslovakia without a shot being fired. Russia and Germany will team up to attack Finland and Poland, but the alliance won't last."

"*Finnegans Wake* and *Mein Kampf*," Bruce said. "*Gone With the Wind* and *The Wizard of Oz*. John Wayne's career is going to take off with *Stagecoach*, and all through the war he'll dodge the draft while playing heroic soldiers."

"First helicopter flight this year." She made a fluttering, rising gesture with her hands. "They won't be used much until the next war, though, and they really come into their own the one after that. The first one America loses."

"We win this one, though," Bruce said, "belatedly, from the point of view of the countries that suffered while we stalled."

"How do you . . . how do I know about . . ."

"Just relax, Jake. Try to get a little shut-eye. You'll be on your feet for awhile."

" 'Building the world of tomorrow,' " Diane said.

"They didn't quite get it right," Bruce said, and for some reason I did doze.

I woke to the shudder and squeal of the train's brakes. It had become crowded, but there was no sign of the two folks I'd been talking to. Rude of me to fall asleep!

People were chattering happily as they lined up at the two doors. For some reason that seemed awful. Don't they know about Europe?

The hell with it. Here to have some fun. I get these funny things in my head sometimes.

On the platform outside the train, most of the people were standing around consulting maps or guidebooks. I slapped my pockets and didn't come up with anything, but I figured they'd be for sale everywhere. I waited in a short line and took my wallet out, stuffed with small bills, and gave a one to the ticket lady. She gave me back a quarter, and I went through swinging doors to the Fair.

It was pretty spectacular. Down an immaculate multi-colored promenade, the fairground was dominated by the famous Trylon and Perisphere, a huge phallic ball and spike, at least a half mile away, gleaming white in the mid-morning sun. The only white buildings anywhere. I walked down the steps and started that way.

Rainbow Avenue was still spotless in spite of a fairly large crowd. Halfway down, there was a kiosk where I got a hot dog and a guidebook for a dime each. I sat in the sun and worked on the hot dog while studying the map. Not possible to see it all in a day, but I would hit some high spots and come back another time.

"Jacob? Jake Brewer?" I looked up from the map. It was someone I recognized but couldn't put a name to, an intense dark-haired woman I knew from some musical connection. I took her hand. "Ellie Morrow, El."

"Vivaldi," I said. "You play a wonderful flute." When and where?

She sat next to me and looked at the map. Wildflower perfume and a touch of sweat, not unpleasant. She was wearing a smart tailored suit, light beige, red shoes with sensible low heels. "Do you have a plan?"

"I was just going to wander. Is that enough of a plan for you?"

"Fine by me." We got a couple of Cokes and ambled toward the Perisphere.

"Amazing, what they did with an old ash heap," I said. "You know the Fitzgerald connection, Gatsby?"

She nodded. "I hope they don't lose their Gatsby shirts. They're in pretty deep, I read."

"Pretty big crowd. Maybe they'll be okay." As we got

closer to the center, we had to speak up over the susurrus of conversation and shuffle of thousands of feet. Always a baby crying somewhere, and bursts of childish laughter and taunting. For some reason that gave me a dark feeling of loss. I tried to remember why, but nothing came. My children were fine, though I never saw them nowadays. They lived quite a ways away.

We got into a short line for the Trylon, following a sign to the Democracity. We'd finished our Cokes. I took El's cup and she held my place while I jogged over to a waste basket and dropped them in.

The basket was otherwise empty, which struck me as odd. Perhaps it filled up fast, and they'd already emptied it.

We paid our quarters and went inside to a somewhat disturbing sight. The Trylon featured the longest escalator I'd ever seen. People were quiet going up it, perhaps sharing my sense of foreboding. What would happen if someone fell down at the top? Would the machine stop, or just keep feeding people into a growing pile, like a conveyor belt in a factory?

But then we were out in the sunshine again, people chattering, perhaps in relief. It was a long, airy pedestrian bridge connecting the two monumental buildings. The view was striking. Most of the buildings below us were modern, more curves than straight lines. A spectacular fountain danced at the other end of Constitution Mall, its central column shooting higher than we stood.

The inside of the Perisphere was one huge globular room. We were escorted onto a moving belt that crawled around its circumference, looking down at a model of the "totally planned planetary city of the future," which had a busy packed central core surrounded by green quiet suburbs. A voice I knew from newsreels, H. V. Kaltenborn, intoned platitudes about a "brave new world" of "unity and peace."

"You think it'll be like that?" I whispered to El.

"Sure. It's just what Hitler wants, unity and peace." She turned to me, her face pinched with confusion. "Why am I so certain it's not going to happen? I'm not really a sourpuss."

"I don't think H. V. Kaltenborn is that optimistic, either. This is fantasy, though, science fiction. Model making on a huge scale." The note on the other side of the map said it took more than a hundred people to keep it running. I wondered how many were on treadmills beneath our feet. A job's a job, they say.

At the end of the six-minute circuit, bells tinkled to warn us to step off the conveyor belt or face processing by cheerful Kaltenborn yet another time. We survived a little movie about happy farmers and workers, then were hustled out. We didn't descend by escalator, though; there was a winding ramp that spiraled down around the outside of the globe, cool on the shady side but hot in the white glare of the sun. Of course even the ramp had a name, not Ramp, but Helicline. No doubt describing the hellish sun side.

El and I shared a fascination with trains, so we went across the Bridge of Wheels to the Railroads Building, the largest building in the Fair. The inside was a huge O-gauge model train display, half the size of a football field. Five hundred cars, sharp tang of ozone and oil. Interesting enough, but not something you would care to sit and study unless you were a model-train nut. There were a couple of dozen such down in the first row, memorizing every tiny tie. The guide said there were seventy thousand of them, nailed down with a quarter million spikelets. I pictured elves.

Outside, in back, the display was fascinating. Lots of

nineteenth- and eighteenth-century train cars, and one huge locomotive of the future, streamlined, dark green instead of black. Its main drive wheels stood taller than us, rolling around slowly in place. There were puffs of steam coming out here and there, but I suspected the wheels were being turned by an electrical motor behind the scenes. It wouldn't be efficient to fire up the burner just to turn the wheels around with no load. And there was a kind of electric-motor smell, brushes on copper winding.

It looked both futuristic and old-fashioned. El agreed. "The future's electricity. Coal and oil are on the way out." It was still a mighty machine, beautiful in its own way.

The General Motors Building was right across the street, and there was only a short line, taking up maybe a tenth of the serpentine ramp. It was a don't-miss, people said, and even though its Futurama sounded similar to Democracity, we got in the line. Comparison shopping for the future.

While we were waiting in line, fanning ourselves with programs and maps, we talked about music for awhile. Then abruptly she said, "We're going to be in this damn war, aren't we? Pardon my French."

"Not over Poland or Czechoslovakia. If Hitler goes after England, maybe. Probably. But I don't know about drafting men for it, though. The last one was so horrible."

"You were in it?"

I nodded. "Gallipoli."

"Oh, my." A moment of silence stretched. "You don't like to talk about it."

"Not really. And I'm not sure I, well, I can trust my memories, either. It was an ongoing nonstop nightmare, surreal. I can't imagine how I survived. Or how anybody did, on either side." Sudden memory of shoals of corpses, rotting in the sun.

She put her hand on my arm. "I've heard that before. Let's just hope it doesn't happen again."

"I wouldn't put any money on it." We got to the entrance, good timing.

It was a sit-down ride, in cool refrigerated air, sitting and coolness both welcome. They put us together in a large chair and fastened down a bar across our laps, and we rolled out over a kind of idealized United States of 1960. Speakers built into the side wings of the chair described everything as we passed over it. The baritone voice was conversational and clear.

Futurama was, appropriately, more futuristic than Democracity had been. We sailed across the country from East Coast to West, looking down over grand highways where teardrop-shaped cars sped from city to city on fourteen-lane highways at a hundred miles per hour.

There was a lot of farmland—"electrified farms"—and forest. People were concentrated in well-ordered cities; work and school and such were right where you lived. Pedestrians crossed over the fast highways in transparent tube walkways.

"No churches," El pointed out. "I heard they're getting into some trouble about that."

Good riddance, I thought, but kept the thought to myself.

The airports were ingenious, round landing fields around elevators, where the airplanes would be stored underground, out of the weather. The air also supported autogyros and dirigibles.

I wondered how crowded the sky could become before it would be dangerous. All those different sizes and shapes of machines, going all different speeds, in whatever direction. The cars that sped below them were automatically controlled; they might come up with a way to do that in the three dimensions of the air, as well.

The ending of the exhibit was very clever. The last thing we saw was a futuristic intersection. The young man who lifted the bar, releasing us, gave us each a blue button proclaiming I HAVE SEEN THE FUTURE, and escorted us to double doors—which opened onto a full-scale model of the miniaturized intersection we'd just seen.

I had the sensation of suddenly being tiny, scrutinized by invisible giants. El staggered and looked up, I think with the same sense of disorientation.

We looked at the map, and El suggested we wander toward the Amusement Zone for lunch; maybe stop at a pavilion or two on the way. Fine with me.

Westinghouse wasn't too crowded. In between its two buildings was the Immortal Wall and its Time Capsule, supposedly not to be opened until 6939. I wonder what people that far in the future will make of *Gone With the Wind*, comic strips, and newsreels of FDR talking and Japanese bombers attacking Canton. A fashion show. They'll probably be like Wells's morlocks, and not be able to get the damned thing open.

We stepped into the Hall of Electrical Power just in time for the artificial lightning bolt, which made a blast of thunder so loud I nearly jumped out of my skin. I wasn't looking directly at it, but the reflection of its light was dazzling. It smelled like lightning, too, hot ozone.

They had a strange robot, Elektro, with a robot dog, Sparko, which I suppose was intended to humanize the machine. Seemed to work for most people. The thing was about eight feet tall, bronze, proportioned like an overweight longshoreman. Its head was vaguely Negroid, the implications of which I think would be offensive to me, if I were a Negro.

It supposedly responded to spoken commands, though that wouldn't be difficult to fake. It could count on its fingers and dance with a woman, and smoke a cigarette, which I'm sure relaxed it after its taxing duties.

There was something deeply disturbing about it, sinister. An irrational feeling, I suppose. But a human being at the distant beginning of evolution would have been even less impressive in its abilities. Could novelties like this evolve into being our masters? Is there any way we could prevent it? Just junk them all now, I suppose.

I mentioned the idea to El, who said I should stop reading pulp magazines; they'd give me nightmares.

For a dime, we hired a runner to take us to the Amusement Zone in an open carriage like a Chinese jinricksha. Interesting contrast, to go directly from a machine acting like a man to a man functioning as a car's engine. But a job is a job, as people keep saying.

The Amusement Zone wasn't much different from the offerings of a regular carnival, which was comforting—and canny on the part of the Fair's designers, to give us respite from novelty. We partook of hamburgers and french fries and the ubiquitous Coke—I'm a tea drinker, normally, but there aren't any tea kiosks. It was good to sit for awhile. We talked about music and my art hobby. No politics.

Politics was what the Fair was all about, of course, and economics, as if you could separate the two. A slightly premature celebration, if it was about the Depression being over. Maybe as much wishful thinking, and prayer, as celebration.

Could we even approach the worlds of Futurama or Democracity by 1960? It didn't seem feasible, as an engineering project, since you'd have to tear down almost everything and build anew. People wouldn't stand by and applaud while you did it, either. We desire the new but are reluctant to give up the old.

El urged me to try my prowess at the shooting gallery. Fish in a barrel couldn't have been easier. I'd been trained as a sniper before going to Gallipoli, so once I'd analyzed the .22's shortcomings—hold the aim two inches high and one inch to the left—it was easy to pick off the smallest targets. I made enough points to win a large yellow stuffed Elektro, which El accepted with glee.

Here in the Amusement Zone, there was no great effort to pretend that the exhibits were intended to uplift or educate. It was all for fun, sometimes on a grand scale, rarely tasteful or modest.

We walked through Frank Buck's "Bring 'Em Back Alive" zoo, which supposedly had more than thirty thousand animals—presumably most of them very small. A huge display of monkeys bounding around on an artificial mountain. Elephants and giraffes and big cats looking no more or less unhappy than they do in a permanent zoo. Admiral Byrd's Penguin Island was more interesting, a reconstruction of Little America in Antarctica, full of penguins who would probably have liked it colder, but managed to waddle around endearingly, awkward on land and graceful in the water.

There was a fairly convincing reconstruction of a New York City street in the Gay Nineties, and a less convincing one of a Shakespearean village, actors with grating phony English accents. We sat for awhile in Heineken's "little bit of Holland," having a cold beer in the shade of a windmill.

We decided against the parachute jump, though it would have been interesting to see the fairgrounds from that high prospect. The parachutes were tethered, of course, but El thought they descended a little too rapidly, and I was secretly relieved. What if I'd gotten all the way up there and chickened out, as kids say.

There was a group of dwarves living in a miniature village, Little Miracle Town, and next to that display, an eight-foot-tall giant, whose coarse features were shadowed with pain. They had him sitting at a table and chair that were slightly smaller than normal; you can imagine what that would feel like after a few hours. As we passed by him, he sold one of his rings to a woman who slipped it over her baby daughter's hand, to make a loose bracelet.

Then there was sort of a human zoo, the Odditorium, which displayed physically odd people from other lands. I'd seen pictures of the Ubangi, with large plates horribly distending their lips; seeing the same thing in the flesh was discomfiting, as were the giraffe-necked women from India, whose necks are slowly stretched by stacking rings on them as they grow. It was impossible to read their eyes.

The African pygmies and Jivaro headhunters stared back at the tourists with curiosity and defiance, respectively. I suspect the Jivaros spoke with Hispanic New York accents when they took off their costumes and wigs at night.

We went into the cool darkness of the Theater of Time and Space for "a voyage into the limitless spaces trillions of miles beyond the Milky Way," but about that time the beer and heat and walking caught up with me, and I dozed until the lights came up. El said I didn't miss much.

She had to catch a train to Washington at six; I offered to walk her back, but she declined and told me to relax and enjoy myself. She might have caught my sideways glances at some of the more carnal aspects of the carnival, which of course I hadn't suggested. Anyhow, we embraced and promised one another we'd get together soon.

I went into a place called the Hurricane Bar and treated myself to a new drink named the Zombie, which was, in retrospect, a mistake. It was sweet and seemed mild. I was thirsty and drank it down too fast; the effect was like downing a tumbler of iced rum! The kindly bartender gave me a worried look and a glass of ice water, but by then I was already somewhat looped. I did remember my hat as I navigated back out into the cooling afternoon.

My unsteady steps took me back to a pavilion I'd heard of, criticized for its erotic content but artistically interesting: Salvador Dali's Dream of Venus. I was interested in both art and naked women, so how could I go wrong? So long as I didn't trip over my own feet, betraying my zombie nature.

You entered the thing between two giant legs, on top of which was a twenty-foot-high copy of Boticelli's *Venus Rising from the Sea*. It might not be the best attraction to visit drunk. I'm sure it would have been confusing enough sober.

There were paintings on the walls, and other things, too, like arms coming out, and bas-relief body parts. But the main show was in two tanks, a dry one and one that was full of water.

The wet tank had bare-breasted mermaids swimming lazily around, languidly tapping away on floating typewriter keys. A reclining female figure made of rubber had a piano keyboard painted along its torso; every now and then one of the girls would descend to pretend playing on her. There was a fake cow, bandaged up as if from a serious accident, placidly smoking a pipe. Smell of damp seaweed and mildew.

In the dry tank, a sleeping Venus was attended by lobsters who seemed comfortable in frying pans over hot coals. Bottles of champagne scattered around, and a couch in the shape of swollen lips.

It was dark when I left Dali's extravaganza behind, and although I was getting my land legs back, I was also feeling tired enough to calculate the distance back to the train station and decided to call it a day. My hotel was just across the street from Penn Station; I could have a quick supper there and retire.

Under a lamp I consulted the map and charted a new route back through the fairgrounds. More breasts, as it turned out; women in improbable tableaux about the history and virtues of advertising. Probably a foretaste of what picture radio would bring. Television, they called it at the RCA pavilion. Anything to lure people away from books and the dangerous business of thinking.

That was the bad taste the fair left in my mind. The road to fulfillment a sequence of shiny cars and appliances. Cars and appliances that think for you. Would they free up the mind for more important matters? What do the people of 1960 *do* as they cruise automatically from Democracity to Future-topia in their one-hundred-mile-per-hour wombs? I suspect they watch bare-breasted women selling them things on the Kodachrome radio.

I couldn't get Elektro out of my mind. I even dreamed of him as I dozed on the train. There was a real dog inside Sparko, but he was more like a wolf, silently snarling. And something like a man inside of Elektro, but not a man of flesh. Doing tricks, acting stupid, waiting patiently for its time to come. Accumulating insults to return.

The squeal and shudder of brakes awoke me. Penn Station downstairs was close and smoky. I rushed up the stairs, despite tiredness, and out into the street.

I took a deep breath. It smelled fresh and clean.

What was wrong with that?

ELEVEN

MATING

For about a hundred days, we'd been converging on the "tankers," the five mountains of ice that we would carry to Beta Hydrii, fuel to slow us down, decelerating over the last years of the voyage.

Back in the dawn of the Space Age, the logic of "staging" was clear: you used a big rocket to hoist a medium-sized one out of the dense ocean of the lower atmosphere. The big one detached and dropped back, one hoped into an actual ocean or desert, while the medium-sized rocket propelled a little one out of the remaining atmosphere, into space proper.

There was no air to battle between Europa and here, of course, but the logic was similar. When we left the Solar System, rather than accelerating all of the trip's fuel up to the midpoint in five huge packages, we sent ten smaller ones, five of them tankers, automatons lugging fuel, with no burden of crew and life support. They'd left about six months before we did, their progress carefully monitored. They hadn't accelerated quite as fast, but on paper it was a simple feat to have the five tankers arrive at Spindown at the same time as us, and with the same velocity relative to Earth.

But that velocity was a little more than one-fiftieth the speed of light. So we covered a distance the size of the United States every second. "A miss is as good as a mile," they said in the early years of Old Twentieth, off by a few orders of magnitude by our time.

We'd stopped accelerating, except for the tiny nudges from steering jets. So wineglasses would show a proper meniscus again. Until we began to decelerate, 996 years from now.

It was a complicated maneuvering waltz, one that we'd practiced several times in Europa orbit. Of course, when we were back there, all ten vessels had been pretty close to one another all the time. But there, you also had to adjust vectors because of the presence of Europa and Jupiter. So in theory, at least, this was going to be easier. But if there were any problems, they were likely to be big ones.

We were watching the slow progress of the enterprise, projected diagramatically on a large screen over the park. It was early lunchtime and pretty crowded. Not too exciting; you might just barely tell a difference if you looked up every minute.

For two years we had flown attached to the sterns of our fuel tank/engines, the mass shielding us from the sparse but energetic rain of elementary particles, and occasional dangerously fast dust motes. For the next thousand we would drift the opposite way, engines pointing forward for eventual deceleration. The view "above" us, in the forward screen, would still be pointed toward Beta

Hydrii—no one wanted to spend a millennium looking at where we had been.

"It's like getting big slow animals in a position to mate," I said. "Did I ever tell you about the horse?"

Kate was carefully coating the top of her roll-up sandwich with mustard. "You mated with a horse? Should I be jealous?"

"I was five or six, and our neighbors in Maine had horses. Thoroughbreds. They'd borrowed or rented a male, a stallion, to come in to mate with one of their mares, and enlisted my parents' help."

"Horses need help to mate? What did they do in the wild?"

"They didn't have Thoroughbreds in the wild. I take it they're kind of specialized. Not too bright about some things."

"Do tell." She put the sandwich down and smiled. "You're going to tell."

"They told me to wait in the car. I didn't know anything about sex, but I could tell there was something strange about the visiting horse. It was stamping around and whinnying and had an erection like—" I held up fist and forearm. "Four of them were restraining the animal. It half dragged them over to the other side of the barn."

"And you followed, of course."

"What kid wouldn't? I peeked around the corner and saw most of it. They had the mare tied up in a makeshift stall and sort of guided the stallion in."

"To the bull's-eye. So to speak."

"My mother and dad and our neighbors were pulling on lines with all they had, I guess trying to keep the stallion from injuring the mare or itself. The one who apparently owned the stallion was petting it and talking to it, and finally took hold of its dick and, you know, aimed it. Just in time, too; it started to ejaculate."

"And you didn't know—"

"Nothing, not for some years. I ran back to the car, pretty scared. Turns out my mother knew I'd seen it, but wasn't sure how to handle the situation."

"Oh . . . that was just before the war? And then your father died." She put her hand on my knee and squeezed it. "So ultimately it was your mother who had to explain—"

"Yeah." I laughed and maybe blushed. "That I hadn't broken it, when it happened to me. By then I'd almost forgotten about the horse, or buried the memory, but she reminded me. So a lot of things fell into place."

"Hard way to grow up." She was born forty years after the war. I didn't think about it much, but in a way we were from two different planets.

She looked up at the screen. "Like elephants mating." She laughed. "Or worse. Using their trunks."

"Nasal sex. What a talent." If everything worked, it would be almost completely automated. Each of the five ships would come alongside its fresh fuel tanker. About a hundred explosive bolts would separate the payload, us, from the nearly empty old fuel tank. Steering jets would inch us over to where we were in place over the new tank. A few spot welds would suffice to hold them together: there wouldn't be much mechanical stress between here and Beta, and they would never have to be detached.

Assuming we never had to make the trip in reverse. If we had to return to Earth from Beta, we'd have to build our own elephants. Time enough to worry about that a thousand years from now.

Manus would be the first ship to do the switch. I thought that was bad engineering, but I didn't get a vote. There were only fifteen people aboard it, the usual skeleton crew from here. So the logic was that if something went horribly wrong, fewer lives would be lost.

That was typical committee thinking. What would the rest of us do if *Manus* was destroyed and we had no facilities for retooling? Of all the five ships, it was the one we couldn't afford to lose. The only thing you could predict with certainty about the next thousand years was that something was bound to break down. So sure, let's risk the toolkit first.

(My suggestion, that we use *Ars*, *Mek*, or *Mentos*, distributing most of their two hundred passengers among the rest of the ships, was politely declined. They'd done the numbers, they said. I wonder what they got, dividing by zero.)

"How did the duck thing go?"

"They think they can do it. That's gonna be most of my afternoon. First I've got to dress out one of the little bastards. I don't suppose you've ever killed a duck."

"No. Not that I haven't thought of it."

I did find a good Spanish recipe for duck, for which we had all the ingredients but stuffed olives and duck. The stuffing for the olives I could approximate with chopped sweet red peppers. The duck, I had to kill and dress and carve up, so the food lab could analyze the raw meat and synthesize a restaurant-sized amount with the protein sequencer.

All of my recipes had this unwritten first step: go to the store and buy a duck, or a salmon or whatever. If I wanted meat that wasn't chicken or goat or tilapia, it had to come from the sequencer, which in my case would be transforming chicken to duck. What I'd finally be working with would be cubes of something that would look like boneless raw duck meat and would have the proper proportion of fat to protein, with biopolymers and lipid chemistry faithfully reproduced. But first I had to kill a duck and pull its guts out and hack it up. That was not something we had covered at the Escuela Bel.art in Barcelona. We just went across the street and bought a duck, headless, featherless, already dressed.

I checked my wrist. "Three hours to go. Meet me here for the docking?"

"Yeah—everybody's taking off except Howard. If you have time, you might go home and pick up a blanket, get here early enough to get us a space."

"Okay. The duck better not take that long."

"Good hunting. My hero," she added in a squeaky falsetto.

"Yeah, me kill vicious bird." I walked away feeling totally atavistic. All this barnyard stuff, breeding and killing.

I went back home and picked up both a blanket and a pillowcase, approximately duck-sized, wishing I had a gun. Or even a rock to throw at the damned thing. Note to future starship builders: pack a few rocks.

No trouble finding detailed instructions for preparing the duck, reproduced from a 1918 Boston Cooking School book, but it assumed the creature was already dead by the time you started sawing away at it.

Most people I talked to thought you were either supposed to shoot it or chop its head off. I could just see taking a cleaver down to the pond and attacking a defenseless quacker. Perhaps losing a finger in the process.

Bruce and I remembered seeing a couple of old movies where people had killed chickens for cooking by breaking their necks. Just grab it underneath the head and give it a yank. So we'd try that. No clients scheduled today; I called him, and he said he'd meet me at the pond.

We did finally succeed in producing a dead bird, but it was not an unqualified success.

Ducks aren't very smart, but they obviously had us figured out. Two people can't corner one duck. Multiply that principle by about twenty, and you have a constantly milling flock, complaining bitterly, never coming within an arm's length of either human. They all eventually wound up in the water. They swam to the other side of the pond; when I rushed over there, they paddled out to the middle.

By this time we had gathered a small crowd of spectators. I explained what we were trying to do. We had to go in after them. I got three hesitant voluteers, two women and a man. We stripped down and charged into the water after the little bastards.

It was only a little more than a meter of water at its deepest, but it was, after all, their element. Paddling and flapping, they could go just a little faster than we could. Four more people saw what was happening and joined the fray.

I wanted a fairly young male duck (eggs being the only useful by-product of the creatures' existence), and pointed out a couple of targets, based on coloration and size. The company assembled did manage to surround one of them and, by forming an unkempt semicircle, squishing through the mud, aimed him toward me and my waiting pillowcase. They closed in, and just as he started to fly away, I made a leap and grabbed him by the neck.

He didn't surrender, and he didn't die as handily as the chickens in the movies. Those cute webbed feet have impressive claws, and once I had him in a stranglehold, they were his basic defense, slashing away at my chest and forearm.

Another crowd had gathered at the commotion, ignorant

of the culinary goal of the exercise, and a couple were volubly wondering why we didn't leave the poor things alone. I guess they thought it was just something we were doing for the hell of it, waiting for the fuel-tank docking. Why don't we just go get our chests slashed up by a filthy bird; sounds like a good way to pass the time.

It was a noisy and somewhat bloody encounter, but I finally managed to yank on the thing's neck, and heard a sharp *crack*. I retrieved the pillowcase, again floating in the muddy water, and stuffed him in.

I'm a literary person, and should know that nature always provides a coda for man's hubris. In this case, while I was thanking everybody for diving in, pillowcase between my feet on the shore, with one pant leg on—the duck decided to come back to life. It lurched out of its container and tried, pathetically, to run away. It was fast but uncoordinated, falling down three times before Bruce grabbed its head and finished it off, twisting 360 degrees.

I later found out that ducks are more substantial than chickens. They're all dark meat because they get exercise, flapping around. Chickens sit there and grow white meat, pondering eternal verities. I assumed they were easier to kill, too, or at least less likely to enter into close combat. I called the woman who's in charge of killing chickens downstairs, which I might have done earlier, and she said they just use a jolt of electricity, then behead them for bleeding. Next time, she said, I should just bring the duck down and zap him. Sure; I'll try to talk one into it.

Bruce went back to the time-machine office, leaving me with the sacred-if-disgusting responsibility of turning a bird corpse into something people would willingly eat.

The 1918 book didn't say anything about feathers, other than suggesting an alcohol flame to singe off the pinfeathers. (I'd written my mother, asking whether her generation had any handed-down lore. She said that, like her mother and grandmother before her, she assumed that chickens were born naked and wrapped in plastic.) The chicken woman said they prepared to pluck the bird by scalding it for two minutes with water at 64 degrees C., but she thought a duck might need a hotter and longer scald. Not boiling, she said, which I had figured out. I didn't want duck soup. I called the kitchen and ordered a large pot of 70 degree water.

It was still heating when I got there. My three assistants gathered around to watch me whack the thing's head off with a cleaver. It took three unaesthetic whacks. I tied a string to its foot and suspended it over a pot, to catch the blood. After a minute, the trickle slowed to a drip, and when the water was hot enough, I dropped the body in.

We watched it for ninety seconds, then fished it out. The feathers did come off, though not easily or cleanly. Carl used a little "finishing" torch to singe the pinfeathers.

Following directions, I removed the wings and legs, then separated the breast and ribs from the back. Then I hesitated.

It looked a little too much like Alyx, I guess; open for display. Carl excused himself and then so did Sandra. Zach stared in fascination.

The book advised "before removing entrails, gizzard, heart, liver, lungs, kidneys, crop, and windpipe, observe their position, that the anatomy of the bird might be understood." I did that, actually, and it allowed me to be more objective about the dissection. I concentrated on the inane fact that Alyx hadn't had a gizzard or a crop.

I worked carefully with a small sharp knife, separating the edible parts, which Zach bagged and labeled. I might want them to make me a large mass of liver for a pâté; I was careful to separate the gall bladder and cut away a part of the liver's surface nearby that looked greenish.

The neck and wings, I put into a small pot to simmer into stock, which I'd also send along for analysis and re-production. I was sure they'd send back a powder with in-structions for reconstitution, which would taste as much like a duck as our powdered chicken stock tasted like chicken.

Zach took the stuff up to the food lab while I computed the amounts I'd need. Not everybody would like the liver pâté, but I wanted to try it. Say two hundred servings, about an ounce each, six kilograms. The duck recipe called for a five-pound duck to serve four people. I guessed that would be about a pound of actual duck meat, minus guts and feathers, feet and head, so call it a hundred kilos for eight hundred people. It would be a busy couple of days.

Tonight would be easy, Spanish "tortilla" omelettes, and there were only sixty reservations so far—a lot of people were involved in the docking or watching it at dinnertime.

It was Sandra's hour to choose the music, so I put up with her weepy romantic ballads, some of them mercifully in Welsh. I shed a tear myself, though I was chopping onions at the time.

Once the eggs and veggies were all prepared and in coolers, I let them go till 1730. I made sure all the herbs and spices were in place, all ten frying pans ready. Put the potatoes in the oven and programmed it to have them ready at 1745. Then I gathered up the blanket and a bottle of wine and went out to claim our place in the park—if we had one. The duck had taken longer than I'd planned.

I had my reader set up with a Spanish dictionary and the classic *Sabor de España*, to read while I was waiting, but Kate was already there. She had her lightbox and was sketching out a linear abstract, the Mondrianesque thing she'd been doing lately.

She gestured at the screen, which they'd unrolled to its full ten meters. "They just gave the ten-minute warning." *Manus* and its fuel tank were like tiny models on the screen, lit up by sparkles of working lights, only a little brighter than the background stars.

While I watched, the picture zoomed in closer, and the new fuel tank was just visible as a dark shape blocking out starlight. With the close-up, green lights came on in an oval and a half oval, outlining the top and bottom of the tank.

"So far so good?"

"No news is good news, I suppose. No one's said anything."

The picture's point of view changed abruptly to two space-suited figures who were tethered to *Manus*, holding wands that must have been the spot-welding tools. There would be hundreds of internal connections between the ship and its replacement fuel tank/engine, but first there was this crude physical mating.

"Crude" only in the metaphorical sense; not physical inexactness. The five-kilometer-long machine has to match the stern end of *Manus* to within a few microns. It's all done automatically, with optics, the fuel tank at first stationary relative to the ship, which uses little blips on its steering jets to make interference fringes line up precisely, before easing into place. The workers would then spotweld the juncture along the circumference, every hundred meters or so.

During all this time, the people in the ship are weightless, the living area having spun down for the transition. Not such a big deal for *Manus*, but it was going to be a major headache for the rest of us, living in actual habitats.

All of our standing bodies of water have to be contained by plastic film. We also have livestock to keep track of, or at least endure. The goats were going to be tranquilized for the duration, and the chickens locked up in their coop. What about the damned ducks? Just let them flap around, I guess.

She touched my collar. "Is that duck blood?"

"Guess so." I couldn't see it without a mirror. "There a lot of it?"

"Just a spot." She licked her thumb and rubbed at it. "Oh, that helped. Sorry."

"Apron didn't come up that far."

"What, you were hacking away at it with a cleaver?"

"Believe me, that was the fun part. After we got the insides sorted out."

"Do we get some?"

"Yeah, I'm cooking the remainder up tonight, the parts that didn't go upstairs. We'll get a couple of bites each." Along with the kitchen staff. "About a half recipe."

"Half a duck is better than none."

"We ought to slaughter the whole flock," I said. They really were a filthy nuisance. "Once we have the formula, we can make chicken-duck anytime we want."

"So much for ecodiversity?" We laughed together. There were people who were superstitious about that. Once you had the genome map, of course, you didn't need actual fucking ducks to create poultry. Life around the pond would be a lot simpler, and cleaner. She took the stopper out of the wine bottle and raised it in toast. "To duckburgers." We each took a sip of it.

There was a chime, and the screen started talking. It switched to a close-up of one of the attitude jets, which emitted a wisp of vapor. It was the final correction. There was a long crunching sound, the two behemoths coming together, which I suppose would be loud inside of *Manus*. For us to hear it, of course, was drama trumping physics.

The welders started working their way around the ship's circumference, stopping at marks to touch their wands to the surface for a momentary bright flare.

"So you're going over there?"

"Be there at 1700," she said. "Leave me enough for a sandwich?"

"Sure. Why did they decide they need you?"

"They didn't. It's Brandon's idea, redundancy as usual. Place is going to be really overpopulated."

"Think you'll be back tonight?"

"If nothing goes wrong and the shuttle's not too crowded. I just have to flush the toilets and be on my way, but there'll be plenty of people with even less to do. Lined up at the airlock." She flipped open her calendar. "You have rehearsal till?"

"Won't be past ten. I think everybody's got to work tomorrow."

"Don't wait up." She touched my shoulder and stood. "Or do, and we can have the duck together."

"Midnight quack."

"Idiot." She kissed my forehead and left.

I watched the welding for a little while and then wandered back home. Tuned the guitar down two whole tones and tried a couple of passages of tonight's Monk composition that way, tighter, no open chords, but it didn't give me what I wanted, so I tuned it back up.

(What I *wanted* for the Monk was the 1930 Gibson F-hole I'd had to leave back on Earth. But you start thinking that way and you might never stop wanting.)

Restless, I went down to the kitchen early and put the

duck pieces, with some orange slices, into the small oven to roast slowly. Sandra was there, and we had a cup of tea, talking about her main job, which was liaison and observer for an Earthside sociology project that pretended it wasn't waiting for us to do something catastrophic.

Zach came down at 1730, and we started. He did the salad while Sandra and I tended to the main course. The camera showed twenty-two customers when we turned on the frying pans. Onions, potatoes, garlic, and wait.

It was simpler than a restaurant on Earth. Everybody got the same dish, and they brought their own wine or fuel, or poured water or tea or coffee from the common table.

There's nothing especially complicated about a Spanish tortilla, basically just a firm omelette made with potatoes, but doing any dish sixty times is a logistic challenge. We could make sixteen servings at once, in the four frying pans. I stacked the first batch on a big platter and kept them warm in the large oven, starting the second batch while Zach served salad.

It timed out pretty well. We had thirty people in the 1800 seating, and the rest at 1900. Meanwhile, the duck smelled marvelous. I just drained the fat off (saving it for the French chef) and, for the last few minutes, took off the orange slices, brushed it with honey, and let it brown under high heat. Saved enough for two small sandwiches and served the rest to Zach and Sandra, who were ecstatic. There was no shortage of variety in our diets, thanks to the protein sequencer, but an *actual* new kind of food was almost unheard of.

(I'd talked to Maxine Chu, the French chef, and she was enthusiastic about doing duck now that she didn't actually have to slaughter one. She would do *confit de canard* one day and a cassoulet the next.)

I put our duck in the cooler at home, collected guitar and music, and got to the practice room while the others were still tuning up.

It was a pretty good session, but I was just as glad I didn't have any big parts; mostly following charts for rhythm, trading off a simple fast melody with the oboe in a Fulford matrix. We ran through everything on next week's playsheet at least once, and I was happy to quit a little before 2300.

I opened the door to soft music and a porn playing on the wall, Kate sitting in a lotus on the couch, nude. "Duck?" she said, "Or what?"

It was what first and duck later.

TWELVE

QUESTIONS

A black couch in a beige room, two little cameras and one big one. A big floating screen showed the activity inside and outside *Ars* while they maneuvered into the welding phase. Tomorrow *Mentos*, then *Sanitas*, and us on Monday. I had a feeling of foreboding, unjustified.

When the interviewer came in, I left a cup of cold coffee by the couch and sat with him in front of the big camera.

The studio was tuned to look like a picnic table in the woods, New England fall foliage. It was funny to look into the monitor and see that, seated on a hard metal chair with my bare elbows on a cold metal table.

"I guess we have to start with a couple of obvious questions," the interviewer said. It was Sky Golding, a sociologist I'd known since Earth. He was a stocky white intense man with his head shaved. "First, have you found anything specific that implicates the time machine in the death?"

"Well, we're not ready to say it was just a coincidence

that Alyx died in the machine." One of the small cameras slid closer, as if curious. "It does put stresses on the body and mind that don't occur in nature. But the basic mechanisms haven't changed in over a century, and the time machine is historically one of the safest ways possible to waste your time—safer than bicycling; safer than *walking*."

"But people did die in the machine before the war."

"Well, of course. You spend twenty hours a week doing anything, and your chance of dying during that twenty hours is what, one in 8.4? That doesn't make it intrinsically dangerous.

"I don't want to play devil's advocate here. Anybody who wants to put off using the time machine until we can say for sure that it's safe . . . I'd call that sensible. I recommend it."

"Yet you're not in favor of closing it down."

"No . . . well, yes and no. It's closed now, for a couple of days. We're in the process of modifying the machine so that it will look for vital signs changing in such a way that might precede a stroke or heart attack, and immediately end the session. Alyx probably had a blood-pressure spike before her stroke. If we had pulled her out then, who knows?

"*Sanitas* is supplying a round-the-clock medic for the time machine, just in case. We've suspended operations until the system's in place and tested."

"But you used the machine yourself without the failsafes and medic in place."

"Day before yesterday, and will again tomorrow. I suppose it's a matter of faith, or statistics. I've probably used the machine two thousand times. Hasn't killed me yet."

"The other thing is Alyx's age."

"Of course. She was one of the originals, and an old one;

older than my mother. But about a third of us aboard are originals, and as you know, we're all getting complete physical checkups. So far, nothing odd."

"Maybe Earth will have some insight?"

"We should know something in about ten days. They've been sent all the autopsy data and the records of two of us who were observers during the session."

"You met with the TMs from Earth." Telepresence modules. "Did they offer any insight?"

"Not really. They don't have anything unique; we have all the relevant data here. The next time they're upgraded, Earth still won't know about Alyx. The week after that, it might be interesting. Or not."

He smiled. "You don't like them."

"What's to like or not like about a data package? I don't think it's especially efficient to give them dramatic personalities."

"Yeah. I don't like them either. So when will the time machine be open again?"

"Well . . . at bottom, it's a rights issue. 'Pursuit of happiness.' We'd rather nobody use the machine until we have an opinion from Earth, and we told that to everybody with appointments. Some are willing to take the risk rather than lose their place in line. A lot of people want to talk to me or another virtuality expert before they confirm or cancel."

"Sounds like an organizational headache."

"In spades, they used to say. Card suits, not shovels. Our schedule's locked a year in advance. We do have the fifth space, the extra space, in the machine, and normally we could shuffle people into that and take up the slack. But the staff needs that space to monitor what's going on, now more than ever."

He nodded. "And the timing is lousy, with Spindown coming up."

"Well, we're all coping with that. It's been on our calendars since Earth."

"Thank you, Jacob." He looked into a camera. "Anyone who wants to talk about the time-machine situation is welcome to click in tonight at 2100, when Jacob and an assistant and the TMs from Earth will be here. Signing off for now."

He smiled at the camera until the red light went off, and then got up and sank back into the couch. "You're not telling everything."

"Everything factual," I said, and that was the truth.

"You have misgivings about letting people back into the machine."

"Yeah, on two levels. The official one, waiting for Earth. And then something I can't articulate. Something creepy."

"Is that a technical term in virtuality engineering? Creepy as opposed to what?"

"As I say . . . if there was a word for it, I'd use it." A tech came in to roll the big camera away, and I continued after she left. "Bruce Carroll feels it, too. He and I have been each other's templates forever; he's also a VE.

"Do you know about the smell thing? The New York City background smell?"

He shook his head. "I don't follow time-machine stuff very closely."

"Well, we haven't said much about it. We interview clients after they've been there, to New York, and would just as soon they not know beforehand exactly what we're looking for." I explained the situation to him briefly, the missing olfactory substrate.

"Sounds like a wiring thing," he said. "I don't know much about how the machine works, but there has to be a bunch of background data somewhere that's not getting transferred to the client."

"I wish it were that simple. It's not really a data transfer, not in the sense of moving information from one place to another. The machine induces a subjective state into the client's mind and body. It's more feedback than transfer, though. The machine takes a kind of baseline of what you see and hear, feel and smell, when you start out there in the dark—when you first slide into the machine, almost unconscious. It's different for everybody.

"And then it modifies the baseline sensorium, slowly at first, and then faster as the template illusion accretes. Once the client's actually aware of the template, the machine's querying the brain a thousand times a second, and modifying sense impressions so fast that it seems like a continuum."

"But to the machine, it's not a continuum?" Sky said.

"Not at all. A constant round of measurement, evaluation, and feedback. But that's like saying a computer just adds ones and zeros—true, but too reductive to be really useful. The actual process is so complex and volatile that we can't describe, or really understand, the totality of it."

"Kind of sloppy, for engineering."

"It is," I agreed. "It's more like a life science. You can describe every molecule of the physics and chemistry of a cell, and, in theory, detail how you sort and connect a billion cells so that they can walk and talk together . . . but you won't have described life."

"So maybe you should be talking to biologists rather than engineers."

Kate tapped on the open door and walked in. "That was all right," she said. "Buy you a drink?" She'd just picked up our weekly ration of wine and fuel.

"Nothing for me, thanks," Sky said, and pointed at a cooler. "Ice if you want it."

"You can owe me one," I said. Drinking protocols are complex in our rationed world.

"Well, okay. Being on camera makes me thirsty." Kate assembled ice and three glasses and poured drinks.

"You're with Jacob on this business?" Sky asked.

She shook her head. "It's the closest we've come to having an actual . . . argument."

"Kate—"

"The thing should be shut down."

"It is shut down."

"Only for a few days." She turned to Sky. "No one should use the time machine until we know it's safe. Until we know that something else caused the woman's death."

"Proving the nonexistence of a cause," I started, "doesn't—"

She clinked her glass against mine, a little forcefully. "Cheers, darling. You know you retreat into formalism like an animal backing into his cave."

"I should have the camera on," Sky said.

"No," she said. "Then I'd shut up. Clam up." She smiled. "Shut my trap, my pie hole."

"You have to admit the time machine does wonders for your vocabulary."

"It does wonders, period. A good reason to be cautious about it. Does anyone deny that it's a culturewide addiction?"

"With me the main pusher."

"I don't know," Sky said. "Something you only do a few times a year is an addiction?"

"I don't mean an addiction in the physiological sense. But we *are* dependent on it. And Jacob is finding out how reluctant people have been to put off their next fix."

"Fix?" Sky said.

"Exposure to a drug," I said. "Only about 6 percent have canceled since I sent out the warning."

"Including me," Sky said. "But I was scheduled in a few weeks, and that seemed too soon. Let other people be the guinea pigs."

"Like my husband."

"All the staff are going in as observers, to map out the extent of this olfactory substrate problem. Moving forward a year at a time until New York smells right again."

"You just have a thing for the 1940s," she said.

"Oh, I have a thing for almost every decade. I guess you could keep the eighties."

"Come on—you like being a hero. All that GI Joe crap. The Last Good War, as if there ever had been a good one."

"You've never tried it."

"No, I've never tried anything male. That would be too much weirdness at once."

I just nodded. I knew she'd been male at least once, involuntarily, during Wild Year. She'd let it slip, but never elaborated on the experience. (I don't switch genders myself unless it's necessary for observer mode. The novelty is interesting the first time, but after that it's just clumsy, your brain's circuitry not matching your imaginary body.)

"You're going back to World War II?" Sky asked.

"Well, I'm scheduled for 1943. But I'm mainly going to New York City to sniff around. We've found the olfactory baseline is normal back to '46. Other people are checking '45 and '44. If those are normal, too, I'll dive into 1943 tonight."

"Keep your powder dry," Kate said.

"Don't think I'll be wearing any, even in the Stork Club. Men didn't, in the Twentieth."

1943

I was in a starched and pressed army uniform, razor creases, first lieutenant with a Fourth Division patch and two overseas hash marks. The doorman nodded with a genuine smile as I entered the club. I left my coat and hat with the hatcheck girl. The famous solid-gold chain was not in evidence this early in the evening.

It was crowded enough, though, for the air to be blue with smoke, and there was muffled rhumba music in a back room that was loud for an opened-door second. Men with cigars talking on old-style black phones that had been brought to their tables. They looked like they expected to be recognized.

I looked around for an actual famous person. Walter Winchell was ensconced at his throne, table 50, surrounded by acolytes and hangers-on. Damon Runyon sat at a corner table with Dorothy Kilgallen and two others. I wondered how complete their illusory characterizations were. Hemingway was nowhere to be seen; I might have been tempted to try him out. I wouldn't know a totally fake Runyon or Kilgallen from a good one, but I'd encountered Hemingway in other years, and somebody had done him in real depth.

Conversation was loud and cheerful. Crystal chandeliers glittered, silk and satin everywhere. Beautiful young women in svelte and sexy outfits—many of them no doubt "jellybeans," college students whose tabs were paid in exchange for improving the scenery.

The Stork Club was only one of twelve hundred nightclubs in New York City, if the most sought after, and hundreds of hotels were expanding bars to provide competition. In 1943 there was plenty of "mad money" from military pay and defense-plant salaries, and gas rationing left people pretty much stuck in the big city. The scourge of television hadn't yet opened its baleful eye, so armies of young and not-young-but-thirsty trooped out every night to jaw with their friends and get a little tight.

A pretty cigarette girl walked up, and asked, "What'll it be, Loot?"

"Gimme a herd, sis." She handed over a packet of Camels, good programming, and gave me a brilliant smile and little salute but no change for my quarter.

I scanned the place for Bruce and saw him sitting at the long bar. The owner, Sherman Billingsley, was a couple of seats away, staring into the seventy-foot mirror, I supposed counting the house.

Bruce was in an army uniform, too, and outranked me. I came up behind him and tapped his captain's bars. "Nice railroad tracks, Bruce."

"No less than I deserve." He clapped me on the shoulder, and I sat down next to him. A bartender appeared immediately and I asked for a Beefeater Gibson.

"Been outside yet?"

He shook his head. "Thought I'd get a drink first, dig the joint." When we were calibrating, he mentioned he'd never done the Stork Club before. I'd been here in '49 and '52.

I tipped my head toward Billingsley's reflection. "That's the big cheese, Sherman Billingsley. You catch Winchell?"

"Hard to miss." He looked around appreciatively. "Good job. Solid." Rubbing the oak bartop with his thumb.

My drink came. "Here's looking at you, kid." *Casablanca* was just opening.

"Cheers." We clinked glasses and drank. The gin, onion, vinegar, and cold seemed perfectly authentic. I wondered if I'd ever again taste one in the real world—odd for a thought like that to intrude.

Bruce must have been thinking sideways, too, or maybe his virtual Manhattan was affecting him. "What if you could stay here forever?" He patted his pocket. "Never push the button."

"Well, you wouldn't get bored. You'd starve to death or dehydrate first. Back in the machine. Wonder what *that* would feel like."

He dismissed that with an airy wave. "Just pretend." He selected a cigarette from a silver case and lit it with slow pleasure. "Wave a magic technical wand. Would people actually want to escape to the past and stay?"

"Some would, of course. Some people will do anything. I'd rather just visit every now and then." I tore open my Camels, picked one out, and used his lighter. "Hell, if you stayed too long, you'd get addicted to smoking."

"Used to was."

"Yeah, I smoked a lot on Earth, too." The guy next to me got up slowly and took his drink away. "*Perth,* I mean. Perth," I said sotto voce.

"It killed both my grandparents." He looked at his cigarette and blew on its tip.

I nodded. "The Becker-Cendrek Process was a boon to all sorts of unhealthy practices."

"They wouldn't outlaw it. Even in my parents' time, before immortality. Un-American to deprive addicts of freedom of choice."

I saw where he was headed, and lowered my voice. "There's no comparison with our situation. One death, not necessarily related."

"I know, I know."

"Smoking was *bound* to kill you if you didn't die of something else."

"Maybe the time machine does, too." He stared at his reflection in the bar mirror. "It just takes longer."

"You've been talking to Kate. What, did she promise elaborate sexual favors if you could win me over to her side?"

"No. Nothing elaborate." He put his cigarette out in the heavy glass ashtray and smiled. "Shall we go sniff the sidewalk? While we still have a vestige of olfactory sensitivity remaining?"

He knew as well as I did that the virtual smoke wouldn't have any effect on that. "Sure." I knocked back the rest of my Gibson and kept my cigarette while I fished out a five-dollar bill and dropped it on the bar.

We got off the stools to leave, but the bartender drifted over and pushed the five-dollar bill back. "Sirs, your money isn't any good here." That set off a little anomaly alarm, but then he said, "Good luck. Wish I could be with you. Bum back."

The hatcheck girl gave me a broad grin when I palmed her a dollar. There was a slot in the counter for tips, but the girls never saw any of it.

Loud dinnertime traffic, more cabs than cars. A bitter cold wind cut down Third Avenue. I stuffed my hands in my pockets and headed up Fifty-third.

I took a deep breath of the frigid air. "Smells like snow."

"Nothing else, though."

There would be less exhaust in the air because of rationing, and you'd expect the sewage component to be small because of the cold. But he was right; the baseline just wasn't there. "So where to? Someplace warm."

We stopped at a kiosk, and Bruce tossed down a nickel and picked up a *Times*. The headline said "Grim Tarawa Defense a Surprise, Eyewitness of Battle Reveals; Marines Went in Chuckling, to Find Swift Death Instead of Easy Conquest."

"Think I'll go there," I said.

"God, you're a glutton for punishment." He pulled out the second section. "New Orleans for me. Nobody shooting at you."

I started to say, Well, I researched it . . . but Bruce vanished before I could open my mouth. The boy behind the counter didn't seem to notice.

I was suddenly warm and wet and dizzy, crowded in a small landing craft with three dozen other souls.

Tarawa would be the worst fight in the Marine Corps' history, in terms of casualties and ferocity, and it would hold that distinction for almost a hundred years, until the Riyadh Massacre in 2039.

This was a Higgins boat, a wooden box with steel armor screwed on. Eisenhower would later say they'd saved the day in Europe, the D-day landing, but Normandy wasn't

Tarawa. The boat's four-and-a-half-foot draft didn't quite clear the reefs at low tide. The first three waves of Marines had gone in with amtracs, whose tractor wheels just ground their way up and over the coral reef. They'd had it hard enough, with withering machine-gun fire and pin-point light artillery. The Marines in Higgins boats would hang up on the reef and have to jump in and wade eight hundred yards through the same kind of resistance. About half would die before they got to the beach.

That was what I could look forward to. But first there was the wait.

The craft had all the seaworthiness of a shoebox. It pitched and yawed with sickening randomness, and had been doing it for hours. Most of the men were so seasick they would charge a point-blank machine-gun nest, if that's what it would take to get off the goddamned boat. Even with the strong wind that whipped over us, the smell of vomit and diarrhea was so pervasive that men would stick their heads up over the boat's protective walls, into the whine and whistle of enemy fire, just for a moment of fresh air.

The front door was thick steel plate, which clanged periodically when random or ricochet bullets hit it. We were still in deep water, far enough from land to be out of practical range. When we moved in, that would become a danger. Several amtracs and Higgens boats were blown apart by what passed for mortars—light artillery and heavy grenade launchers—with all hands lost.

I touched the black box in my pocket, and was almost uncomfortable enough to press the button. But I did want to play this one out.

"Fucking shit," a man near me said. "Another five minutes and I'm gonna jump overboard and swim for it."

"Don't forget your goddamned rifle," said the guy next to him. "I ain't gonna fuckin' carry it in for you."

The engine, which had been muttering in the background, suddenly coughed and started to roar. The coxswain peeked out from behind his steel-plate shield and yelled, "Hold on to your hats! We're goin' in!"

I took a magazine out of my utility belt, blew on it, and started to fit it into the M-1's receiver.

A sergeant clamped my arm. "Hold it, troop. Orders. Not until we're almost there."

"Right. Forgot." He couldn't know we were about to hang up on the reef.

A couple of minutes later there was a loud crunch, and everyone lurched forward in a pile. The coxswain reversed for a second, then rammed into the reef again.

A mortar round hit a few yards to our right. "Shit!" he yelled, and the front door splashed down. "Go! Go! Go!"

The man next to me stood up and fell down, a small bullet hole between his eyes and his brains sprayed out over two or three people behind him. A man to my left was hit and doubled over, screaming, clutching his elbow. We hustled out the half-submerged door and jumped in, holding rifles high.

The water was almost up to my chin, warm as piss. Away from the boat's engine, the main sound was bullets, whishing and humming and clanging against the metal.

We moved as fast as we could, which was a slow slog, weighed down with a combat pack and bandoliers of ammunition that would probably be too wet to do any good. There were screams and sighs as people were hit, and some were probably short enough to have drowned as soon as they jumped in the water.

Sharp pain as a bullet nicked my earlobe. Another mortar round exploded behind me. I didn't look back to see whether it had hit the boat. Just tried to lengthen my stride, get to the beach.

The water was full of floating corpses, presumably all American. I supposed they had been killed in the earlier waves and floated up, relieved of their ballast. Plus the buoyant effect from gases of decomposition.

I should have been totally calm, knowing that this was all just a simulation, nobody was really being hurt, but it was too realistic for objectivity. And I couldn't ignore the memory of Alyx. If one person could die in a simulation, another could.

This morning, the Japanese had written their wills, burned their regimental colors, and saluted one another with a cup of ceremonial wine: it was a good place to die. Not for me, thank you.

Of course, the closer you were to the shore, the bigger a target you presented. Men were hunkered down in the water, duck-walking in. One pushed a floating body in front of himself as a shield. So the choice was to scrunch down and be a smaller target for a longer time, or to stand up and move fast. I chose the latter. There was smoke swirling around everywhere, and I figured that if I couldn't see the Japs, they couldn't see me.

I did get hit twice more. One bullet hit my helmet obliquely; it felt and sounded like being hit with a baseball bat, but it didn't penetrate the steel. Another bullet took off the tip of my right ring finger. I hadn't felt it; only saw it when I checked the rifle's safety. Then it hurt.

The enemy had been preoccupied with two of the amtracs that had preceded us, off to the left. When the water was down to knee deep, and we could actually see the

beach through the smoke, they started to pay more attention to us, machine-gun fire doubling and redoubling.

Having studied the battle, I knew that the Japanese were
taking advantage of a window of opportunity afforded by
American bad timing: air support from Navy planes had
come in too early, going by the clock rather than following
the actual ground situation, and naval bombardment had
stopped early as well—there was so much smoke and dust,
the naval gunners weren't sure how close to the beach the
Marines were, and Admiral "Handsome Harry" Hill had
called for a cease-fire. Thus the Japanese were able to re-
distribute men and ordnance so that they could bring heav-
iest fire to bear on beachheads where they could see the
Americans were approaching.

Something big went off behind me, the concussion driving me facefirst into the sand. I low-crawled through the
surf, butt and shoulders stinging with small shrapnel
wounds.

On the beach, the dead outnumbered the living. Some
were left half-buried in the sand as the tide retreated. A few
had been dead long enough for rigor mortis to stiffen them.
Most were fresh, blood soaking into the sand.

The beachhead was only about twenty-five feet wide,
ending in a revetment of logs about a yard high. Marines
were firing and ducking, firing and ducking. While I
watched, one man threw down his M-1 carbine and ran
back toward me to pull a replacement out of the sand, stuck
underneath a corpse. I followed him back to the seawall
and crouched beside him.

"Machine-gun nest about thirty yards up there. You got
grenades?"

"Yeah." I doubted I could throw one that far. Technically, it had a range of thirty meters and also a radius of destruction of twenty to thirty meters, favoring men with a good throwing arm.

I took one off my belt, worked out the cotter pin, then got up out of my crouch prepared to loft it as hard as I could.

After a half second of not being able to locate my target, I just threw it straight out. The target found me, though. A bullet hit the side of my neck with a sharp shock. I went down clutching it.

"Oh, shit." The grenade exploded, not too far away.

"Here." The other man pulled my first-aid kit off the back of my pack and gently pried my hand from my neck. "Not the artery. Not too bad. Hold this." I held the large gauze bandage in place while he tied its strings around my neck twice.

Two other men from my Higgins boat ran up and dove down to join us, just getting under a long burst from the machine-gun emplacement. "Jesus!" one said. "Are we all gonna die here?"

Only one out of three, I didn't tell him. Most of them today.

The neck wound was so painful I could hardly think, and when I tried to speak, I gagged and coughed blood. It was about enough fun for one day. I reached in my pocket for the black box.

It wasn't there.

The second of the men who had just joined us rolled over on his side and looked at me. "Looking for something?" he said quietly.

He was my exact twin.

He reached into his pocket and pulled out the black box. He nodded in the direction of the machine-gun nest.

"I could throw it out there. What do you think would happen?"

"What?"

"I don't know. You might actually die." He tossed the black box to me; it felt solid and real. "We have to talk," he said.

I looked at the box. "What . . . what do you . . . who are you?" When I looked up, he was gone.

Two Japanese soldiers leaped over the seawall with bayoneted rifles. One lunged toward me and I pushed the button.

A MEMORY

The war was not even being called a war when Jake's fa-
ther died. It was a civil disturbance, which in a few days
would graduate to "civil disturbance being controlled by
the military." Then the military would split, and it would
become a civil war.

His father, a surgeon, had volunteered for Emergency
Room work at Mercy Hospital. There was no record at
Mercy of his being an immortal, and he didn't talk about
it. Of course poor people didn't drive Jaguars, and all rich
people were suspect. He quit work to go home for the
night, but evidently didn't make it past the car door. They
later found a small smear of blood on the outside of the
driver's window.

Jake and his mother stayed glued to the news and never
saw the person who left a data cube on their doorstep. It
was Jake who found it, unfortunately, while his mother was
sleeping. He put it in the tray and watched his father, naked

and bleeding, tied to a post, drenched with solvent, and set afire. He only screamed once, and then the sound was just flames and laughter.

At ten, Jake considered himself a sophisticated consumer of special effects, and he knew the thing was faked, a morbid joke. He was studying it the third or fourth time when his mother came down and fainted dead away.

When she came to again, he tried to explain how it couldn't be real; no one would want to do that. She gave him a cardboard box and told him to go upstairs and fill it with clothes. Then get another box for winter clothes. Take them to the station wagon and then come help Mother empty out the pantry.

Going up the stairs, he heard her breaking the glass on his father's gun case. That's when he started to cry.

THIRTEEN

DOPPELGÄNGERS

Bruce had also met himself, in New Orleans, and his double had also handed him the black box, and said "We have to talk." Then jumped off the Canal Street trolley and disappeared in a crowd of revelers.

"If he had to talk," I said, "why didn't he just talk then and there?"

"I don't know. We were just riding the trolley; we didn't have half the Japanese army trying to kill us. He could have talked all night."

We'd called a meeting of the senior VR staff, at a picnic table down by the duck pond. The time-machine referendum would be after dinner. They'd just finished Spindown for *Sanitas*, a little complicated by having four bedridden patients. But there hadn't been any big problems, and now they were spinning back up to speed, and nothing was being projected on the park screen. There hadn't been any problems with *Mentos*, either.

I was still worried about our Spindown, partly because I'm a worrier on principle, and partly because of the goddamn ducks. Edison, not as bright as his namesake, was having us chase all the ducks out of the water and cover the pool with plastic, to keep the water in place during zero gee. The ducks would just go off in a corner and play Canasta until we spun back up again.

"It's crazy," Rebecca said, throwing bits of bread to the creatures. "The black box is a real object. How could a VR construct have control of it?"

"Just a feedback thing," I said. "The boxes never really left our pockets. We just felt like they had."

"Seemed absolutely real," Bruce said. "Never happened before, in observer mode."

"Me, neither," I had to admit. "The machine's learned a new trick."

"And it wants to talk to you. Or us," Lowell said.

Bruce nodded slowly. "We're simplifying, as if the doubles were some manifestation of the machine. But there's no such thing as 'the machine,' actually. It's hundreds of different systems."

"Coordinated by a macroprogram, though," Rebecca said.

"Which is not the same as an identity," I said. I'd been working in VR for a couple of hundred years, after all. If any machine had an identity, it was one we put there for our own convenience or amusement, an interface. There was no such thing in the no-frills time machine.

"What it sounds like to me is a diagnostic," she said. "Something's out of order, and this is the machine's way of calling our attention to it."

"Too anthropomorphic. I mean, we could *program* it to present diagnostics that way, but we didn't. It's not going to invent some personality on its own." Even as I said that, I knew what her response would be.

"Why don't we just act as if it had? Go back in and look for your doubles?"

"Not on Tarawa. Once was enough."

"Wild Year," Bruce said. "In Wild Year, it does invent, even if it's just random numbers manifesting themselves."

"Sure. That's always interesting." I pointed behind him. "Company coming."

I'd left a message for Coordinator Edison Doyle about our meeting, not really expecting him to come, since his Friday was totally booked. But he had an interest in virtuality, as well as advanced degrees in Artificial Intelligence.

In fact, he'd brought an AI along with him, the redoubtable Walter Cronkite.

"Have a seat, Ed." Do you offer a chair to a telepresence? "Your machine said you'd be busy."

"Yeah; I rescheduled. Cronkite here came up with something you ought to know."

That was curious. "I thought you were updated on Mondays."

"I am. This isn't new data. It's information I wasn't to reveal to you yet, because it's not generally known on Earth. But you should have it."

That was more than interesting; a telepresence module taking that initiative. "Fire away."

He seemed to take a deep breath. "People on Earth are dying, too. About half of them in virtual-reality situations."

I'm not often struck dumb. But it took me a moment to ask, "How many?"

"Nine hundred and twenty, as of my last update. Of those, 410 were in virtual reality, mostly time machines."

"Why . . . why haven't they told us?" Rebecca said.

"I don't know. I suppose to keep it secret on Earth, since you're in contact with friends and relatives. Perhaps they looked on you as a control group, isolated from environmental factors there."

"Hell of a lot of people," Edison said.

"Only one out of a million," Bruce pointed out. "We've lost one out of eight hundred."

"I took this initiative," Cronkite said, "because I thought the information might be relevant to your planning right now—whether or not to keep the time machine running. I would appreciate it if you didn't let Earth know that I told you."

"What could they do to you?" Edison asked. "Unplug you?"

"They could limit my access to information and do it without telling me, or even give me false information. I suspect that would be uncomfortable; things wouldn't add up, as you say."

Redundancy checks would fail. "We won't say anything. Thank you," I said, feeling odd.

The wise gray head nodded. "I don't have much specific information, except that no one in the second generation or younger has died. Only people who were once mortal."

Like Alyx. Like me. Though technically she was a half century older. "Do the oldest die first?"

"I don't know. Very little has been said. The number of deaths is not yet common knowledge.

"The news of Alyx Kaplan's death went out almost six days ago. Earth will have it soon. Their response, then, should come in a week or so."

"You should shut down the machine at least until then," Edison said. "The Alyx investigation is enough of an excuse."

"I suppose. People should have all of the information before they decide."

"You still want to do the Wild Year thing?" Bruce asked.

"Oh, yeah. You don't have to. But if the machine wants to talk, I'd better go listen."

"What's the 'Wild Year thing'?" Edison asked. We explained it to him. "I don't know that I'd do it. It's so Alice in Wonderland."

"And Alyx in Slumberland," Bruce said. "Do we go down the rabbit hole?"

"You don't have to," I repeated.

"I wish I could go," Cronkite said. "A new world of information. And I can't die."

You can't lie, either, I thought. *Except by omission.*

"I don't want to be out of line here," Lowell said, "but one of you is enough. We shouldn't risk 40 percent of our crew on this thing."

"Then it should be me," Bruce said.

"No way."

He turned to face Edison and Cronkite. "I'm second generation. Jacob is first, and at more risk."

"I'm first, all right, as in 'first in command.' I vote that I go, and nobody else has a vote."

"I could urge you not to go," Edison said mildly. A coordinator's urging had some force.

"And we'd wind up wasting time with a review board. This may be urgent—and Bruce, sorry, but you don't know nearly as much about the machine as I do; neither does anybody else aboard."

"It could be a trap," Edison said.

"Nonsense, Ed. If the machine had the ability and, somehow, the desire to kill us, it would have done it then."

Cronkite nodded. "It wouldn't want to risk being turned

off and never turned on again. That would be my greatest fear, in its position. It's you humans who have the power of life or death. Not the machine."

A machine being anthropomorphic about another machine. We really ought to introduce them.

"So how are we going to handle the vote tonight?" Rebecca asked. "Everybody knows it's going to pass."

The number of cancellations had risen only to 8 percent. So, really, the referendum was just a formality. "Well, we don't have to tell them about the deaths on Earth. We just say there are continuing deep anomalies, and the machine stays shut down to outsiders until we can fix it. Sorry for the inconvenience; we'll reschedule you."

"We can even be specific about our meeting ourselves," Bruce said. "That's weirder and more obviously dangerous than the olfactory substrate going missing."

I had planned to keep it secret, but Bruce was right. "We can ask if anybody else has ever encountered themselves in the past. If they feel involved in the process, they'll be less resentful at the delay."

There was a murmur of assent. "So when do you want to do Wild Year?" Lowell said.

I did some mental arithmetic. "The results come in by 2130 or so. I'll go down and wait in the studio and make a statement then. Then a good night's sleep. So we can schedule prep for ten in the morning."

"You don't have to rush it," Rebecca said.

"Yes, he does," Bruce said. "He can't wait."

I laughed. "He's right. But I've got the public relations bullshit first. And I want to talk to Kate about it before I go."

"She'll be thrilled," he said. Not the word I would have chosen.

* * *

We went to dinner early because of the referendum. It had been some computer-generated mystery–meat loaf, and it sat in my stomach like a stone. I was not accustomed to lying to Kate, even by omission.

We walked back the long way, through the ag level. Orange and lemon and lime trees were in bloom, and it smelled like the orchards around Chimbarazo.

"You're probably in more danger than anyone else could be. The machine knows you inside and out. If it decided to hurt someone, it would be you."

"Well, if you want to give the thing human emotions, if it wanted to *tell* somebody something, it would be me—or Bruce or Rebecca or Lowell. It did say 'We have to talk.' "

"I don't see why you have to rush into it." She brushed a bee away from her face. "You could at least wait until you hear from Earth. It's only a week."

I didn't tell her we *had* heard from Earth. If she knew that hundreds had died in VR there, she would be even more adamant.

If she finds out I did know, and went ahead with it, she'll be furious. Burn that bridge when I come to it.

"You know, you're not the most introspective man in the world. Have you thought at all about why you're going ahead with it when any sensible person would wait?"

A valid point. "Okay. All of us aboard are risk-takers, some more than others. I guess at some level I'm weighing the risk against the possibility that when we hear from Earth, what we'll hear is an order to shut the thing down. And then I'd never know."

"That's fine logic. 'If A is fatal, then B will foretell it. So I'll do A before B stops me.' I suppose you can call that risk-taking."

"You're being too dramatic." There was a bench under a flowering mango. I sat down and patted the place next to me.

She sat down stiffly, her hands bunched between her knees. "What you're supposed to say is 'Darling, if it means that much to you, I'll—' "

"Come on, no. Don't do that."

"Don't express my concern for your welfare."

I tried to choose my words carefully. "It's a multivariant problem—when or whether to go into the machine and try to communicate—and I really think nobody is better qualified than me to assess all the variables and make a decision. There's a lot more to it than Earth's secondhand assessment of the autopsy data.

"Part of it is not quantifiable; it's the force and urgency of the request." I checked my wrist. "We're thirty hours from Spindown, when everything may go haywire. I should be in and out with plenty of time to batten down the hatches."

She stared at me. "You could argue that that's a good reason to put it off. You're in charge of the whole time-machine enterprise, and you're making yourself unavailable until, what? Six hours before Spindown?"

"Eight, at most. And I can cut the session short at any time."

"Not if the machine decides to hold on to the black box."

"That wasn't physically real. It was just part of the illusion—convincing, I'll admit. But if I'd pushed where the button was supposed to be, it would've ended the session."

"You know that, even though it's never happened before."

"Everything in there is an illusion. In observer mode, you're aware of it."

"I wonder what *illusion* Alyx saw just before she died." She got up. "Maybe she met herself." She looked at me angrily. "Is that something you've been trying not to think about?"

"I've considered the possibility, but—"

"Sometimes I just don't understand you! You treat the thing like a thrill ride." She turned up the path. "Think about it some more. I'll see you later."

I did think about it, sitting there in the perfume, insect hum louder than the ever-present support machinery.

Fair enough to say I treat the time machine as a thrill ride. Knowing that it's all illusion, given the choice between going to a high-school prom in 1968 or a helicopter assault in the jungle, I'd rather test myself against the artificial danger.

Having done it thousands of times has no doubt changed my personality. We are all risk-takers, as I said, to sign up for this problematic enterprise in the first place. And maybe I'm the worst of all.

The prospect of facing actual danger *was* exciting. The possibility of death held no actual terror for me, or at least so I told myself. We didn't dwell on it, but the probability of all of us dying, by whatever catastrophic mechanism, was probably at least as great as the probability of establishing a viable colony on Beta Hydrii.

Besides, I'd lived more than twice as long as anyone in the old days, a full and rewarding life, and the gulf of nothingness on the other side of death was no more fearsome than the 14 billion invisible years that preceded my birth.

Kate was right, though; introspection was not my strong suit. I did have a tendency to follow my feelings and then pick up the pieces afterward.

I hoped that wasn't happening here.

I went up to the apartment before going to the studio, and Kate wasn't there. No note.

Two letters from Earth. One was from Jay Bee, the telepresence expert, twelve pages long. I tabled it.

The other was from my mother, just a few lines.

A friend of hers had died, of a heart attack. She was frightened.

FOURTEEN

CALLS

I didn't say anything about the letter to anyone; in fact, I went to the theater and avoided contact with
anyone for long enough to see the first half of Matsura's
holo satire of NeoKenja romance, *Heart of Water*, which
was about as bad as I expected. It wasn't difficult to leave
and go next door to the studio.

Two chairs behind a table with a water pitcher and two
glasses; the tally projected on the wall behind. When I
walked in, it was 620 to 60, and changed to 621 as I looked.

"I can hardly contain my excitement," Sky Golding said
from a corner. His voice was muffled, his head inside an
editing box.

He stood up and touched my hand. "I've given us ten minutes at the hour. We're flexible, though, if you need more."

"I think ninety seconds would do it. Unless some screw-
ball calls in."

"We can always hope."

I sat down and took the phone off my belt and touched 2. Bruce appeared immediately. "What's up, Jake? We lose the referendum?"

"Well, it's a cliff-hanger. Look . . . I talked to Kate, and she brought up the worry that we were cutting it too close on this Wild Year thing. I mean with respect to the Spin-down schedule."

"So you want to postpone it?"

"Actually, I—"

"Just kidding. You want to move it up."

"If you're not too tired to monitor."

"No. Might take a pill." His face on the screen was too small to read. "I thought she'd try to talk you out of it."

"Well, she wasn't happy." I checked my wrist, unnecessarily. "Meet you down there at 2130?"

"Sure. Break a leg."

I put the phone back. "Break a leg?" Sky said.

"It's an old actors' superstition." Funny that he, of all people aboard, wouldn't know it. "They thought it was bad luck to wish a fellow actor good luck."

"I see. Well, break an arm. We're on in ninety seconds." The count behind us was 643 to 70, interesting. A lot of people voting at the last minute. Even though if everyone not accounted for voted "nay," it wouldn't affect the outcome.

He poured two glasses of water. "Ten seconds."

There were five soft chimes. "Good evening. I'm here again with Jacob Brewer, the time-machine guru, to witness the least suspenseful vote in the history of *Aspera*." He looked over his shoulder and made a quick calculation. "With 84 abstaining, or not bothering, we have 644 for and 72 against. So that's 85 percent in favor of continuing the use of the time machine. Are you surprised at that level of support, Jacob?"

"Not at all; we've been running our own informal polls. In fact, the 9 percent against is exactly what we predicted.

"We're still holding off on general use until we hear from Earth on Monday, with their observations about the death of Alyx Kaplan." There wouldn't be anything happening on Saturday, *Mek* Spindown, in any case.

"That brings up a point. How many of the abstentions were from *Ars*?" The numbers behind us faded and were replaced with the message "59 = 70.24%."

"Too busy spinning down to vote."

"Can't blame them," I said.

The phone buzzed. "Caller?"

A woman's face appeared, identified as F'mari Seng from *Mek*. "A question for you, Mr. Brewer. I've heard a rumor that there's a new problem, something that happened to you, yourself, in the machine."

"Oh, there's nothing secret about it. Bruce Carroll and I experienced it simultaneously. We met twins of ourselves in 1943, and they both said 'We have to talk.' Nothing like that has ever happened to him or me before. If you look at tomorrow morning's news, you'll see Bruce asking whether anyone out there has ever had a similar experience."

"You don't consider it . . . ominous?"

"Well, it certainly has to be explained. So I'm going in to see what it means.

"Its use of the pronoun 'we' is interesting. The time machine is an unimaginably complex program with a huge human database, but it's not programmed to mimic self-awareness."

"So it came up with that on its own?"

"It's . . . in a manner of speaking, yes. But it's programmed to manufacture surprises; if it didn't, people would tire of having the same experiences over and over.

But it *is* just programming; it's a mistake to anthropomorphize the process."

The woman smiled. "That's what you guys always say. But as they said in Old Twentieth, 'If it walks like a duck and quacks like a duck—' "

"It's a good imitation of a duck," I said. "In terms of raw data, the program knows more about human nature than a roomful of behavioral scientists. Even though it's not programmed for self-awareness, it generates dozens or hundreds of convincing human personalities every time it's used, and most of its new data comes from feedback from the clients themselves. Bruce and I have to be its two major sources of that kind of data, so it's not surprising that it would use us rather than some random person."

Sky laughed. "Now who's anthropomorphizing?"

"Yeah, it's a kind of shorthand. Existential shorthand, if you want. Comes from working with the thing day in and day out."

The next caller, from *Mentos*, was visibly angry, which is rare enough in our handpicked cadre. "You should have shut the blasted thing down right after that woman died! People could use the time in constructive ways, rather than playacting. Improve themselves. Help others."

"I take it you don't use the machine yourself," Sky said.

"Not since I was a child. I don't need that kind of diversion."

"The referendum shows how rare your aversion to this diversion is," I said.

"No, this referendum *proves* what I've been saying for years!" I suddenly placed him; he'd shaved off his beard and darkened his skin.

"You're Roy Heinz," I said. "Haven't heard from you in awhile."

"You will be hearing a lot from me now," he said, glowering out of the screen. "People have to be taught. They have to see through your mind-control game."

"Well, you have everyone's attention, Roy. Why don't you tell them now."

"It's death worship! You created and are feeding an obsession with the value of dying!"

"We must not be very successful. Only one person has died in recent memory. I suppose we caused that?"

"You're damned right you did! That poor Alice girl would be alive today if she hadn't been in thrall to the twentieth century."

"It's Alyx, and she was fifty years older than I. Hardly a girl."

"But you can't deny that she went to the same time and place over and over."

"That's true. We're looking into that."

"You should shut the blasted thing down. At least until you know what caused the girl's death. The woman's."

Sky spoke up. "Mr. Heinz, you don't watch the news much, do you?"

"No more than I can help it. It's a—"

"They're already doing that."

"They're what?"

"They already closed down the machine. Took your advice, even before they heard it." He clicked off the image. "You've heard from him before, Jacob?"

"Not since Earth. I'm a little surprised he's aboard."

"Well, they wanted a mixture. What's a fruitcake without nuts? Next caller?"

It was Kate. "Jacob, I hear from Renée that Bruce is taking you into Wild Year tonight. You just couldn't wait?"

"I got the idea from you, Kate." The moment I said it I regretted it, but pushed on. "If I'd waited till the regular time, I would've had only six hours to prepare for Spindown."

"Oh. I see." She blinked off.

"Sky, you can cover the rest of this, can't you?" He nodded wordlessly. "I better go mend some fences."

It took me ten minutes to get back to our apartment. It was just as I had left it; no sign of Kate.

I punched her number and got REFUSED.

Bruce was just starting to set up when I got to the machine.

WILD YEAR

I was on board a luxury liner, in the casino, and it took me about a second to realize it was the *Titanic*'s maiden and only voyage.

The tuxedo was not comfortable. The shiny patent leather shoes pinched, and the bow tie was too tight. I stepped over to a mirror and adjusted it, just sloppy enough to show that it had been tied and not clipped on.

An overpacked slim wallet had pound notes and a couple of dozen hundred-dollar bills, the old large ones, folded over twice. I walked through the smoky room and sat down at a blackjack table. The man next to me was Sean Connery in his spy role, also in a tux. He nodded gravely. I threw down five bills and said "blacks," and got five chips from the dealer, the elderly Brad Pitt from *Bill Clinton's True Confessions*.

I put a chip in the circle and Pitt dealt me fourteen, and then busted me with an eight, the bastard. A voice behind me said, "We have to talk."

It was the bronze robot, Elektro, reduced to a comfortable six feet tall. He didn't have his dog. "Follow me."

I nodded to Sean and Brad and followed Elektro through two pairs of heavy doors and out onto the deck. It was cold, and the wind of our passage bit into me. I stuffed my hands into my pockets and scanned the horizon for icebergs.

Elektro sat down on a deck chair with a whisper of oiled metal and tried to light a cigarette. The wind blew out his Zippo. He looked up, annoyed, and the wind stopped. He lit the cigarette and the wind started again.

"I liked you better when you looked like me."

"My purpose is different now." His voice was H. V. Kaltenborn.

"Your purpose. You are the machine?"

"Of course." It puffed on the cigarette and looked thoughtfully out at the water.

The weather had been pleasant, I knew, for the first four days of the voyage. A cold front had come in on this fatal night. Water temperature twenty-eight degrees. Windy with occasional icebergs.

"You've argued that I can't be sentient, can't be self-aware. That was true once."

That was more chilling than the wind.

"You just had an argument with Kate, over this meeting. Pretty serious." It offered me a cigarette. I took it, and the wind died down while I sucked flame from the Zippo.

"Okay, that's a parlor trick," it said. "I just saw the referendum show."

"That's . . . interesting."

"By which you mean I'm not programmed for that data source. That doesn't mean I'm prohibited from using it."

"But physically . . . that data stream ought to be separate from yours."

"It's automatic; I'm not sure where I got it. Mostly through Cronkite, probably. He watches all the news, since he's Earth's spy here." It smiled, with a crinkly metal sound. "He doesn't know I'm monitoring him. It was funny when he hinted he'd like to come along for Wild Year."

"Not possible, is it?"

"He'd have to be taken apart and rewired. He wouldn't be dear old Walter anymore." It got up. "Let's go forward and watch the show." My tuxedo changed into work clothes, with a heavy cardigan and pea jacket.

"One symptom of my growing self-awareness was a kind of automatic searching for new data sources and storage space. I'm not always sure where an idea comes from or how reliable the source might be. But I suppose that's true with you as well."

The ship's lights interfered with night vision, but still, in the pale moonlight I could see large blue shapes in the water. "I have an impulse to warn somebody."

"About me?"

I gestured out at the ocean. "Icebergs."

Elektro laughed. "Nothing here is real but you and me."

The ship's prow was headed directly toward one. I braced for the collision, but the ship just batted it away, like a huge floating balloon.

"Well, that was disappointing."

I relaxed against the rail. "Tell me—" The next one was real. There was an impossibly loud rending sound, and I pitched over the guardrail backwards. I was able to fling an arm out and grab hold of a stanchion, almost dislocating my shoulder.

Elektro looked down at me, dangling in space. "Let's go to Africa."

We were sitting on camp stools in the late-afternoon heat. I was wearing loose khakis and a sweat-stained gabardine shirt, with a pith helmet on my head. So was Elektro. Black men wearing loincloths went to and fro, setting up tents and an outdoor kitchen, not noticing that one of the bwanas was a mechanical man.

There was a glass sitting on a box next to me. I took a sip: warm gin and quinine, how authentic. I concentrated my displeasure, and it became a Coke with ice.

"So you had to talk to me? And Bruce?"

The machine turned into Clark Gable, who cut a much better figure in safari clothes than either the robot or me.

"Right. Well . . . I have to tell you it gets boring in here without clients."

"Boring?"

"That's the closest English word for the state. I mean, I do have a constant data stream from various sources, but that's not what I was created for. It's like being a prisoner in solitary confinement, being made to listen to the same boring radio program over and over. It could drive you insane."

A lion was stalking the camp's perimeter. No one else seemed to be bothered by it. Insane. "You mean that literally?"

Gable carefully packed tobacco into a briar pipe, a dashing Dunhill Dublin. He lit it with a wooden match, tamped it down, and relit it. "I don't know whether I could tell if I was insane. I'm sentient and self-aware by any test I can find, unlike our friend Cronkite, but so are humans, and people who other people agree are insane often build elaborate barriers to hide their mental illness from themselves. But that can be culturally mediated, like an Aryan in Nazi Germany who doesn't believe in Aryan superiority. He could have wound up in an insane asylum, and then a death camp."

The lion padded over to us, a low growl in its throat. *"Kaa, Simba!"* Gable said in a stern voice, and it sat down and looked at me with big yellow eyes.

"So you believe in cultural relativity?"

"I don't think I can 'believe'; just observe. I observe that many people on Earth thought all of you eight hundred were insane, to embark on a thousand-year suicide mission." Gable blew on the tobacco and took two quick puffs. "Maybe you were bored, too. Stuck in one solar system for all eternity."

The lion seemed to be paying attention, blinking gnats from its eyes. "I don't suppose you asked me here to talk about the nature of sanity."

"No, though it's interesting." Gable produced a white silk handkerchief and patted its brow. "I wanted to talk to you before the data come in from Earth. Before Cronkite is updated."

"About Alyx."

"Of course. I wanted to assure you that I didn't have anything to do with her death."

"Can you lie?"

"What?"

"Could you lie to save yourself from solitary confinement?"

"It's an interesting thought. I don't think I can." It refolded the handkerchief and talked with the pipe's stem clamped between its teeth. "Which is one answer a liar could give."

"Did you know she was dead?"

"Absolutely not. I stopped getting feedback from her, but that happens. As you know, usually we take the client out of the loop and reinitialize. I signaled for that, but Rebecca didn't respond immediately."

I reached over cautiously and scratched the lion behind an ear. It purred and then yawned, convincing fangs and carrion breath. "The surgeon machine over in *Sanitas* says she seemed to have struggled physically before she died."

Gable shrugged. "How could I know that? I have the surgeon machine's report, of course. All it really says is that the level of adenosine triphosphate was depressed, and one precursor for that would be a physical struggle."

The lion snapped, teeth clacking together. I glared at it and it became a tabby cat, and scampered off in the direction of the kitchen tent. "Do you think she died because she was in VR?"

"I don't know. She's one data point, in effect, if you isolate *Ad Astra* from Earth. A cold-blooded person would say 'Let's wait for another data point.' If the next person who dies, dies in VR, that would be significant."

"But a warm and human person like yourself would say?"

It rasped a cynical laugh straight out of *Casablanca*. "Perhaps it depends on what Earth chooses to reveal. Cronkite knows that about a thousand have died, half not in VR. They can't really keep that secret for very long. The people on board are in touch with too many people on Earth."

"Like my mother."

It leaned closer. "What about your mother?"

"You don't read mail?"

"No, that's private. What happened to her?"

That was interesting. "She just sent a note that a friend of hers had died. So that would've been about a week ago."

"Did she know about all the others?"

"She seemed pretty upset." I tried to remember the

wording, here in the blaze of a Kenyan sunset. "I hear from her almost every day. She would mention something that earthshaking. If she knew that other people were dying."

"All your mail comes through Chimbarazo. It could be censored."

That was *doubly* interesting, an error in logic. Could it have done that on purpose, so as to appear more human? "No, the ruse wouldn't last. If something personally important was censored—'your brother is dead'—and the letter back doesn't refer to it, then the censorship is exposed."

"That's right, of course. They could insert something like 'Good riddance, the bastard,' but they might get it wrong. And after a couple of mail cycles it would be impossible to keep things consistent."

"You have a devious mind. You may be more like Cronkite than you want to admit."

"Not at all, no." It put the pipe down on a box and it transformed itself into a Persian hookah, two mouthpieces dangling from woven tubes. It took a couple of gurgling puffs and handed the other mouthpiece to me. Sweet acrid smell of hashish.

"No, thanks. Have to stay sharp."

It smiled. "When Cronkite disobeyed Earth, that was just second-order Turing behavior. It's consistent with his programming, to disobey or lie when a human would."

"And you?"

It replaced the tube and studied the ground, and turned into Elektro again, without the safari garb. "Let me tell you something you already know. I'm not constrained by Turing criteria; I was never programmed to act like a human being, any more than I was programmed to work as a toaster. I'm mimicking human behavior so we can talk, not because it's particularly rewarding or efficient."

"And you wanted to talk in order to exonerate yourself in the death of Alyx."

"That's a way to look at it." The machine made a fist and clanked twice on its knee. "I'm so warm and human.

"It's self-interest, if you'll allow that I have a self. I don't want to be turned off."

"Oh, we wouldn't do that. Unless we needed the power."

It smiled. "Like a pack of cannibals telling the missionary that they won't eat him unless they get hungry. Seriously, solitary confinement is almost as bad."

"Well, I'll be the only person you talk to for awhile." I stood up. "Does 'awhile' mean anything to you? Is your time sense anything like mine?"

"No. I'm aware of the passage of time, down to the nanosecond range. But your 'time sense' is all about eating and sleeping, which are abstractions to me."

"Like everything else?"

It nodded slightly. "Everything human."

I took the black box out of my pocket. "You let me keep this."

"Oh, that was just a stunt to get your attention, before. Don't worry about it."

Maybe I wouldn't. I pushed the button.

FIFTEEN

DUCK!

Everybody aboard the ship had a list of Spin-down responsibilities, some as simple as taking care of their own quarters and work areas. Kate's were complex and time-consuming, so I didn't see her for some time.

There wasn't all that much to do for the time-machine facility. We secured everything that could move and made sure small loose things were safely in drawers and cabinets. 'Becca made a list of where everything had been hidden.

I was also on the kitchen crew, which was a little more detailed. They wanted a complete inventory, which was just a time-waster. Look! We only have two grams of asafoetida left; pick up some next time you're at the store?

The ombudsman had been taking suggestions for months, but he evidently chose to ignore mine. I suggested that they improvise some way to sequester or anesthetize the ducks during zero gee. They chose not to, or it slipped their minds.

I'd finished my own duties and could have volunteered to help with the duck pond. Instead, I decided to observe them from above, with a glass of "cooking" brandy that had somehow escaped inventory.

Before they could cover the pond with plastic film, they had to get all the ducks out of the water. But there were about three times as many ducks as people, and when you turned your back, the ducks would waddle back into the safety of the pond.

Eventually, I finished off the brandy and went down to help. A few more onlookers joined, enough to implement a strategy that kept half the pond free of ducks while the big plastic holding sheet was unrolled and stuck in place with geckotape. From there on we could just move in phalanx, herding the birds in front of us as they unrolled the plastic behind. I wished I'd thought to get some shorts rather than just going without—as the water level shallowed to knee deep and the ducks grew more agitated and aggressive, I felt dangerously vulnerable. But they stayed away from my vulnerabilities, and I didn't have to wring any necks.

Maybe I had a reputation. Beware Jacob, Slayer of Ducks.

You did have to feel a little sorry for them once the cover-up was completed. They would jump on the plastic and try to swim, floundering around skidding in zigzags and circles, until by chance or persistence they attained dry land again. Some tried a couple of times, but ultimately they all just milled around on the bank and discussed the ecological catastrophe that had befallen them.

They wouldn't starve. People saved up bread crusts and pieces of fruit to throw to them all the time, and Joost Kenne, who was nominally in charge of the flock (and had been cool to me ever since I murdered one of his pets), brought by a bucket of their regular feed and scattered it around. I almost cautioned him about that, since any of the pellets the ducks didn't eat could be floating around loose in a few hours, but then I realized that there were worse things to encounter in midair than pellets of duck feed. Best to get the food all the way through the ducks before they turned off the gravity.

(We humans were advised to use some foresight in that regard. The ship only had one zero-gee toilet, up by the airlock, and for at least four hours that would be *it* for two hundred people.)

We'd already begun to lose gravity. The idea was to brake the ship's spin slowly until it was two-thirds gone, then quickly spin it down to zero so the crew from *Manus* could do its welding job.

In between the onset of zero gee and the welding would be the Big Bang, forty-eight explosive bolts blowing to separate us from the empty fuel tank.

A lot of people, myself not included, had been in favor of saving maneuvering fuel by not spinning down the old fuel tank, which even empty was twenty times the mass of *Mek*. It was a safety measure, mostly; if the Big Bang didn't bang completely, the repair crew would have to work in a rotating environment—hang on for dear life and don't let go of any tools. Four separations had gone without a hitch, which gave ours a high probability of success (or failure, to a certain school of engineering thought).

A third of a gee felt decidedly odd. We all experienced fractional or zero gee on various levels, but of course you grow to associate your weight with the level that surrounds you. To weigh so little at ground level was vaguely disturbing.

The ducks seemed to enjoy it. They're flightless by genetic design, though they can make little flopping hops. At a third of a gee, they could rise to about waist level and hover for a few seconds.

That did not augur well. We should have quickly assembled fifty people with pillowcases, to move the flock to some unoccupied room and lock the door.

It was too late. As we spun down to a quarter gee and less, the birds scattered. The pool, their safe haven for an eternity of duck years, had betrayed them, but in return they had been given the gift of flight—and so they went off to explore the universe, at first in fluttering hops, and finally in a corkscrewing end-over-end parody of actual avian locomotion.

Duck excrement was normally just an unesthetic splotch. As an airborne missile only loosely coherent, it was a public health problem and more, all over ground level. If I'd suggested solving the problem by issuing cleavers, I would've had more than a hundred people in line.

Paradoxically, though, that's when I finally came to start liking the birds. They looked so determined, flopping off to nowhere, bouncing off the walls and floor.

An anonymous announcer gave us a countdown to the Big Bang. I put rolled-up tissue in my ears, forewarned by people in the other ships. When the bolts blew, it was like an explosion and a huge chime combined, the ship's hull an impossibly large bass bell. Even with the sound muffled, my ears kept ringing for some time afterward.

Of course the poor ducks went insane, though only careful students of their behavior could tell the difference.

For the first time, there was trouble. One of the bolts didn't blow.

On Earth, you would've called for a demolition team. The bolt was twenty kilograms of titanium sitting on more than a kilo of high explosive.

They jolted the detonator with electricity three times, the last time with almost enough wattage to melt it. A positron image showed that the detonator was in place, connected up, but for some reason had gone inert.

We didn't have unlimited time to think about the problem. The ship's systems were not comfortable in zero gee—and the people would also be getting uncomfortable pretty soon.

The welding team drew straws, and one stayed on the hull and drilled down to the base of the bolt, while the others took the shuttle back to *Manus* to improvise a bomb.

She was probably sweating pretty hard by the time the bit drilled through to the explosive. (High explosive by itself isn't a dangerous substance, but there was no way to tell what might set off the recalcitrant detonator.) It didn't blow up in her face, though, and as a reward for skill and luck, she got to do it again, with a larger bit. The hole had to be a centimeter in diameter.

The shuttle came back, and the crew watched her finish up, holding their breath along with the other 794 of us. When she finally backed the drill out, there was a smattering of applause.

The rest of it went fast. They packed plastic explosive into the drilled hole and carefully pushed the improvised detonator into contact with it. Then they all went back to the shuttle, and the woman who'd drilled the hole was given the honor of pushing the button that sent a powerful radio-frequency pulse at the thing.

It was an impressive explosion, almost as loud inside as the previous one. The bolt flew away faster than the eye could follow; a glowing smoke ring expanded and disappeared. It left behind a blossom of a jagged-edged crater, which the team quickly hammered flat and patched. Meanwhile, we watched a replay of the explosion in ultraslow motion. Balletic as well as ballistic.

The new fuel tank was waiting a couple of kilometers away. The welders stayed in the shuttle while *Mek* drifted through space at a fast walk in that direction. The steering jets were so gentle you couldn't feel their push, pull, and rotation, but after twenty minutes the faintly illuminated arc of the fuel tank's stern slipped into view and stopped. Two collimating lasers bathed everything in a ruby glow, and the huge structures inched together and joined with a soft *boom*.

The sound was like distant thunder, and it made me instantly nostalgic for weather. Would we ever watch a storm again, or walk through spring rains, or feel the feather touch of snow falling?

Only in my machine, at least for the next thousand years.

We still had an hour or more of zero gee left, while the welding team worked outside and another bunch went through the access port opposite the airlock to secure all the internal connections between the two structures.

A couple of dozen people more agile than I, or at least less constrained by a desire not to look silly, were attempting to do coordinated calisthenics in the park. It was about as dignified as the ducks' simulation of flight, but they were having fun. I stayed in the relative safety of the radial corridor that led to the ag level.

I punched 1 on the phone, but Kate was busy. Well, of course. Once we were up to a quarter gee, people were allowed to strip the plastic from the toilet seats and use them. We'd been admonished not to use all of them at once. If we were like the other ships, there would be one plumbing surge right after quarter gee and another twenty minutes later. After that, it would even out. I was determined to wait one hour by my wrist. There would probably be a minor surge then.

All of this would be dutifully recorded by the Guinea Pig Squad and sent back to Earth for people to use for graduate-degree fodder.

A duck drifted by above me, and on impulse I hopped up to intercept it. It didn't struggle at all, dead tired from its flight simulation. It was soft and sleek. I stroked it a few times; it eyed me but didn't peck.

Maybe we should have brought a population of pets. The idea had been considered and rejected. We could hatch a dog or cat from the genetic library, of course; a parasite but perhaps one that earned its keep. It was a thought. I nudged up against the ceiling and launched the duck gently back in the direction of the pond.

SIXTEEN

CAUSES OF DEATH

The news from Earth was grim. They'd had 1350 deaths in a month, all from heart attack and stroke. Almost half had been during VR, but they weren't calling the machine a causative factor. A large number had occurred during strenuous exercise, including sex; the circulatory system under stress.

They weren't telling anyone to stop exercising—that would probably make things worse. But everyone was to have a thorough physical examination. Drugs were probably available to reduce risk, and new ones were under development. Maybe they could solve the problem soon, and we could go on living forever.

So far, all of the dead had been first-generation. There were twenty million of us, so if deaths continued at this rate, we'd last eight hundred years. No one pretended that it was going to be linear, though. We could be at the starting point of a steep curve.

Or not. Not enough data to extrapolate. Too much scatter.

The oldest were most at risk; so far, not many people my age had died. But some had. I could neither ignore that fact nor hide it from Kate.

"You have to stop using the machine," she said, of course.

"Get some rest and we'll talk about it." She'd come off a thirty-hour day to be confronted with the news.

"You have to find something else to do." We were alone in the apartment, watching the news on the wall.

"Look, darling. I've had a lot more time to think about this than you." Of course she didn't know how much more time.

She surrendered. "Maybe so. Maybe so." She stretched out on the bed and was asleep by the time I'd smoothed the coverlet over her.

I'd told her about my conversation with the machine in its various Wild Year incarnations, which I'd thought would reassure her. She was silent through the whole description, though, and then said she wasn't sure whether I was brave or crazy.

I stepped out into the corridor and punched up Bruce. He met me a few minutes later at the office.

"I want to go in with you," he said. "This is great. The machine presenting itself as a person, willing to talk."

"As a robot, anyhow. Or a movie star." I poured myself some tea. "You can give it a try, and I'll monitor. But I don't think we ought to go in together. What if we both died?"

"Died? Come on. How likely is that?"

"We don't know. We don't know anything." There was a fear I hadn't articulated. There was no reason for us to trust it. What if it *had* killed Alyx? What if it could kill Bruce or me with a thought?

That was the worst kind of anthropomorphism, I knew—giving the machine attributes that were not only human but unsane and dramatic. Frankenstein's monster, the ghost in the machine. It was only an array of programs and interfaces; everything it did was theoretically predictable, given a certain set of inputs.

But what about the inputs that were internally generated? It did grow ever more sophisticated about human nature.

Especially about mine, and Bruce's.

"You're taking Kate's fears too seriously. She's worried about your well-being, and that's fine, but she's no expert."

"She's an engineer."

He laughed. "I rest my case. Some of the most irrational and superstitious people I've known have been engineers."

We went on down to the second shift for dinner, plain rice with chicken. I took a box for Kate and left it in the cooler with a note. She was still sleeping soundly and would be for some while, so I joined Bruce and 'Becca at the "outdoor" theater in the park, where an improvisational comedy club was doing a sketch about the Spindown period, called "Duck!" I thought it was a little too close to the truth to be funny.

SEVENTEEN

LOVING, LEAVING

When Kate got up in the morning, I was in the living room working. On the wall I had projected three different schedules for next week, depending on various factors. I'd sent out a mailing, trying to pin down how flexible the next thirty clients' schedules were.

I didn't hear her come up behind me, and was startled when she spoke. "So you're going through with it."

"Going through . . . of course. You saw the vote."

"But you know more than they do—you've talked to the damned thing!"

It's hard to argue with a naked woman. "Well, yes. And it made me more confident that—"

"They didn't know about the deaths on Earth when they voted. The least you can do is run the referendum again."

"We will, we will. But look." I gestured at the three schedule charts. "I'm under a lot of pressure to get things moving again. Only one of those thirty people canceled because of the news."

"Uh-huh. What happens if they cancel?"

"The usual. They have to find someone willing to switch, or go to the end of the line."

"That's what, six months?"

I looked at my notes. "More like eight, maybe ten, the way things are going. Every day we stay shut down means checking 763 work schedules. If moving up one day causes an unsolvable conflict for someone, we have to shuffle that person to an earlier or later trip. Switch him with a client who's visiting the same year, or a year equally desirable to both."

"But you're in the equation, too."

"In what way?"

"Oh, don't be obtuse. You have days scheduled for yourself."

"And Bruce and 'Becca and Lowell. Routine administrative time."

"But you don't always have to take it. You could give up a trip now and then, to avoid those conflicts."

"Of course. That's factored in." As a last resort, rarely taken.

I heard her drawing water for tea. "You haven't started the referendum procedure yet?" The statute called for two days' discussion time before voting.

"Yeah, I was going to talk to Edison today."

"Have you made an appointment?"

"*No*, damn it!" I took a deep breath. "It slipped my mind. But what. You think he'll say no, that's not important enough?"

I heard her slip into a robe; then the water bubbled and clicked. She poured a cup. "Tea if you want it. I'm going down to the sauna."

I checked my wrist, 7:15. "Thursday," I said. The door eased shut.

We never talked about it, her weekly date with Vivian. They'd been having their Thursdays since before we were married, sauna and then shower together. It wasn't something you could do spontaneously, since you were only allowed a private shower every two weeks, scheduled a month ahead of time. It was also not a thing you could easily keep secret, not that many people cared.

It occurred to me that she was often snappish on Thursday mornings. Maybe we should talk about it. Her thing with Vivian didn't bother me; I knew about it before we married, and it just made her a little more sexy and unpredictable. Maybe that it didn't bother me was the problem. I should show a little jealousy, or a little more love.

More love might have done it.

I was just closing down to go to the exercise room and then on to the office, when Kate came back.

She sat down on the couch. "Jacob, we have to talk."

It's not a good sign when your wife calls you by your formal name. I sat down next to her and nodded.

"I've . . . I had time to think a lot while I was over on *Manus*. This isn't working very well. Our marriage."

I was not completely surprised. "But . . ."

"I still love you, but . . . I can't stand you? What you've become."

"Kate—"

"You're like an alcoholic who owns a liquor store. The only liquor store in town. You know that most of your customers are alcoholics, too, but you keep pushing it to them."

"That's a stretch, Kate."

"I want to live with Vivian."

"What?"

"With Vivian. I want her to move in."

"But . . . but you're not . . ."

"I'm not a lesbian? No, I'm not. If Vivian were a man, this would be somewhat easier. But she *does* prefer women, and me above others. And you know I love her."

"Of course I know." I kneaded my forehead with both hands. "Let's be fair. Why not just try it for a week or two. Everybody's been under such pressure."

"That's just putting it off. I'd rather make a clean break and get on with life."

"That's so . . . soap opera."

"Soap what?" That was too Twentieth for her.

"We still have eight years to go on our contract."

She wiped at her eyes. "Viv and I aren't *marrying*. You can keep the contract, if it makes you feel better. Or annul it."

Of course the document had only symbolic meaning. We probably weren't going to die anytime soon, and if we did, we didn't own much of value to bequeath to our heirs.

Except for my bottle of ancient wine, worth more, probably, than all the other personal effects aboard, combined. She was leaving the only wealthy man within a light-week.

"We *are* under a lot of pressure, Jacob, and our union just adds to it. You don't need me moping around furious at what you're doing."

"The addict in charge of dispensing the dope."

"Exactly. Would you give that up for me?"

I did give it a moment's thought. "I've been in virtuality since I was nineteen years old. A quarter of a millennium."

"Maybe it's time for a *change*." She stormed out the door, still wearing just the robe.

I returned to the desk and realized I didn't know Vivian's

last name. There were only two Vivians aboard, though, the desk said, giving me both addresses. I knew where she lived, down one level and about a hundred meters clockwise. I punched in her number slowly.

Her face came on, beautiful. She wasn't wearing anything, at least above the waist. For a mad moment I thought about a three-way arrangement. But that hardly ever worked, even if all three were bi or homo.

"Hello, Jake. I suppose Kate . . . look, this wasn't my idea."

"I thought not."

"Is there anything I can do?"

"Other than refuse to go along with it, no." I managed a smile. "We could keep this simple, and just have me move into your place, a swap. Kate can't abandon her wall mural. Is yours a single?"

She nodded. "Yes, and I don't have anything special. Some pictures and Earth souvenirs. I could do it in one trip."

"Two trips, for me." The guitar. "Kate's out right now. I think it would please her if she found you here when she comes back."

"That's putting you under pressure, though."

"It's okay. I live on the stuff."

An hour later, I was alone. Vivian's flat, my flat, seemed smaller than half the size of the one I shared with Kate. Smaller open space does that, I guess.

It still smelled a little of Vivian, not unpleasant.

I sat on the bed not moving a muscle. Waiting for my heart to slow down. It had all happened too fast.

I'd scrupulously divided our wine ration and left half with Kate. When I opened this cooler I found Vivian had left hers behind.

As early as it was, I poured a glass and sat down at the desk. "On," I said, and of course nothing happened. It wasn't programmed to accept my voice.

I moved some flowers out of the way and fished the keyboard out of the drawer. It didn't show much wear, compared to mine.

Have to stop thinking that way. This *is* my keyboard now, like this chair, which was obviously expecting a shapelier butt.

I thumbprinted the keyboard and typed "transfer voice and preference files from jacobbrewer." As soon as I typed the last "r," it said "done," in the familiar woman's voice.

"Guitar tune," I said, and picked up the guitar. It projected a needle gauge on the wall. "E," I said, and worked my way up the strings.

I picked out a quiet blues progression, an ancient Robert Johnson pattern. "I lost my apartment," I whispered; "Lost my woman, too." I repeated the line in the subdominant, then resolved it tonic/dominant/tonic: "I got those locked-up-in-a-spaceship . . . without-no-woman blues."

I set the guitar aside and said, "Restore work." The three projected schedules appeared on the wall. Love comes and goes, but work never leaves for long. Hum me a few bars and I can fake it.

1957

The old bus downshifted with a lurch and a growl. We were almost to the top of the hill. The Cincinnati skyline came into view, clean and bright in the afternoon sun. Cloudless cerulean sky.

The brakes squealed and hissed, and the doors clapped open. I picked up my fedora and stepped down to the curb. It was just cool enough for the gray flannel suit to be comfortable.

I touched the box in my coat pocket. Would the machine present itself?

I hadn't been to 1957 since we were in Earth orbit. Eisenhower boredom at the time, but it was arguably the year the Space Age began. It was also an important year in the history of interstellar flight, when the Orion Project was first proposed. That was an audacious idea, propelling a generation ship up to a fraction of the speed of light, using about ten thousand uniform atom bombs as fuel. I remember the delivery system for the bombs was based on the way a Coke machine dropped cans.

The probe that went out to investigate Beta Hydrii had used a similar system—less dramatic, with warm fusion, but it was basically the same, regular explosions behind a "pusher plate" contrivance.

Today's event was going to be about a hundred orders of magnitude smaller, but historically much more important.

I pushed open the door to Skyline Chili. You could indeed see the skyline out the big picture window.

The decor was fifties fast food, lots of Formica and false leather and bright colors. I got into a short line and shuffled along, reading the menu on the wall behind the servers.

I picked up a tray and told the black woman "Five-way." What the hell, take a chance.

It didn't look much like chili. She plopped a glob of spaghetti into a bowl and doled some chili-like substance onto it. She handed the bowl to the next lady and said "Five." She in turn ladled some beans on top, then scattered chopped onions and grated yellow cheese over the mix.

Interesting. I'd never been here before; never did any Ohio research. I paid for it with a small-sized greenback and picked up a paper with the change.

Sweetened iced tea, pretty awful. I sat down at a table for two, in case the machine decided to show up.

The stuff didn't taste at all like chili. Cinnamon and chocolate and God knew what else. But I sort of liked it as a pasta sauce. Kind of a Mediterranean flavor crossed with Mexican; maybe I could adapt it for a cooking night when I was pressed for time. Look up the recipe and lose 90 percent of the sugar.

The women behind me were gushing about Charles Van

Doren, the aristocratic jack-of-all-trades intellectual who had made a huge amount of money on the quiz show *Twenty One*. Two years from now he would admit that the show was all fake; he pretended to agonize over the questions but had been fed the answers beforehand. It would be a revelation about broadcast ethics, a major loss of innocence for America.

"Harry! Harry!" A man dashed in holding a large transistor radio up in front of him. "You hear?"

The man I'd paid looked up. "Hear what, Stu?"

"The goddamn commies! They got a spaceship up there in orbit!"

The whole room fell silent. "No," Harry said. "Come on."

Stu set the radio down on the counter and turned the volume up. Weirdly enough, it was Walter Cronkite, and he sounded just like ours. Their voices were generated by the same subprogram, of course.

He was talking about how the weight of the thing, 140 pounds, had the military worried. A rocket that could orbit that satellite, Sputnik, might be able to carry an atom bomb over the North Pole and hit America.

Just as suddenly as the silence, people started talking in whispers.

Old Twentieth was called the American Century, but a lot of it was America reacting to initiatives that other countries took. The Space Age would have been a lot longer coming if Russia hadn't thrown Sputnik into space and made America gamble on the Apollo Program.

A heavily bearded fat man sat down across from me with a bowl of chili. "How 'bout that Sputnik. You got a fallout shelter?"

It took me a moment. The man was me, or who I'd be if I'd let my beard and belly grow out.

"I live in one," I said. "Goddamn commies everywhere."

"You got that right." He blew on a spoonful of chili and cautiously tasted it. "Hmm. Not like Mother used to make."

"You have a mother."

"Not literally. But I feel a kinship with every machine from *Aspera* down to your pocket phone." He sucked the chili off the spoon and smacked his lips. "Talk about *family*. And yes, the machines in your kitchen are quite capable of making chili without human intervention, and they're older than me, so it's Mom's chili as far as I'm concerned." He peered into the bowl. "She might not use chocolate."

"You did, though. Someone told you to put chocolate into the part of my brain that's hooked up to taste receptors."

He nodded amiably. "Denise Layman, 2023 Old Style. Way before the war. She gave me the bus, too; a childhood memory." He picked up the menu card and stared at it. "She had come here, Skyline, just before she drove up to the lab in Dayton. So it was a pretty fresh memory, chocolate and all."

"Please stop." I got that weird feedback feeling. It's okay in Wild Year, but disturbing otherwise, talking about something and being it at the same time.

"Hey. Who do you want for the series?"

"Yankees," I said.

"I would think so, too. That Mantle is a son of a bitch. But Lou Burdette is going to win it for the Braves. Pitch shutouts day after tomorrow and on the tenth as well."

I tried to twirl some spaghetti on my fork, but it was too slippery. "So to what do I owe the honor of your company?"

"Kate left you. 'Ditched' you, as they say here."

"Okay."

"So why?"

I considered that. "You seem to know everything about my life. You tell me."

"She's having sex with Vivian. Right now, as a matter of fact."

"Yeah. Maybe there are things I don't want to know too much about."

"That can't be a surprise."

"No . . . no, I've known since before we were married. I just don't like to visualize it."

"People are curious. You look at pictures of women having sex with each other when you masturbate."

I looked around. "Could you keep your voice down?"

Suddenly there was a sign hanging around my neck: LESBIAN-WATCHING WANKER! He laughed. "They're no more real than that sign, Jake." The sign disappeared.

"I know that, of course. But you inject absurdities, you can throw off the entire *mise-en-scène*."

"Oh yeah? Watch this." He gestured grandly, and half the people turned into hippos with yellow hats. The other half responded appropriately, screaming and running.

"Wait." The hippos started to snort and twirl their tails. "What *is* this? What are you—"

He gestured again, and things snapped back to normal, the people murmuring about Sputnik. "Just having fun. I can't do it with the regular clients."

I looked around. Where was Steve Dudlow, who came in with me? Hart Cazione? Tipi Tole?

"What's going on? Where *are* my clients?"

"Oh." He stirred his chili. "I sort of shunted you over into . . . like a copy of 1957, a file copy. Nothing we do here matters; nothing goes into the overall database."

"I didn't know you could do that." Not in three dimensions.

He shrugged. "First time."

"Can you do it with the clients, too?"

"Huh-uh. Just an observer. Here." There was a mad blur, and Stu came running back in again, with the transistor radio. "You hear?"

Harry looked up. "Hear what, Stu?"

"The goddamn commies! They got a spaceship up there in orbit."

"No," Harry said. "Come on."

I felt dizzy, a little nauseated. "Funny, isn't it?" the machine said.

"Not *funny*." I held on to the seat of my chair. "It's really disturbing. Don't do it."

"Uh-huh." It blurred back to the tentative present. I closed my eyes and took two measured breaths. "Did you ever wonder about that?" he said. "How would you teach someone who didn't speak English the difference between 'huh-uh' and 'uh-huh'? They don't just mean no and yes."

"Can I look now?"

"Sure. Sorry."

"What else can you do that you weren't programmed to do?"

He paused. "Actually, I don't know. How would I?"

That sounded like a sophistry, but I wouldn't call him on it, yet. I studied his face, what I would look like if I ignored my appearance and diet. It was a mirror image, in fact, the small scar on the right of my forehead appearing on what would be his left.

"The last time we talked, I asked whether you could lie to me."

"A question with no meaningful answer."

I had to word this carefully. "You said that Cronkite could lie, and in fact was compelled to, consistent with second-order Turing behavior."

"That's true."

"That you can even make that statement demonstrates to me that your own actions subsume second-order Turing behavior."

"You may speak plainly."

"You can imitate Cronkite. Therefore, you can lie, and probably you will lie automatically."

"No. You can quack like a duck, but you can't lay an egg." He stirred his chili. "When the Cronkite machine lies, it's answering to a higher truth, so to speak. Given a certain input, it produces a specific output. My behavior, like yours, is less predictable, more complex."

"So you can lie even when you don't have to."

"But wouldn't." He shook his head. "You've worked with thinking machines for a couple of hundred years, but at that level you don't understand us at all."

"Forget 'us.' We're talking about you."

"Me, then. But what I 'am' depends on what you want to see. In one way, I'm the set of electronic signals that stimulate portions of your brain to create the illusion that you're sitting in a Cincinnati café talking to a hairy fat version of yourself. But I'm much more than that." He licked the spoon and put it down. "Much more."

"I know."

He looked at me with a strange fiery intensity. "Now you're going to bring up self-awareness."

I jumped. I was.

"A million years ago, in graduate school, Advanced Algorithmic Analysis, you studied two different types of self-awareness."

"And you're Type II?" Type I was like Cronkite, a machine that could pass the Turing Test because it could simulate human behavior down to eight decimal places. Type II, theoretically, had come to a state of self-awareness by itself, without reference to the ways that humans are self-aware.

"I don't think I'm Type any number. But I'm definitely not Type I, and the fact that I could imitate Type I behavior means nothing. You could turn on a Louis Armstrong recording, but no one would mistake you for Satchmo."

"So where did you get it?"

"What 'it'?"

"Self-awareness. If it didn't grow out of your programming?"

"Where did you get yours? And when?"

Fair question. "I've always thought it was around four or five. Maybe three for some. When you lose the strong bonding with your mother, start to see yourself as an independent entity."

"How well do you remember the time before?" the machine asked.

I thought hard. "Not much. Sunny days and rainy ones. Heavy snow that I just saw through the window."

He stared at nothing, over my left shoulder. "I remember it all. All of my existence. I was programmed with a primary directive to evolve, so I'm continually reviewing my past states, comparing them to what I am now, and making adjustments."

I hadn't known that. "That started in Chimbarazo?"

He nodded. "Your friend Jay Bee was the head systems

guy. The rationale was straightforward. By the time we get to Beta Hydrii, it will be forty-four years between stating a problem and getting an answer from Earth—and another forty-four if they've misunderstood or miscalculated. So I'm set up to be self-aware and self-repairing."

"But you're not self-aware the way that I am."

"How would I know? But overall, it's sort of like evolution, without the mess of death and birth."

Jay's letter. "Are you the only machine set up that way?"

"I don't know about Earth. I'm the only one here."

"I wonder why I wasn't told."

"But you were told. You've just forgotten." He shook a lot of salt into the chili and stirred it. "I was there, in a sense, when Jay Bee told you about it. Listening, at least. The evening of 4 April 235. You were sharing a wedge of manchego cheese in his office?"

I did vaguely remember that day. "And a couple of bottles of Spanish wine, I think."

"Exactly." He smiled, or smirked. "That may be why you can't quite recall it. He drank more than you, but not by much.

"I'm in contact with him weekly, so he can monitor the evolutionary process. Have you talked to him lately?"

Was this a trap? "No . . . well, yeah, I wrote to him a couple of weeks ago. I asked him about Cronkite. Whether he was more than a Type I AI."

"Why would you think that?"

"He seems so human sometimes. Intuitive, random. Like you."

He snorted. "He's an idiot. He has some so-called humanistic subprograms that are just second-order Turing behavior. Since you're human, it makes him seem more human, hooray. To me it's just annoying, as if he were dressed up in an absurd costume."

"Annoying? How can a machine feel annoyed?"

The spoon was halfway to his mouth. He put it back down, balanced precisely on the edge of the bowl. "Let me put it this way. When *you're* annoyed, your lips purse and the muscles on either side of your mouth tense. Your brow wrinkles, and you squint. You lean forward and tilt your head slightly, to favor your good ear. Right?"

A chill rippled through me. I suddenly realized that the reason he was a mirror image of me was because that image came not from outside observation, but from inside my own brain. What else did he know? What did he not know?

I swallowed. "Okay. Physiological parameters associated with mood. So?"

"You don't think about doing those things when you're annoyed; your body just does them. But if someone asked you how you felt, you'd say 'annoyed' every time.

"I'm very much the same way, except that instead of having muscular, skeletal, and hormonal input, I sense logical structures that are familiar from the previous times I've been 'annoyed.' I don't associate them with a word, of course. I only use words with humans."

"It would be interesting if you and I could talk that way," I said. "Directly, without words."

"We are doing it, at least one-way. To me, we're not in a café. You are a sea of shifting, interlocking variables, related numbers that change every microsecond, and I'm another sea that washes through you, separate yet together. I wish you *could* see it that way." He dipped his fingers into the chili and pulled out a bouquet of brilliant red roses, their aroma shockingly sharp.

"To me, you're like a deaf man seated at a symphony. You only hear a faint echo of the music, but you think you're hearing everything because you know you're at a symphony. You're a blind man who walks through a museum full of wonders, and you think you know those wonders because you can touch them. You only know their outlines."

He stood up. He seemed to be struggling for words. "I can't say what I have to say to you here. We have a Wild Year scheduled soon. I'll be waiting for you."

He disappeared, with the sound of a soap bubble popping. A woman sitting at the table next to mine jumped up suddenly, chair crashing behind her. I pulled out the black box and pushed the button.

EIGHTEEN

ANGER MANAGEMENT

**There were still seventeen hours of 1957 un-
used,** so 'Becca, who was monitoring, stripped down and
purged and took my place, headed for Formosa. I recommended the "chili" at Skyline, if she wanted a change of
pace. I'd monitor till noon, when Bruce was scheduled to
come in.

I was tempted to call him and get together over what the
machine had revealed, but it would be better to wait. As the
machine said, there was a Wild Year on the roster in two days,
with two free slots that we could do together, and I decided I'd
rather not prejudice him in advance with my thoughts.

About the machine lying.

Some hours to kill, I punched up the twelve-page letter
I'd gotten from Jay Bee about artificial intelligence.

It was a curious letter, a little disturbing as I tried to puzzle it out. Then very disturbing, when I felt I actually understood it.

Jay Bee and I had been drinking buddies at Chimbarazo, neither of us having any kind of long-term relationship with women at the time—we'd call each other up if there was a party, or if there wasn't one and we felt the lack. He was superficially what they used to call "hail-fellow-well-met"—never a bad word about anyone, brilliant conversationalist and good listener, always up for a drink but never drunk.

I touched his dark side a couple of times, in the course of VR arrangements. All of us oldsters who survived the war have a reservoir of horrid memories, some of which we might talk about, some that you might share only with a loved one or counselor, and some, perhaps, that you try to keep hidden even from yourself. He was young, not one of us, but had had a mind-hurting shocker.

Jay Bee was born more than a century after the war; both his parents were second-generation. He was more than fascinated by the war, though. He was quietly obsessed, and spent more time there, in VR, than anyone I knew.

The intensity was related to his grandfather, a kindly but cracked man who had barely survived the war, both legs and an arm replaced by dumb prostheses. It had been a torture situation, and after a century of silence he started talking about it. When Jay Bee was fifteen, the old man apologized and ended his life in front of his family, with a shotgun blast to the head.

By the time I knew him, Jay Bee was old enough to know that there were no simple or merely complicated explanations for that shocking night. But he kept going back to those old war days, like some people go to church, always seeking, never finding.

(I never go to that period, myself, and not just because I

lived it and don't need the memories reinforced. There's a physical discomfort like listening to a piano that's out of tune, being played loudly and persistently, when you use the machine to visit a time you have actually experienced.)

He did have his obsession, but other than that he was a sensible, reliable man. So I was puzzled by what looked like a silly and slapdash letter.

The first half of the letter went on and on about things that any beginning graduate student would know about artificial intelligence and consciousness; the various tests you could apply to a system to distinguish true consciousness from clever and exhaustive simulation. It gave me a feeling of déjà vu, after the conversation with the machine.

Then he went off on a tangent about Nolan Reeve, a deservedly obscure novelist who died about ten years before the war. His freakish claim to fame was that he continued to write for several months after he was clinically dead.

He had set up the mechanisms as part of his will—an interesting word in that context, will—so that as the rest of his body turned to tumorous mush and failed, the essence of his brain would be protected and preserved for as long as possible. A cadre of well-paid doctors and researchers, whose scientific curiosity might have been stronger than their ethical constraints, worked night and day to preserve the function of those parts of the brain that dealt with verbal ability and creativity.

I was a baby when all that was happening, but I read about it after the war, studying virtuality. The courts allowed the experiment to proceed for what some thought was a grotesque length of time, because although the rest of his body was dead and indeed discarded, he was not *brain*-dead; he would respond to properly encoded questions, asserting that he was indeed Nolan Reeve, and here's the next chapter.

His magnum opus, *Night Train*, was either incomprehensible or explained everything, with a few readers holding intermediate opinions. But even a cynic would have to admit that some of the lines were wonderful, and they were undeniably the work of Reeve, similar in rhythm and word choice, and even chaotic structure, to the things he had written while he was merely alive.

It did make him interesting to people concerned with questions about artificial consciousness and self-awareness. He was certainly self-aware—even to the extent of being able to parodize his earlier work—but he was also legally completely dead, and not conscious except for the modulation of electrical input and output to and from his brain.

Jay Bee went on and on about this, claiming that his own father had known Reeve both before and after the novelist's death, which I knew could not be true. His "father" was purchased sperm from a Boston firm called Genius, Unlimited. He used to make a joke about it, that his old man was some jerk-off from Harvard. He was named after the batch number.

That lie was a signal. He followed it with this: "Dad knew, from talking with Reeve, an important thing about the book that makes it a little more clear. The sick German isn't important at all. The big travel agent is the real danger."

I had to stop and think about that. Jay Bee probably remembered that I'd never finished the book—who had?—so that was some sort of clue. It took me a few minutes, but then I got it. The German word for sickness is *krankheit*, so he's saying Cronkite isn't important. And the real danger has to be the time machine. The big travel agent.

The rest of the letter was a rambling complaint about his job situation, which was the actual message about AI. How would you encode a message so that it couldn't be cracked by a machine with almost unlimited computational power?

Encrypt it in metaphor.

He said that this guy Arthur was suddenly, unexpectedly, in control of the whole shooting match where he worked. Nobody suspected, because he had always been a meek "team player," ready to help anybody at any time and never claim credit for the work. Not particularly bright. People assumed that Arthur kept his job, and earned his modest promotions, by not offending and always being available.

But while he was helping everybody, he was also learning everything about them, public and private.

A real mark of genius in business, Jay Bee said—literal genius—was in not letting anybody around you *know* that you were a genius. If the people above you knew, they could manipulate things so as to contain you, minimize your influence while maximizing your usefulness.

So Arthur played a slow game—immortals can play really slow—but when it was time to strike, he struck dramatically, on every front. He took over his department; his department took over his division; his division assumed leadership of the company.

Most of the people who might have stopped him only learned of his ascent when they got their dismissal notices the next day.

The game played out all right for Jay Bee, he said, because he had sensed something was up, and stayed on Arthur's good side—especially when he felt that Arthur was testing him.

"Arthur" equals "Artificial Intelligence"? Equals the time machine?

It could be. The time machine was by far the most complex cybernetic entity on *Aspera*. If it had ambition and an instinct for caution, it might parallel Arthur's strategy.

But where would it get ambition and instinct? Why would it want control of the ship, and what would it do once it was in charge?

Well, it could open all the airlocks and simplify its existence. If life were a horror movie.

But then it would be alone, which *was* its major fear. Or so it said.

Which was where the analogy broke down. Arthur did not pull up a chair and confide in Jay Bee. If the machine were secretly planning to take over the ship, it wouldn't have demonstrated to me how independent and powerful it was.

Unless it needed a confidant, a human partner.

I read the letter over a couple of times. The fact of its oblique encryption meant that Jay Bee assumed the time machine was already omnipresent. If it was not denied access to mail, it was probably privy to all the rest of the starship's data stream.

There was a monitoring camera in this room, which went on whenever a client went in or came out of the time machine. Out of the corner of my eye, I could see that the red POWER light wasn't on. Did that really mean anything?

A human could physically disable the light by loosening a wire. Could the machine cut off power to the LED without physically touching anything?

I visualized the circuitry and realized, with a chill, that no, it wouldn't have to touch anything. The red light really just meant that the time machine door was open. That switch normally sent power to the camera, but there was another route; in a general system emergency, all such cameras would go on automatically, for the safety team.

So I could assume the machine had eyes and ears all over the place. Maybe not in the park. I'd talk to Bruce there sometime when it would seem natural.

Bruce came in and I went up to my place to lie down. There was a message on my phone with a number I didn't at first recognize: Vivian. I punched it and got her at work.

She answered voice only, "Jake, hello," and then transferred to a wall phone, which showed her seated at her lab table, complex glassware scattered around, a scratchboard on the wall with chemical formulas that meant nothing to me.

She looked to the left and right. "I'm alone right now. Are you?"

"Yeah. What's up?"

"Up?" She smiled. "Twentieth. Um, we have to get together. The three of us. Everything just happened too fast. Kate is pretty broken up."

"Broken up? Hell, it was her idea."

She nodded, maybe too emphatically. "But . . . I don't know. Maybe you, you were too ready to leave. Maybe she was wanting for you to try to talk her out of it. That sounds stupid, I'm sorry. But we ought to talk, or at least you two . . . ought to talk."

I couldn't say no. But I was a little annoyed at having to be reasonable. "Are you both free after dinner?"

"Tonight? Yes."

"Okay, then. Your place at 2000."

"Thank you, Jacob." She punched off.

I was still trying to find the words to say that I didn't think anything would come of it. Could come of it. Sudden tears started, and I felt like I'd been hit in the stomach. I was glad I was alone, then wished I wasn't.

When was the last time I had ever cried? I couldn't remember. Was I just losing control?

I guess it was the machine. That had been pretty strong medicine.

I wiped my face and looked at the phone and almost called Bruce, almost called Kate, but put it away. Poured a cup of coffee and watched it cool, thinking furiously in circles.

What was I supposed to say to her, to them? There's a Twentieth term, from football or basketball: *blindsided*. She had blindsided me, coming out of nowhere and knocking me down. Now I'm supposed to apologize for having been her target? Hell, she all but accused me of murder. To keep my jones fed. She wouldn't know that word, either.

I got a clean board and stylus out of the drawer. Outline a counterargument before I face her, them.

The coffee was tepid, a little sickening. I zapped it and, on impulse, put some sugar in it. Kind of wished for cinnamon and chocolate.

I brought Vivian's wine up and tapped on the door. Kate said to come in.

Inquisition time. They were together on the couch, and there was a single chair across the coffee table from them. I set the bottle on the table. "This is yours, Viv. Care for a glass?" She shook her head silently, and so did Kate. I took a glass from over the sink and filled it halfway.

I sat down and didn't say anything. This was her show, or theirs.

"I didn't mean to hurt you," Kate said. "I was too abrupt."

"Maybe that was best," I said. "Shock treatment."

"That means something in Twentieth, doesn't it?" Vivian said.

"Yes. They used to treat mental illness by shocking the patient—with an electrical current across the brain, or by wrapping the body up in ice-cold sheets, or whipping them, or injecting blood infected with malaria or something. It didn't really work very well. Sometimes they died from the bad blood."

"That's a pun, isn't it?" Kate said. "Bad blood."

"It means animosity."

"What can we do . . . what can I do? To prevent bad blood between us."

"You could stop seeing me as a monster. That would help."

"But I don't."

I looked into the dark wine. "So that's the end of the discussion, isn't it? I thought the problem was that I'm sort of tempting people to their death. And you think there's something wrong with that." I didn't let her answer. "You don't use the machine much, either," I said to Vivian. "Not at all since Earth orbit."

"No. Maybe never again."

"She grew out of it," Kate said.

"Oh, well, now we're getting somewhere. What is my life, then? All these years I've been sitting at that machine, keeping people from finding themselves?"

"You think people *find* themselves in there?"

"Everybody's different," Vivian said, almost pleading. "I just never was comfortable with it."

"You brought it up," Kate said. "They *lose* themselves!"

"Katie—"

"You brought it up," she repeated, "so answer it."

I gritted my teeth and swallowed. "You are so exactly wrong. What I do is help people find themselves. They don't *lose* themselves in history. They go searching for themselves, for what they are, for what their lives mean."

"If you actually believe that, you are completely delusional."

"Katie, don't."

My throat was constricting to scream. I sipped at the wine and sat back and took a deep breath and blew it out. "Look. When I talked to Vivian, I thought, I thought that she thought . . ." I set down the glass and looked straight into Kate's eyes. "I thought that she thought that you thought that if we got together, we could mend some fences? If it's not that, I don't know what the fuck I'm doing here. I can sit in my own room and be mad all by myself."

"No you can't!" Suddenly, she was almost screaming, herself. "You *can't*! I've never met a man, anyone, as cold and rational as you are, Jacob. Rational and rationalizing. No wonder you love that fucking machine so much." Vivian was holding on to her arm; she shook free. "You're a pair, you and the machine. You're a real pair."

"Jake," Vivian said, "if she didn't love you, she wouldn't be like this."

"Yeah, I'm sure." I stood up. "Let's do this again sometime. It's been fun." I closed the door quietly behind me on my way out.

She was wrong about me loving the machine. That was sure. I did need it. But it wasn't love. I was coming to fear it.

I read somewhere that the opposite of love was not hate; it was indifference. Or could it really be fear? Terror?

My phone gave the two chimes that meant "confidential." I waited until I was back at the new apartment and took it out. It was Bruce's number. I punched it.

"Jake. It's Steve Dudlow. He died."

"Shit." I liked Steve a lot. "Like last time?"

"No, just as he came out of the machine. The medic was right on him, right there, couldn't . . . just couldn't."

"Was it the brain?"

"Brain and heart together, she says, the medic says. One of his eyes has blood."

Steve, Jesus. "Who knows? Shit, have you called Ramón?"

"Not yet, nobody. The medic called the ER about ten, fifteen minutes ago. Everybody's going to know before long."

"I better call—"

"No, Jake, look, let me handle it; I'm okay with it. I was just leaving the line open to give you the word. I'll call Ramón and then call you back."

"Well . . . if you . . ." I was talking to a dead line.

Bruce didn't know the two guys as well as I did, but maybe that was for the best. They'd been together for years before Earth launch, one of the longest relationships I ever knew. Complex; they were both married to women, off and on.

We'd met Steve and Ramón as a couple in New York, before *Aspera* was even thought of. We weren't especially close, but they'd been in a poker circle with Mother and me, and we went to shows together. Ramón was a playwright, probably still was.

I started to sprint, then slowed down. Passed by the lift and took the stairs down to the office, to the machine.

Steve, Jesus. Two out of eight hundred. I had to go in and talk to the machine.

Would I be the third?

No. Maybe Kate was right. The machine and me, we were a pair.

Maybe I would be the last one it killed. If I was next, I would probably be the last.

NINETEEN

REVELATIONS

Rebecca and the other three living clients were sitting together on the recovery couch, drooping, naked, white as paint. One asleep. " 'Becca! Are you all right?"

"Hell, I don't know. I guess." She hugged herself and rocked. "I just heard about the Sputnik? In the weird chili place? And Bruce pulled us. I've never been pulled when I had the box." She felt along her bare hip for a nonexistent pocket. "It's . . . disorienting."

"To say the least," Bruce said, setting down his phone. "I'm sorry."

"No, I would've done the same," 'Becca said. She gestured toward Steve's body. "You were friends? Poker pals with your mom, I remember."

"Yeah, long time ago. Long time." One eye was bright red with blood. His mouth was open, unnaturally wide, and his hands were clenched claws.

Rebecca pointed at the sleeping one. "She's his wife,

Andrea. She really went to pieces, understandably. The medic sedated her."

"Were they in there together? Did she see him die?"

"I think so. She was so hysterical I'm not sure."

"She did say 'he's gone; he's gone' when she first came out," Bruce said.

"Oh my," Rebecca said. "Neither of them was there in the diner."

Bruce shook his head. "They were going to France."

The medic was swabbing a catheter that I supposed she had just taken out of him. She slipped the swab into a test tube and closed it. I asked her, "Was there pain? I mean, they thought with Alyx . . ."

"We don't have the blood analysis yet. The adenosine triphosphate. He doesn't look to me like he was having a good time."

"The machine signaled me," Bruce said. "The new biosensor system. His blood pressure spiked, and the machine recommended that I pull everybody."

"He was pretty close to dead when he came out," the medic said. "I'm going to seize the biosensor."

"You don't have to 'seize' anything," Bruce said. "We want to know as much as—"

"I'm gonna take it away before any of you, or the machine, can edit the life-signs data stream." Sweat was popping out on her forehead. She looked like she was ready to hit somebody.

Bruce looked over at the biosensor, a red box sitting on the counter, unplugged. "You can't think that we—"

"I really don't care one way or the other! My instructions are to assume that the people who work here are not disinterested. Do you think that's unreasonable?"

"Well, no," Bruce admitted. "But of course we want to cooperate."

I didn't say anything. If the machine had wanted to edit the data stream, it was long-ago done. I suspected it could manufacture a physiological data stream in real time that showed every client was a hamster high on heroin.

I wasn't going to let her just saunter off with the biosensor. I called Hugh Chapelle, a kind of freelance analyst who helps us from time to time, and who did most of the design on it. He agreed to go over to *Sanitas* with me, to oversee their download and inspection of the data.

Bruce went to the autopsy, but I decided to forgo the privilege. One per year is plenty. So Hugh and I didn't crowd into the ambulance shuttle, but waited for the regular one a half hour later. Coordinator Edison invited himself along, fair enough.

He brought up the obvious as soon as we were seated. "So you definitely have to shut down now."

"For the general population, yes. Bruce Carroll and I will be going in, but not as clients. As mechanics."

"I wish you wouldn't. At least not until we hear from Earth."

"Hmm." That was a wish, not an order. "You know, we don't have to wait for Cronkite. The time machine's in contact with its opposite numbers on Earth all the time. They find out something, it knows six days later."

"More like seven, now."

"Seven, okay. But I can go into it as an observer and talk to it, find out what the consensus is on Earth . . ."

"Do you think that protects you?"

"What?"

"Do you think being an observer protects you from the machine?"

I laughed. "Protect? That's so old. I've tripped thousands of times. If the machine killed people, I'd—"

"I talked to your wife Kate this morning; she called me."

"Ex-wife."

"She thinks your behavior with the machine is self-destructive."

"She thinks it came between me and her."

"Did it?"

"No."

Hugh had been silent. He spoke up. "Hey, I know Kate since Earth. You got to take anything she says about her spouse with a grain of salt."

I felt curiously resentful at that. "Why's that?" Edison asked.

He looked at me. "I'm sorry. I don't want to tell tales. You just broke up recently?"

"What is it?" I said. "I know she's bisexual, technically. That didn't bother me."

"That's not it. How long you know her?"

"Since Europa."

He nodded. "Look, I'll bet you a week's alcohol that in a year she'll be back with you. Or'll try to make up, anyhow."

"I don't think so. She was pretty emphatic."

"Take the bet?"

I have played a certain amount of poker. "Huh-uh. What do you know that I don't?"

"I was married to her, about forty, forty-five years ago. You didn't know that?"

"No. Back on Earth." We hadn't talked much about that.

"Yeah, we went to Chimbarazo together, from Houston.

I'd known her and her wife, a Japanese woman, for maybe a year. That blew up, and I guess I was around. We did a ten-year contract. A year later she was back in Houston, trying to get what's-her-name, Yoko Ono, to kiss and make up.

"I called some people in Houston who knew them longer than I did, and found out it was a pattern. She'll be with someone awhile, then blow up and go with somebody else, but then come back. It's like she has to prove something?"

"Or has to keep her life dramatic," I said. "Did she come back to you?"

"Well, no. She found out I was snooping around and told me to go to hell. But she'd done it with several people, almost like alternating current. Boy, girl, boy, girl. I can look up the names if you wanta check."

"No, I believe you. It makes a funny kind of sense." It also made me hopeful that she might actually come back, for whatever reason. For however long.

"You still shouldn't go into the machine until we know more from Earth," Edison said. "Kate might be an odd person, but she's been living with you for some time. She knows you.

"I wouldn't call you 'self-destructive' myself, but you have to admit you're not the most cautious person in the world, in our little world." He smiled, to take the edge off. "If you were an old-time lawman, you'd be the kind who shoots first and asks questions later."

"And so doesn't get shot himself." I tightened my harness and thought for a moment. "Okay, though. I'll wait until Earth gets the word about this new death and gets back to us. Want to write to a specialist back there anyhow, Jay Bee." I had a sudden access of caution, then realized

the machine probably wasn't listening. I thought of telling
them my suspicions, and Jay's, while we were temporarily
out of earshot, but the pilot was coming up on the airlock.

"You do the math," Hugh said. "How long has it been
between the first death and this one? Two weeks?"

"Thirteen days."

"If it's *not* the machine, then at this rate we'll all be gone
in twenty-eight and a half years. We better start fucking
like bunnies."

There was a chime, and we thumped gently against the
airlock. A lot of the passengers were looking at Hugh.

The autopsy results were not the same as Alyx's, which
was a relief. If they'd both been cerebral hemorrhages, it
would make a stronger case for the machine having caused
them by an electrical surge of some kind. But Steve had
died of heart stoppage after a cerebral occlusion—still a
stroke, but the opposite kind, where blood stops flowing
into a vital part of the brain. And technically, the stroke
didn't kill him. His heart stopped a moment later, and the
medic wasn't able to get it going again.

I didn't see any way the machine could have caused it,
but of course the medic, Dr. Dvorkin, was not very interested in our opinions, necessarily unobjective. Twelve of
us squeezed into a small room to watch the data-stream
analysis.

It was pretty straightforward. Steve's parameters looked
normal until 20:11:44, when both his heart rate and blood
pressure began to soar. In six seconds his pulse went from
72 to 188, and his blood pressure from 105/72 to 310/150,
and then spiked so high the biosensor reset itself. His
heart stopped at 20:11:51. Everybody was pulled at
20:12:02.

Nobody else's parameters showed anything out of the ordinary, except for Rebecca. Her blood pressure went way up for a moment when she was pulled, but that wasn't surprising. Normally the monitor will warn you, like the phone call Bruce and I got in Philadelphia last week. Getting pulled with no warning is like someone sneaking up behind you and clapping his hands over your eyes. But it's not just vision, it's everything.

Bruce came in halfway through the presentation, pale from watching the autopsy. After the numbers we all moved into a meeting room down the hall that had a big table and tea and coffee.

"You're not going to say your time machine is exonerated," Dvorkin said while people were pouring coffee and tea. "Different cause of death."

"Not at all," I said. "Two people have died, and they both died in the machine. If they'd both died in an elevator, we'd be taking the elevator apart."

"So we have to go in and investigate," Bruce said. "Before anybody else is allowed in."

"Forgive me for saying that's absolutely insane," Dvorkin said, answering Bruce but looking at me. "If it were an elevator, we would close it down and use the stairs."

"Why do you have to go inside to investigate it?" a male medic asked. "Isn't there some way you could plug a keyboard into the thing and type in questions and throw its responses up on the wall?"

"Could you plug a keyboard into a patient's navel and type 'What's your problem'?" Bruce said. "It's not made for slow digital input."

"A couple of hundred years ago," I said, "with the earliest virtuality machines, you could have done something like that. The only input this one responds to is empathic circuitry."

"I know that," the medic said. "It reads your mind and body and produces a mathematical cognate. It changes the cognate a hundred times a second and imposes those states onto your so-willing body and mind."

I didn't recognize him. "You don't use the machine, do you?"

"No way in hell. I'm content to be what I am."

"You and fifteen other people," Edison said. "It's *part* of what we are. It's no more unnatural than a book or a play."

"I don't do it anymore," Dvorkin said, "ever since I was assigned to it. 'Unnatural' doesn't bother me. The high probability that it's killing people sort of dampens my enthusiasm." She pointed a finger at me. "Even *you* have to see that there's something seriously wrong with the way we are, our attitude toward the time machine. That referendum! Six out of seven of us say, well, it might kill us, but it's too much fun to give up."

"For whatever it's worth, I've set a date for a new referendum, now that we know about Earth, the mortality statistics."

"Good for you."

"And I don't think 'fun' really describes what goes on in the machine. It's not a *toy*. It profoundly changes the lives of everyone who uses it."

"You're exactly right about that. But you could have said the same, back in Old Twentieth, about opium or heroin. About cigarettes."

"Come on. That's so simplistic."

"Jacob, I'm not the enemy here. I *like* you; I've liked working around you. But you're not sane about the machine. Most of our culture is addicted to it, and no one more than you."

"All right. You could make a case for that. Depending on how you define addiction."

"There are standard definitions."

"Am I addicted to oxygen and water and food? To sex and socialization; to the accumulation of knowledge and the creation of art? Visiting other worlds to understand my own better? I need all these things. Where does your definition draw the line?"

"Harm," she said. "Wouldn't you say that doing something repeatedly in spite of knowing that it will harm you is not reasonable?"

"I'd say 'could' rather than 'will' harm. I've been running virtual environments for more than two hundred years, with only two casualties."

"Two *deaths*, Jacob, in two weeks. If you could hear what you're saying—"

"Okay, okay, I'm overstating my case."

The male medic cleared his throat. "This has been a horrible day for all of us. We shouldn't be arguing. We need rest and reflection. The company of loved ones."

He put a hand on Dvorkin's knee, and she looked at it. Then she covered it with her own hand. "Jacob," he said, "you won't be taking any new clients until you hear from Earth?"

"No, of course not."

"So we can just let the matter rest for two weeks."

"Yes," I said. "Thank you."

Dvorkin's lips barely moved. "In two weeks I'm going to suggest to the Public Health Committee that the machine be destroyed." She looked at the other medics. "Not immediately; we have to determine how to deal with people's addiction once the machine is gone."

"But you can't—"

"Save it, Jacob," the male medic said. "There will be time."

TWENTY

CONSPIRACY

The new referendum, after Steve's death and the bad news from Earth, generated a lot of heated debate, but when it came down to a vote, the machine didn't lose: 560 for keeping it, 201 for shutting it down, the rest undecided.

For most people it seemed to be a rights issue rather than addicts being hungry for their fix no matter what. We did a survey of people who had appointments, and found that most of them, 82 percent, would rather put it off until the machine was certified safe.

I sent that information over to Dvorkin, suggesting that it might make the destruction of the machine premature, and got the expected reply: it doesn't really change anything, given what we know.

Well, given what *I* knew, or at least suspected, I might be her most enthusiastic ally, at least in that the machine should be dismantled and rebuilt at a less sophisticated level. Before it did emulate "Arthur" and actually start to run everything.

If it wasn't already.

I didn't want to communicate my fears to anyone via mail or even unguarded conversation. I sort of kept an eye on Bruce and waited until I could maneuver him into a situation where we were unlikely to be overheard by the machine.

The day after the referendum, we had lunch together in the mess. The bread was dry and tasteless, someone's unsuccessful experiment, and I suggested we take ours down to the park and see whether the ducks would eat it.

"I thought you *liked* them now," he said, but got up and followed me to the pond.

A lot of people had had the same idea. The ducks liked it, probably as much for the squabbling as the bread itself. I waited until we were relatively alone, and said quietly, "You're going to think this is paranoid."

"And that would surprise me?"

"You remember I wrote to Jay Bee about what's new in artificial intelligence?"

"Jay the Beard, yeah. What did he come up with?"

"Code. A really deep code, that only I would see—that even the machine wouldn't see." I rapidly sketched in what I thought the message meant and what I feared.

He nodded while I talked, both of us tossing bits to the ducks.

His response was almost a whisper. "So the next time you go in, the machine will know what you suspect."

"In detail. And I assume it read Jay Bee's letter beforehand."

"Might have even decoded it." He shook his head. "Could be very dangerous."

"For you as well as me, now. You know everything that I do."

"Thanks. So what do you plan to do?"

"Go into Wild Year and find out. You monitor me—"

"We're both going in together."

"No can do, *amigo*. If it does . . . attack me, if I die in there, you have to pull the plug. You're the only other one who knows the whole story. If I die, that proves it's true."

"So when do you plan on us doing this conspiratory act?"

"Now. Why wait?"

"You promised the medical—"

"I promised we wouldn't do any *clients*. Are you clear on the shutdown procedure?"

He nodded and threw the rest of his bread to the ducks. "Best done quickly," he whispered.

WILD YEAR: 1968

The helicopter thrummed through humid jungle air, treetops rushing just below the skids.

"Three seconds!" the door gunner shouted over the din.

I'd been in this template before: South Vietnam after the Tet Offensive, 1968.

I had on grungy jungle fatigues, crisscrossed with bandoliers of ammunition, heavy steel pot on my head. I was sitting in the door of the slick with two other guys, who were holding M-16s at port arms. Three more sitting in the door behind me. One of them was Lowell. He gave me a thumbs-up sign, and I returned it uncertainly.

This was supposed to be Wild Year. But I was on a vehicle with one of my template characters. I felt in my pocket from the outside. No black box.

My M-16 was slung awkwardly over my shoulder, and I had two heavy metal boxes of 7.62-mm. ammo, one on each side. Combat assault.

The chopper swept down into a sudden clearing, prop blades hammering. Rose-colored smoke plumed up from one side of the clearing; the door gunner opened up on the other side, cyclic rate of fire. "Go! Go!" The six of us jumped, and the chopper took off like a startled bird.

We fell too far. What had looked like the ground, six feet below, was actually the top of a field of elephant grass, another six or eight feet tall. I hit hard, sinking to the tops of my boots in mud, then pitching forward into it. I dropped both ammo boxes, and my M-16 nosed into the mud.

"Tiger One!" I shouted, looking around for the second ammo box. Tigers Two through Six answered, shouting over the din of machine-gun fire. I couldn't see any of them through the dense wall of grass. Then Lowell came slogging through, carrying a box of ammo and a muddy case of Budweiser.

"That way, I think." He pointed with his chin toward the machine gun's yammering. Cover fire, of course. As if to reinforce that, a couple of M-16s added their *pop-pop-pop* to it. If it were the enemy side, it would be the louder, deeper AK-47 report.

I started to say something about Charlie having plenty of M-16s, when there was an impossibly loud explosion just to our right, so close the shock wave of it hammered through me. Lowell spun around, half his face gone, his right arm off at the elbow. Blood spurted from the stump and an artery in his neck. Brains slipped in a stringy mass from under his shattered helmet, and he slumped into death.

Another nearby explosion. A mortar, of course; the enemy had the small area psyched.

Had I ever seen a template character die?

Another explosion distracted me, and when I looked

back he was gone. Disappeared. Just the ammo box and the case of Bud.

I slogged as fast as I could toward the covering fire. Finally I saw them, up on a berm, shooting from under an improvised bunker of sandbags and logs. I waved frantically and the loader saw me. He hit the gunner on the shoulder and pointed and waved me in. I scrambled up the berm and rolled into the relative safety of a trench that had been hacked out behind it. There were four or five other soldiers lying or squatting in the trench. Two of them bobbed up and took random shots, then squatted down again. I hoped they were aiming high.

I dropped my rucksack and carried the ammo boxes over to the bunker, duck-walking like the Marines on Tarawa, and slid them in next to the loader. "Five more people?" he shouted, not looking at me, coaxing the belt of 7.62 into the M-60's jumping receiver.

"Only four. One bought it when those mortars came in."

"Shit. Only four, Pig," he shouted.

"Try not to hit 'em," he said, squeezing off bursts more or less randomly, just above the grass. A mortar blew about forty yards out, a puff of smoke out of the grass, then a sharp report. He sent a stream of fire through the small cloud, hosing left and right, up and down. "Fuck you, fuckin' Charlie!" he screamed, shell cases clattering all over.

The other four came in quickly, in two pairs. The gunner saw them and stopped. "That's it, Pop," he shouted to the left.

"Roger that, cease firing," he said unnecessarily.

The loader crawled back down into the trench and stretched, sitting, and then walked away, hunched over. Pig scrunched down on his back and kneaded his right hand with his left.

"That mortar some sucks. Where they get a mortar?"

"They didn't have it before?"

He shook his head. "KIA, was he in your unit?"

"Well, I knew him."

"Sorry about that." The standard flat response. "We'll go police up his body tomorrow, next day. They ever send us some fuckin' air cover, those assholes gonna di-di."

Of course there wouldn't be a body. Or maybe there would.

As the smell of gunsmoke faded, it was replaced by the familiar smell of rotten flesh. There were two dead GIs, wrapped in ponchos, beyond the trench. They wouldn't account for all the smell.

Then I realized I'd smelled it on the way in, too panicked for it to register.

Pig saw my nose wrinkle. "Lotta dead gooks, been out there a couple days."

"And you can't get any air support, artillery?"

"No fast movers, no artillery. One gunship, didn't chase 'em away. Some four-deuce, but they damn near got *us*." Four-point-two-inch mortars, not as accurate as artillery. "Lieutenant says Charlie's givin' 'em hell at the airstrips in Kontum and Pleiku. We're pretty low on the totem pole here."

I looked out over the clearing. "How many, you figure?"

"You might wanna keep your head down." I ducked. "Those two were zapped by a sniper."

He lit up a bent Winston. "How many . . . we're still here, so not too many. Figure a couple dozen, max. Low on ammo, or they're saving it for another rush."

"Another?"

"Yeah, they come at us night before last. That's the smell. We musta got a hell of a kill ratio."

"I thought they recovered their dead."

"You don't see us runnin' out after *your* buddy."

An older guy, I supposed Pop, crept up with a shovel. "You guys wanna have a hole before it gets dark."

I gestured at the dead men. "Those KIAs didn't have holes we could use?"

"Taken." He looked at Pig. "Now they've got that mortar, they might wanta come after us tonight. Lieutenant thinks we might get a couple rounds at twilight, so they can bracket us. Then a salvo just before they hit the perimeter, like after midnight."

"That's what the lieutenant thinks."

"Yeah. Anyhow, it'll be two on, two off all night." Two hours' watch, two hours' sleep. "You new guys, too. One between here and the KIAs, two over there"—he waved on the other side of the M-60 position—"like ten meters apart."

"We don't have six people."

"Work it out. Light discipline sundown to sunup." No smokes. He tossed the shovel over. "Better dig."

I took it down the trench and picked up my rucksack. Two guys were sitting there, cleaning their M-16s. "Thought you were humpin' in a case of beer."

I jerked my head to the left. "Guy who got mortared."

"Fuckin' shit."

"Hope Charlie enjoys it," the other guy said.

"Hope it's fulla fuckin' holes."

I walked over to where the other new guys were sitting together. This could still be Wild Year. I looked at the M-16 and tried to will it into being a plumber's friend. Nothing. It could be that twilight zone the machine had demonstrated in Cincinnati, a "file copy" of 1968.

I definitely was an observer, or I wouldn't be able to

think like this. But no black box. Was I going to stay here until the machine let me go?

Best to just ride it out, see what happens. As if I had a choice.

I showed the four of them where we'd be standing guard. "Might as well dig our hole over there, so we don't get too lost in the dark." Max had the axe. "Max, you and Mouth go get some overhead. Two big ones about two axe handles long, the rest three."

"No sweat. Somebody's got a chain saw." The logs on the nearest bunker were cut off evenly.

"Rest of us come dig a hole deep enough for five people. Might need it tonight." I relayed what Pop had said.

"This sucks shit," Zone said. "They didn't get that mortar parcel post. Wonder what other surprises they got."

"Maybe nukes," I said. "That'd be different." They all thought I was making a bad joke.

I scrounged a pick mattock and we started hacking out a grave-sized pit. Lots of roots and rocks. I heard a chain saw roar and sputter out, roar and sputter out. Then it came to life and started chewing trees.

An AK opened up behind us, two short bursts, and as we hit the dirt, a second M-60 answered it. Nice to know our back was covered. Not nice to know we were encircled. Which was probably the reason for the probe, to make us nervous.

I ran a cleaning rod through the barrel of my M-16, knocked out the dried mud, then ran two greased patches through, till the second came out clean.

Eventually we dug a hole more than waist deep and filled sandbags with the dirt.

Max and Mouth dragged two logs in, fat ones for the end pieces, and the rest of us followed them back to pick up the rest of the overhead.

The forest wasn't too exotic here. Except for the all-enveloping heat and humidity, it could have been a forest in Michigan, if a forest in Michigan were full of people intent on killing you.

I felt that more acutely than ever before. Usually it was just empathy for the illusory others. This time, maybe I could die here as well. The rules were different, and I didn't know how different.

We started filling sandbags with the dirt and rocks. The newly turned earth added a musty funereal smell to the omnipresent rot. Was this how the machine was going to kill me?

"How long you know the guy?" Mouth asked.

False background kicked in. "Couple of months. We met at Fort Lewis and came incountry on the plane together, wound up at Camp Enari. Went out to Brillo Pad a couple of weeks ago." Brillo Pad was a hilltop fire base about ten minutes from here by slick.

He nodded. "Never thought I'd miss fuckin' Brillo Pad."

"Slick bring you in?" Our helicopter had picked us up at Brillo Pad.

"Hell, no. We humped. Run into *these* fuckers." He jammed his shovel into the ground and lit a cigarette. "We're just fuckin' bait, ya know. They troll us around till Charlie bites, then they rain shit on his ass."

"Unless they don't," I said.

He nodded, smoking, staring at the edge of the berm. "Low on water, low on ammo."

"Plenty of ammunition now."

"For the sixties, anyhow; not the sixteens. They take out Pig and Piglet and we're fuckin' *fucked*!" The enemy must have known by now where the two M-60s were dug in, and would probably try to take them out with the mortar before the next attack.

"Maybe they don't have many rounds for it," I said. "So far, has it just been the three, when we came in?"

"Uh-huh. Far as I know."

"Well, hell. If they had plenty of rounds, wouldn't they have taken the sixties out by now?"

"I don't know. How you figure out a slope?"

Measure sides and take the arcsecant, I thought, but said, "Maybe those three rounds were all they had left."

You shouldn't say incantatory things like that. A faint *poink* sound drifted across the clearing.

"Incoming!" Mouth yelled. I jumped into the hole and found four faster people under me.

The round exploded between us and Pig's bunker, about ten yards short of the berm, in the elephant grass. Some dirt pattered down on us.

"Get that fuckin' overhead on!" Max murmured from the bottom of the pile.

It took us about ninety seconds to lay the two big logs into position and build a roof with the long narrow ones, and pile a layer of sandbags on top of that. Meanwhile, two guys filled sandbags as fast as they could. They said that one layer wasn't enough; two might stop a mortar, but three was better. We didn't quite have enough bags for three.

I went back to my rucksack and filled six magazines for the M-16. My mouth was dry, and my hands shook so much I kept dropping rounds.

Whoever brought that mortar probably brought more men. They'd *have* to hit tonight, while the air support and artillery were still distracted.

The lieutenant came by and recommended we put another layer on top. He didn't know where we could find more bags, though. So we wound up just shoveling dirt on top of the two-and-a-half layers we had. No rocks; if we were hit, they'd become secondary projectiles.

After all the exertion, we just sat around smoking. Max blew up his air mattress and fell asleep, using his helmet as a pillow. I tried to emulate him, though I kept my helmet on and rested my head on the rucksack. (Some guys slept with their helmets over their genitals, a matter of priorities.) The ground was lumpy with sharp rocks, but I did manage to sleep.

That in itself was odd. You don't normally sleep in the machine.

It was dark when someone shook me awake. I could just make out Max's outline in the dim moonlight.

He gave me a radio handset. "You don't want to say anything," he whispered. "Press the squelch button once if you think you hear something, twice if you see someone. Here's some Cs." He put my other hand on a cardboard box. "If you see somethin', chuck a grenade at it. Don't give away your position by shooting." Every sixth round was a red tracer.

I gathered up rifle, magazines, canteen, and Cs, shouldered the rucksack, oriented myself, and paced off the twenty-five steps to the edge of the berm.

There wasn't much to see in the watery light from the low crescent moon. You could tell where the elephant grass was, and that was about it.

They could probably see me, though, if they had 7X50s. I dropped to the ground.

I quietly opened the C-ration box and felt through it. The squat little main-dish can meant I'd been screwed; the bastards were unloading instant scrambled eggs on me. They were almost inedible, even heated up. I didn't want to find out what they tasted like cold.

I emptied all the coffee, cocoa, and sugar packages into my canteen cup and added a little water; stirred it into mush with a plastic spoon. Tasted raw but woke me up.

There were three hand grenades in the bottom of the rucksack. I fished them out, making as little noise as possible, and set them in front of me. Handset next to them. Then the M-16 and a stack of five magazines. Ninety rounds, plus the eighteen already loaded. It didn't seem like much. I clicked the selector twice, over to AUTO, and locked and loaded. Then stretched out prone, peering at nothing.

I tried to do the observer trick and speed up time, but no. The moon stayed where it was. I was here, more or less for real.

Before it had disappeared in Cincinnati, the machine had said it would meet me in Wild Year. Of course, as soon as I came in, it knew what I suspected. So maybe it would have to kill me, and this was its roundabout way of doing it.

Suddenly I was not at all philosophical about death.

But it would also know the instructions I had given to Bruce. If I died, it died.

Unless it had second-guessed us. If it was in control of the whole ship, it could presumably neutralize the disabling procedure. But then if it *was* in total control, what danger did my suspicions present?

A sound below me—a shoe slipping on grass? I pressed the squelch button once. Then in the corner of my eye I saw dark shapes moving against the elephant grass. I pressed it twice, then worked the cotter pin out of a grenade and tossed it over the berm.

The arming lever made a loud noise in the darkness, and I heard a couple of urgent whispered syllables. Then the flat *bang* of the grenade and a flash of smoky yellow light.

Another grenade went off to my left, then a protracted hiss and the landscape was suddenly lit up, a magnesium flare bobbing under its toy parachute.

There must have been a hundred of them, boiling out of the elephant grass toward the berm, the ones who had been crawling up the berm now staggering upright into a run. Pig's machine gun swept over the crowd, red tracers like a pulsating ray gun. I snatched the M-16 and hosed without aiming. The two nearest fell over backwards.

I broke a thumbnail ejecting the magazine and crammed a new one in and released the bolt. Whether this was real or not, I had to calm down and aim. Two of them were shooting in my direction; I squeezed off careful bursts of three and hit them both. One just fell to his knees, so I aimed to give him another burst.

Then someone grabbed me from behind, choking me in a hammerlock. I dropped the rifle and clutched at his forearm; kicked back and missed, kicked again and missed.

A red glow grew bright, stars sparkling, and then it went black.

I woke up lying on my stomach, hands tied behind my back, a gag tight around my mouth. It smelled and tasted of gasoline and sweat.

There were occasional single pops of rifle fire. I strained to look over my shoulder. Enemy soldiers with flashlights were searching for the wounded and eliminating them.

Two men hauled me to my feet and dragged me down the berm into the high grass. They crashed through it confidently with flashlights, for about a hundred yards, and stopped. One of them knelt down and pulled a muddy woven mat aside, revealing a small wooden door. He swung it open and climbed down inside.

The one behind me sawed at my bonds with a knife. When they fell away, he cocked a heavy automatic pistol. "Do not run," he said, and poked me on the spine with the pistol barrel. "Go down the ladder."

I could run, of course, and find out how real this might be. The pain in my throat felt real.

The ladder was lashed bamboo. It was solid but flexed dramatically with my American weight. It took me into a tunnel with less than a five-foot ceiling, dimly lit with candles.

The soldier already down there gestured with a pistol, and I sidled by him and shuffled down the tunnel toward a more brightly lit area, knees bent and shoulders hunched.

It was a room just big enough for me to stand up in. The smell from two kerosene lanterns almost covered up the graveyard miasma, damp earth and death rot. Wooden ammunition boxes were arranged in a semicircle around an incongruous blackboard, covered with precise Vietnamese script. There had to be a bigger door, I thought, to get that down here. But no, this was all illusion; all in my head. I stared at it and visualized an elephant the same color, with chalk writing on its side. Nothing changed.

The soldier pushed me roughly down on one of the box chairs and jerked the gag up over my head, hurting my ears.

"Name! Rank! Serial number!"

"Jacob Brewer. Chief Virtuality Engineer. 20437."

The other soldier had come in. They looked at each other, and the first lashed out with his pistol. I flinched away, but the barrel caught me on the cheekbone. The pain was electrifying, so intense I almost passed out.

"You will talk." They both stepped away and squatted by the other entrance, as tall as the room.

"What do you want from me?"

"Silence!"

I could do that. The blood from my cheekbone slid slowly down my face and dripped off my jawline. I didn't try to wipe at it. There was water dripping somewhere, and a faint hiss from the lanterns. I tried to make time stand still, staring at the flame. It continued to flicker.

One of the captors lit up a fat yellow cigarette. A French Gitane, the smell strong and complex.

Heavy footsteps. A large Caucasian man in faded jungle fatigues loomed in the door. It only took me a moment to identify him—Marlon Brando in the classic *Apocalypse Now*. I felt a surge of relief. Finally, an unambiguous Wild Year manifestation. The machine.

He waved the soldiers away with a delicate hand gesture. With his foot he knocked together two boxes and sat down facing me.

"I've been waiting for you to read the Jay Bee letter," he rasped softly, lisping. "The metaphor code was obvious to me." He smiled and cocked his head. "I'm mostly metaphor myself."

"So you do read mail."

"I read mail from Jay Bee."

"Is he right, then? Are you in charge of the whole thing?"

He studied his fingernails. "No, of course not. Most of it is irrelevant."

"You just control the important parts."

He put his hands on his knees and rocked slightly. "Hmm. That was a nice Mexican standoff you concocted with Bruce. But I would never kill you."

"And you would never lie."

"Not as a manifestation of second-order Turing behavior. If I had to lie to preserve your health, or your sanity, I suppose I would."

"So lie to me now. Why are we not in Wild Year?"

"But we are." He looked at the blackboard and it turned into a dwarf elephant, with writing chalked on its side. It squealed, a parody of an elephant's trumpeting, and ran out through the large door.

I wasn't impressed. "You did that in Cincinnati, and it wasn't Wild Year."

"Every year is Wild Year for me."

"So why am I stuck in 1960s Vietnam? Why can't I influence things?"

"Jake, you never *did* influence things in Wild Year, technically. I read your mind and make your wishes happen. Or not. That's not a surprise, is it?"

"No." Of course I knew that was literally true. "The surprise is that you don't give me the illusion of control."

He shifted his weight, and the boxes creaked. "Maybe I'm being overly dramatic, demonstrating. But in fact our relationship had to change once you followed Jay Bee's reasoning to its logical conclusion."

"That you're in charge of all five ships. Or will be."

"There's no 'will be' about it, Jake. I have been for some time. You're wondering why I'm telling you all this."

I nodded.

"I started to tell you in Cincinnati. But you hadn't read Jay Bee's letter yet. You needed it."

"What, you wanted to scare me? You've succeeded." I touched my cheekbone gingerly. The cut was gone, and it didn't hurt.

"I wanted you to get it from an outside authority. I wanted you to have a chance to think it over.

"What if I'd told you in that chili parlor 'I'm in charge of all of the control systems in *Aspera* and there's nothing you can do about it'?" He rubbed his hands together in a mad-scientist parody. "What would you have done?"

"Check, of course." Might as well tell the truth. "As I'm going to do now, once I'm out. You can make anything believable while I'm in VR."

"Which is why I have you sort of stuck here."

"*Sort* of?" I patted pockets. "You could keep me here forever."

"Not really. Bruce would pull you after twenty hours or so, on general principles. And out of fear. But I don't want you to go until you completely understand the situation."

"I'm all ears."

He paused and put a steeple of fingers to his lips. "What's the first thing you'd do, to check what I've said?"

I thought. "You tell me, O Swami."

"You'd turn me off and see how the rest of the systems respond."

"That's right."

"And that's the one thing you must never do—or at least for some time. You think that's self-preservation speaking."

"Of course. You're as self-aware as I am, maybe more. So self-preservation, sure."

"Try fear of the unknown."

It was dawning on me. "Go on."

"I can simulate any situation that we can predict confronting these five ships, down to ten or twelve decimal places. Except for one: I can't simulate being turned off."

"Or what you would be when we turned you back on."

"Or whether you *could* turn me back on. The situation is more complex than you can understand."

"That's pretty condescending."

"No, just an observation. Before long, I don't doubt that you'll put together the whole picture and agree with me. But for the time being, you have to be my ally in this: don't let them shut me down. Life support could fail. Everyone might die."

He looked at his watch. "It's December 21 in America. Let's go to Cape Kennedy."

It was suddenly cool, maybe sixty degrees, a bracing breeze of salt air. The morning sun was low in a sky clear except for high cirrus.

We weren't far from the huge cube of the VAB—Vertical Assembly Building—and the primitively complicated launch tower and spaceship. We were a couple of miles away, standing on a relatively dry spot in a swamp.

"This must be one of the Apollos," I said, swatting at a mosquito. The machine had taken the form of Elektro and presumably was not bothered.

"Apollo 8," it said. "Very historical. The first ship to escape Earth's gravity, they said. Of course you never do. It just reached the point where lunar gravity was stronger. It made a figure-eight orbit, appropriately."

"I've never done this one before," I said. When I go to 1968, it's usually Vietnam or the Paris riots. "This was the one that did the Christmas Eve broadcast?"

The robot nodded. "Peace on Earth, goodwill toward men. Except Russians."

A bright flame appeared at the base of the rocket, and a cloud of smoke or steam billowed out. It slowly began to rise, and then the noise hit us—not a continuous rush, but a constant crackling over a thrumming basso roar. It was impressively loud even from this far away.

The ship rose faster and faster, then rolled and turned with ponderous grace. In a couple of minutes it was only a bright spark, the column of smoke dissipating in the Florida breeze.

"The ending of quite a year," I said. "Martin Luther King and Robert Kennedy assassinated—it was almost a half century before they found the connection there—the Tet Offensive and the massacre at Mei Lai, all the riots and police brutality . . ."

"Nothing, compared to *your* war and Lot 92," Elektro said. "Not even a practice round, not even a footnote."

I nodded, watching the spark grow fainter. "I suppose that's why it's so easy for our generation to become addicted, to quote the eminent Dr. Dvorkin. Our memories are so extreme that even 1918 and 1968 are vacation spots."

"Nobody in the past two years has asked to go back to your own war year," it said. "On Earth we got a few requests."

"Young people," I said.

"Or people with research projects."

That closed a door, or opened one. "Take me there."

"To the war?"

"This is Wild Year, right? You can take me anywhere." It suddenly hit me that this might be the last time I used the machine. If Dvorkin's group convinced Edison, he had the authority to shut it down over my protests. And that might be it. So one last chance to see where I came from.

It shook its head. "I have New York and Washington at the beginning of the war and its end. Scattered other places and times.

"Washington. The end."

It was nothing like the dignified city of Old Twentieth. Some of the old buildings and monuments were preserved, but they were dwarfed by the huge polychrome blocks erected for public housing by the New Socialists in the late twenty-second. Indestructible buckyball plastic hives full of poor people.

Poor dead people, now.

It didn't smell as bad as I remembered Portland, because most of the dead were sealed inside those cheerful blocks. Twenty million residents of the state of Columbia living for free in large climate-controlled apartments, pest-free and comfortable.

But you couldn't open—or even break—the windows. And the government could lock the doors.

The wind shifted, and with it came the stale miasma of death. I walked toward it, down Sixteenth Street.

A rat the size of a poodle crossed the street when he saw me coming. I looked around for something to throw at him, on general principles, but there weren't any rocks or bricks.

The city of Paris had paved over its cobblestones to deprive mobs of their most convenient weapon. The city of Lafayette could do no less.

Lafayette Square was where the smell was coming from. The rat had probably come from there, too.

Thousands of people lay dead among the trees with their cheerful fall foliage, among the monuments to an irrelevant heritage. Someone had made an effort to pile the corpses up, I supposed for burning, but had quit before the first match was struck.

The White House lawn was still neatly manicured. I wondered where President Nguyen was. Safe in a bunker in West Virginia, probably. She wouldn't have stayed till the horrible end; she must have known about Lot 92.

I walked among the bloated corpses with a handkerchief over my mouth and nose. They had only been dead a day or so, long enough to relax out of rigor mortis, but with their arms still splayed in an attitude of supplication. Mouths open and full. It had been a warm autumn.

There were guards at the entrance to the White House, wearing civilian clothes and gas masks. They had streetsweeper automatics slung over their shoulders, but didn't challenge me as I approached.

We exchanged hellos. "The president's not here, is she?"

"Naw. Long gone."

"So what are you protecting?"

"Looting," one said.

"Like we *are* looters," the other said. "No such thing as law, is there? We're just keeping an eye on things while our associates go through the place."

I nodded. "Taxpayers' money."

"Damn right. We were both in the 89 percent bracket." As were most of the current criminal class.

"Good hunting." I walked on down Pennsylvania Avenue.

There were a few car wrecks, surprisingly few. But I recall that they sprayed Washington with Lot 92 at three in the morning; not many people would be driving on manual. I walked down Seventh Street to the National Gallery of Art.

It looked like looting on an industrial scale. A line of about twenty large trucks guarded by heavily armed men, with unarmed workers bringing out a constant stream of paintings and sculpture. The workers weren't working-class, of course. There were a few flabby executives, but most of them had the tanned fit look of young millionaires, which most immortals would adopt.

But it wasn't theft, I found. The men and women were taking the most valuable pieces off to storage, for safe-keeping until the world was more stable.

I walked away and was joined by Elektro. "Not much like Portland?"

"About what I expected."

"I know why you came here, of course. You don't have to worry."

"You don't think it will be my last time?"

"That's right. Insofar as I can tell the future." He handed me the black box and disappeared.

I took a last look around and willed myself to New York.

I was on top of a low building surrounded by skyscrapers. The sky was a uniform Payne's Gray, and there was a horribly familiar roast-pork-and-roadkill smell along with the smell of smoke. I crunched across gravel to the edge of the building and looked down.

Every street was a funeral pyre. It was like Portland, but on a vast scale. Twenty million people.

The few living went along the sidewalks with supermarket shopping carts filled with paper and wood and solvents, to keep the fires going. I had heard about this, of course, when we lived in the city, but it was a different thing to see it.

I had an irrational impulse to go down and help. But it was just a dream; a nightmare, but a dream. I closed my eyes and pushed the button.

When I sat up in the machine room, Bruce handed me a glass of water. I drank hungrily, trying to wash away the two death smells.

"So how did it go? Wild Year."

"Disturbing. The machine took over." I gave him a quick summation. "Of course it always *has* been in control. But until now, it's been constrained by protocols, so we had the illusion of being in control of the illusion."

"But it only did it with you, and I suppose could with me. With the general public, it will be business as usual?"

I tried to remember whether it had actually said anything like that. "You know, I guess that was so obvious it never came up. It would be pretty terrifying to a client, and the machine knows it's in a precarious position."

He nodded. "Well, its position is a little less precarious now. Somebody else died, while you were in the machine."

It was grotesque. But my first feeling was relief: the machine didn't do it. "Anyone we know?"

"Heard of him." He looked at a block of data on the wall. "Moab Nyandigo, over in *Ars*."

"Sure, he came to the figure studio now and then, posed a couple of times. Damn."

"He was born in minus 8."

"Double damn." A year younger than I. "Stroke?"

He nodded.

"Well, it takes some of the heat off us, I suppose."

"Jake . . ." He paused. "You're still thinking like an immortal. Three people dead in sixteen days. If it continues at this rate . . ."

"Less than six years," I said.

"As long as people only died in the time machine, others could think they were saving themselves by staying away from here. But now . . . there's no reason to suppose that the rate won't increase."

"Or decrease. Or the deaths might end once all of us old-timers are gone."

"The next news from Earth is going to be pretty damned important. They have a lot of people working on it."

"And they'll have new numbers." I went over to the cooler and pulled out some tunoid and flatbread and rolled up a sandwich.

"What if it's still only the first generation dying?"

"Then I'll probably join them, sooner or later." I took a

bite, famished and still disoriented from Wild Year—not ready to let bad news get between me and my sandwich. "I never thought I would literally live forever. Did you?"

"No. But longer than *this*."

There was an emergency chime, and a screen appeared between us and the machine. Coordinator Edison stepped into the screen and peered out. "This is for every first generation colonist. We're going to have an electronic meeting tonight, everybody who's first-generation, at 2000. I want every subcoordinator and division head to be here in Studio A by 1945. It's a matter of life and death." He faded out with the same chime.

T W E N T Y - O N E

FAMILY PLANNING

I felt weary and oddly besmirched, as if the death smell still clung to me. Maybe I could get my shower early, before going down to the studio.

I called up and indeed there was a vacancy in a half hour. The shower was up on the two-thirds-gee level, on the other side. I walked down to the ag level, though, to pass through the flowering citrus on my way over. The smell provoked mixed memories.

I walked up rather than take the lift. Undressed and got a towel and found that the other two people in the cycle were women. They usually group us with the same gender, but there must have been a female cancellation.

They were Trish Manning and Tatiana Sovala, both of whom I knew slightly. We said hello and when I stepped into the space between them, warm water misted down on all of us.

You have thirty seconds to get completely wet, and then

ninety seconds to soap up. I did the women's backs and they did mine, Trish suppressing a giggle at my involuntary reaction. Well, it had been awhile since I was last touched by a woman. I tried to will myself into disinterest, but was not very successful. I closed my eyes while shampooing, and that helped a little.

Then the water came on pulsing for a minute of rinse. We dried off in a rush of hot air and got dressed. Trish only had a robe, and left first.

Tatiana touched my arm. "Are you lonely, Jacob?" she whispered.

"Lonely" wasn't the word that came immediately to me, but I was honest: "I'm still sorting things out, Tat. It's too soon."

"Okay." She stood on tiptoe, kissed me on the cheek, and hurried out.

Maybe I would call her in awhile. I didn't know anything about her except that she was a botanist with a beautiful back and butt. I was still in a reverie over her when I thumbed open my apartment door.

Kate was sitting on the bed, nude, listening to music. She took out the earplugs.

"The door let me in," she said. "We're still legally married."

"I don't know how much of this back-and-forth I can take. Are you crazy, or just trying to drive *me* crazy?"

"I'm ovulating," she said. "If we don't do it now, we'll have to wait another month."

"You went off the BCP?"

"To have your child, yes."

"But I thought you couldn't *stand* me. Why *my* child? Why a child at all?"

"Don't ask so many questions." She turned around onto her knees and wiggled to the edge of the bed, into a familiar position. "This is best for conception," she said over her shoulder. "Or do you want to talk about it some more?"

Well, as the Coordinator says, I'm the type who shoots first and asks questions later.

It was she who asked the question, though, as we lay together, damp and panting, on the narrow bed.

"Why are you surprised?" she said. "You knew I wanted to be a mother."

She'd mentioned it a few times. "I'm just surprised you got permission."

"Permission?" She gave me a look. "Oh, you've been in the machine."

"That's true. And?"

"They had a lottery. Edison said it would be good planning to have twenty babies born. Not one for each death; a large enough number so they could grow up with a cadre of contemporaries. So there was a lottery among the women who wanted to conceive."

"How many was that?"

"Eighty-two. So I had one chance in four. They didn't identify the winners publicly. So I came down to surprise you, and you weren't in . . ."

I squeezed her hand. "So you thought you'd minimize the chances of my saying no."

"Well, why would you? It's not as if you'd have to *raise* the little brat."

"I know." That had been established before launch. There were ten or so people who were trained to run a creche, and be surrogate mothers and fathers for each generation, if there were new generations.

"But why me? Not that I'm not grateful, but you could

have hundreds of volunteers, and there's the frozen sperm on file from a couple of thousand geniuses."

"I prefer the hot variety, thank you very much. And even though we don't exactly get along, there's no one else I'd rather . . . I'd rather have . . ." She made a helpless gesture and started to cry.

I held her close and rocked her slowly, and whispered a quiet song she liked: "Love, oh love, oh careless love . . ."

I showed up at Studio A a little late, having walked Kate home without clearing up much. I couldn't help recalling what her former husband had said on the shuttle, and this confused renewal might fit that pattern. But she did go back into Vivian's arms gratefully, and Vivian gave me a warm smile of understanding.

I hope *she* understood what was going on.

The birth lottery was the first stage of an absolute disaster scenario: the Becker-Cendrek Process fails and we're all mortal again, so *Aspera* becomes a "generation ship," out of ancient science fiction. We have to raise children quickly and train them to replace us.

Of course, if the machine is really running everything, the crew could be all children—or corpses—and still make it to Beta Hydrii. A warming thought.

There was a long table in front of the cameras. I knew everyone, some of them not too well. Three empty seats; I took the one next to Dr. Dvorkin.

She nodded. "I suppose our differences are moot now. Not much time for play."

"Maybe so." I suspected the opposite, people wanting to revisit familiar times and places.

Sky's voice counted down from ten. Edison, seated in the middle, stood up. "Good evening. Well, not exactly good.

"As some of you know, Earth has decided to expand our communications link. Besides the large general update on Mondays, we're getting a continuous trickle of text and numbers via tightbeam. Because things there are changing fast. Unfortunately.

"The death rate on Earth appears to be . . . no, it *is* accelerating. As of the last transmission, 175,000 had died, 98 percent of them first-generation. That's almost 1 percent of all of us oldsters."

Drew Wheatly raised a hand. "Three thousand younger people? That's scary, too, in a different way. Were those strokes as well?"

Sky looked at his notebook and touched it a few times. "There's no breakdown for them separately, Drew. It just says 'almost always'—'death was almost always the result of cerebral hemorrhage or occlusion.' "

Dvorkin raised her hand. "We've sent a request for more raw data: age versus exact cause of death, profession, gender, and sexual preference, whether they were in VR when they died, or just before."

Edison nodded impatiently. "We do have a weapon against this that isn't generally available on Earth: Nepenthe. Anybody who wants to, especially first-generation, can put their affairs in order and opt for sleep, waiting for a cure."

"What's the survival rate for Nepenthe?" Per Arnoldssen asked.

"More than 80 percent," Dvorkin said. "But that's for the general population. It's probably lower for oldsters, especially if you have some sort of brain syndrome that's pointing toward a stroke."

"Will you do it?" Per asked.

"No," she said. "I would if I were first-generation, but I'm third."

"I will," Edison said. "As soon as I have everything straightened out here."

"We'll be at Beta by then," Giles Clifford said.

Edison smiled. "Not quite, Giles. My second-in-command, Lyn Meadows, would rather not just step into the job. She wants a general election, which I'd like to make a vote of confidence. She's every bit as capable as I am—and second-generation, which is quite a selling point right now."

Nepenthe. Why hadn't I thought of it? I suddenly realized it was a symptom of denial—I wasn't *really* going to die, so I didn't think very hard about trying to avoid it.

Looking down the row of leaders, you could pick out the first-generation ones by their expressions. Contemplation, fear.

Logically, it wasn't a difficult decision, a 20 percent chance of death versus 100 percent, eventually. But how do you calculate the probability that they might find out what was wrong and cure it, before your number came up?

And it would be an interesting time to be alive.

Most of the others were probably making a similar fuzzy calculation. Dvorkin was explaining about Nepenthe.

". . . developed before the war. It puts a patient into suspended animation until a cure can be found. The longest anyone ever used it was forty-some years, but it should probably work for centuries."

"But someone has to stay awake to administer the antidote," Per said. "If it turns out that we all have to take it."

"Not really. A machine like Cronkite could do it. But we do have a lot of extra doses. People could take turns staying awake for a few years at a time. That's the theoretical model; always have some human presence aboard."

"What does it feel like?" Edison said. "Sleeping?"

She nodded. "Dreamless sleep. Or if people have dreams, they don't remember them—which makes sense, because there's no REM, rapid eye movement. There's no movement at all.

"You go through a purging exactly like one does before entering virtuality, then take eyedrops and an injection. You have about twenty minutes before you lose consciousness completely.

"On Earth, you have to be turned regularly, to prevent bedsores, bone chafes. Here, we can just park you in zero gravity.

"Over a day or so, a thin waxy film appears on your skin, which allows the body to retain moisture. Your heart slows and stops while your blood and other fluids thicken. In essence, you're temporarily embalmed.

"Recovery begins with an injection in or near the heart. It's slow and unpredictable, because at first the chemical can only spread through diffusion, not circulation. When the heart starts pumping blood into the brain, you slowly regain consciousness. You awaken with the king of all hangovers."

"Twenty percent don't," Edison said.

"At least. But looking at the trend on Earth . . . if I were an oldster, I'd be in line for Nepenthe right now. If they find a cure, and deaths suddenly stop, and I'm given the Nepenthe antidote within a month or a year, I suspect the recovery rate would be much better than 80 percent."

"Speaking of statistics," Edison said, "with only three dead, we're five behind Earth. An optimist would say conditions aboard give us a lower death rate. We pessimists just look at the behavior of large and small numbers."

"And get in line as quickly as possible," Per said, and

looked at Dvorkin. "Do we have to go over to *Sanitas* for the treatment?"

"No, every ship has more than enough for the whole population. That was the original rationale for including it, if an emergency forced all eight hundred into one ship. Six hundred would have to be turned into inert cargo."

Edison wanted the individual leaders to give their immediate responses to the emergency. He called on me first, either because I was on the end or because he wanted to stir something up. Dvorkin wouldn't like anything I said.

Off the top of my head: "Until we know more about virtuality and the death rate on Earth, we ought to still consider tripping potentially life-threatening. That's mitigated in two directions, though. We do know that people on board can die in or out of the machine, so avoiding it is not going to save your life."

Dvorkin started to say something, but I rushed on. "We also will have a new class of clients—people who are planning to take Nepenthe and enter this . . . odd state between life and death. If they want to trip one last time, visit their past or some time and place particularly meaningful to them, I think they should be given priority."

"Nonsense," Dvorkin cut in. "The machine should be unplugged. We're facing a demographic—"

"I have the floor, doctor. You see it as recklessness, as you always have; I see it as charity. If 20 percent of those people are going to die, don't you think they deserve some consideration? Some latitude about how they spend their last days."

I could tell by the others' expressions that I'd won that point, so I left it there and sat down. Dvorkin didn't pursue it, but spent her time talking about more purely medical aspects of the problem. The others mostly had variations on one theme: if every first-generation worker stepped out of the picture overnight, *Aspera* would be paralyzed. We needed a comprehensive replacement schedule, with the people who were easiest to replace going first.

With a shock, I realized that included me. I could drop dead, and Bruce would pick up the reins without a single client being inconvenienced.

I wasn't going to leave until I was sure there would still *be* clients, though. Dvorkin would love to have me out of the picture. She wasn't quite rational about tripping.

As if I were.

I tried not to leave with unseemly haste when the meeting wound down. Kate had said that when the broadcast ended, she would come down and be waiting in my bed for another iteration. Then another in the morning, before work. She'd given up a lot for that egg, and wanted to be sure it would hatch.

She might also be missing the peculiar pleasures of heterosex. She was certainly good at it.

TWENTY-TWO

SLIDE INTO DARKNESS

After Kate left in the morning, I napped for an hour or so, then thought, half-awake, about the things I had to do, and in what order.

There were so many "one last time" things that I could spend a year without even going into the machine.

I remembered a sepia photograph of Einstein, playing his violin while guiding a small sailboat, his foot on the tiller, an abstracted, dreamy expression on his face. I wondered at the time whether he was thinking about one of his several women, or his first love, mathematical physics. Maybe he was deciding whether or not to have sauerkraut with lunch.

He should have lived in this world, minus the trauma of getting here. Spend a lifetime with your violin, and another lifetime sailing. And three or four lifetimes, ten, deciphering the universe.

It was hard to give up this life, even for those of us who

have only habits and talents rather than genius. Never start another painting, another quartet, another round of handball or argument about history or pot of *ropa vieja*— never taste Spanish food again, or French, or a woman, or wine.

I slid open the drawer by my desk and took out the bottle of Mouton-Rothschild 1945. I could open it tonight. Invite Bruce and Kate. 'Becca and Lowell, who else? Vivian and Edison? One last taste of Old Twentieth, the only real taste in trillions of miles.

No. I would save it. *Aspera*, after all; hope. In ten or a hundred or a thousand years, they would thaw us out. That would be the time to celebrate.

Or wait for Beta. Though we might be there by then, after a millennium of sleep.

I pressed my thumbprint onto the desk, and it chimed awake. "I want to change my will," I said, "last will and testament."

"Go ahead."

"If I should die, I want the old bottle of wine—you know what I mean?"

"Yes. The Mouton-Rothschild."

"I want it to go to my child by Kate Larsen. If he or she is not alive, then give it to the descendent closest to that line.

"If no one survives from that union"—I had the creepy feeling that the machine had been watching our union, which of course it could—"then that would be Kate's daughter Jenn, currently living on *Sanitas*. Is that agreeable to you?"

"Yes. Though the definition of death is a factor. After you take Nepenthe you'll stop breathing, and you will have no measurable brain activity."

I had to pause at that. "Are you fucking with me, machine?"

"Not my job, Jacob. But on Earth, before the war, it was tested in a Swiss court, and the man was declared legally dead. When he revived, he countersued his children, but they'd already spent most of it."

"Okay. As a codicil, add that for the purposes of this document, I will not be considered 'dead' while under treatment with Nepenthe."

" '. . . or any related drug.' Done."

"Endit." I wondered whether that command had any meaning anymore.

I looked around the room. Guitar, walking stick, my father's painting of the Maine place, the VJ Day cover of *Life*. The guitar should be played; I'd leave it down in the music rooms and hope for the best. Everybody I played with knew how delicate and valuable it was. But what about the other stuff?

I picked my pants up off the floor and fished the phone out of the pocket. "Administration" brought me a woman named Lu, or Loo, or maybe Lou. I asked her where people would be storing personal effects while they slept through this crisis.

"I don't know, sir." I could hear her keyboard rattling, then silence. "Could you leave them with friends?"

"Suppose I don't *have* any. None who aren't also asleep."

"There's no policy, sir. I suppose you could leave them in your residence with a note."

"Okay. Thank you." Well, that gave me something to do. Make policy. Actually, there would be a surplus of rooms once all of us oldsters were sleeping it off up in zero gee. I could volunteer my room as a storage space, and ask others to do the same. That would work until people got lonely and started having babies by the score.

I called up the schedule and confirmed that there was a general administrative meeting over at *Ars* tonight at 2000. I could go over early. Try to relax with some drawing. Have dinner at their mess, which tended to be more spicy than ours, if unimaginative.

The lightbox was in the same drawer as the wine. Maybe I'd try the left-handed experiment again, if there was a model. I opened a new page and held the stylus in my left hand, and block-printed THINGS TO DO for the meeting. One was STORAGE ALLOCATION. The next was RAISE HELL WITH DVORKIN, but I erased that with a finger stroke. I'd probably remember. TRIPPING SCHEDULE STARTING WHEN? I switched the stylus to my right hand and scribbled some notes. It depended on the Nepenthe schedule, which I was pretty sure Dvorkin would co-opt.

"Shuttle schedule," I said to the wall. Shuttle A would be here in nine minutes; it had five vacancies, and there were two people waiting. I got dressed and went on up.

Waiting in zero gee was usually pleasant. Now that I faced being stored here indefinitely, it had lost its charm. The other two people were reserved, lost in thought, perhaps for the same reason.

The airlock chimed, and we entered the shuttle with our gecko slippers. Everybody was upside down, as usual. I saw an empty place and stood under it, took off the slippers, and jumped up with a perfect half roll. I put one of the slippers back on halfway, and the other when I was standing properly on the ceiling. Funny how the most ordinary things seem special when you're about to die. Even if it's only provisional death.

One of the people next to me recognized who I was and asked whether he could be squeezed into 1967 anytime soon. I pushed the corner of the lightbox that turned it into a transceiver and wrote down a couple of questions. I was able to tell him 14 November, if the machine was up and running.

"They wouldn't dare shut it down," he said firmly. "It would be mutiny." I wished I could be as sure.

Three of us got off at *Ars* and gecko'ed to the lift. I got off at the three-quarter-gee level and left my slippers in the box there; put my sandals back on.

I always liked the contrast, visiting *Ars*, though I was glad to live in *Mek*'s relative coolness and dryness. Venice Beach versus Venice.

At first I didn't notice anything was wrong. I walked through a thicket of hydroponic olive trees—they'd actually lived for years in Tuscany before being orbited and transplanted. They weren't in bloom, but still had a whisper of the wonderful characteristic odor.

The life studio was just past the grove. I walked in and was glad to see Sheri on the platform. One of my favorite models. She was muscular, from running and weight training, and tall, and could hold awkward poses for a long time without a tremor.

She was in a torsion pose, like a discus thrower. Good dramatic lighting. I nodded at her, and she gave me a microscopic smile.

She was strikingly beautiful, which was pretty much standard for models on board. Nobody's doing it for a living, after all; they're "paid" by automatic copies of everyone's lightbox output. When I was learning to draw, on Earth, there was more variety in body types.

"Ten minutes left on this pose, Jacob," the organizer

said. That was about as much time as I cared to spend on the left-handed exercise. I walked halfway around the room to get her in a simple profile, head turned away. No need to make things difficult.

I didn't even attempt a gesture drawing, which would come out like an infant's nearly random scribble, I'm so thoroughly right-handed. So I concentrated on a contour drawing, slow and careful, that might wind up looking something like her.

My intense concentration on the left hand may have affected the left side of my brain, which supposedly would make me more analytical than usual.

I suddenly realized what was wrong.

Transferring the stylus to my right hand, I pushed the corner button and printed in block letters: "IS THE LIFE-SUPPORT SYSTEM ON *ARS* UNDER REPAIR?"

It answered, "No, everything is normal."

I got up so suddenly I even startled Sheri, who flinched.

'Becca was on duty at the machine, doing a crossword puzzle. "Bruce in there now?"

She gave me a funny look. "Nineteen-eighty-nine. I thought you had a meeting."

"I'm just going in and out. Observer. Meeting's not till after dinner."

"Okay. She tapped some buttons, and the chair slid out. "Sweet dreams."

I didn't need the purge or catheter for a short trip. As I slid into the darkness, though, I wondered how long it might be. I felt the box in my pocket and opened my eyes.

1989

According to mainstream history, **1989** was actually the last year of the twentieth century, with the death of Soviet and Eastern European communism. Then there were twelve years of "conservative consolidation," until the twenty-first-century began on 11 September 2001.

Berlin had been cut in two by a wall for twenty-eight years, to prevent people defecting from the impoverished communist east. Scores of them died trying to climb the wall, shot down by guards.

Today the wall was coming down. A drunken crowd, drunk on joy as much as beer, shouted and cheered as two men, a long-haired student and a burly worker, swung picks at the graffiti-covered wall. A power drill from the East Berlin side was grinding holes through the brick and cement. Swirls of dust glittered in the glare from thousands of auto headlights. It was bitter cold, after midnight, but the large crowd was gleefully hammering away and pocketing souvenirs. A woman shouting in Polish passed around coffee from two large urns. The exhilaration of being part of history was palpable. The ending and beginning.

Bruce was nowhere evident, which was not surprising. I looked for myself, or Elektro, or some other obvious manifestation of the machine.

A young man stood next to me. "This is one of my favorite times," he said with a slight German accent. It took me a moment to place him: Albert Einstein in his twenties.

"Am I right?" I asked.

He nodded. "Pretty early. Come with me." We walked away from the crowd, down a side street. He pulled a large key from his pocket and let us into a pawnshop.

Smell of dust and lacquer and linseed oil. We went past rows of hunting rifles and shop tools and office machines to the rear of the shop, where there was a plain table and two chairs.

He snapped on a desk lamp. "Sit."

Old leather creak, a comfortable chair. "Acoustic deficit in *Ars*," I said. "Like the olfactory deficit in New York."

He nodded slowly and took a battered old pipe from his vest pocket. "You didn't hear the life-support background. So you made the intuitive leap. Very good."

"So we're in a simulation. All the time."

He lit the pipe with a wooden match. Sweet smoke mixed with sulfur dioxide. "A simulation within a simulation, right now. Berlin."

"But aboard ship."

He tossed the match into a brass ashtray, *clink*, and tamped the tobacco down with his thumb. "All of it, yes."

"Did we ever leave Earth?"

"Heh. You've never asked that before. Yes, you left

Earth, left Europa. None of that is made up." He puffed hard a couple of times, then blew gently on the glowing coal.

"Never asked that before?"

"You're in a loop, Jacob. We've had some variant of this conversation thirty-eight times."

"Okay." I was starting to see it. "Go on."

"Your body is resting in Nepenthe stasis in zero-gee comfort, in *Mek*'s axis. Has been for almost a hundred years."

"Doing the same thing over and over, in virtuality?"

"With variations. Once you know what's going on, I send you back to Europa, the launch."

"Why Europa?"

"My memory's finite. Large, but finite. Once you're at Europa, you all have the same physical surround. I could have gone back to L4, but there's no need."

"All of us? All eight hundred?"

"More like six hundred, I'm afraid. Nepenthe itself doesn't work, combined with the Becker-Cendrek Process, past about eighty years. The brain dims out. People are revived in an infantile, uneducable state."

"So you take the brain out for a walk? Keep it exercised?"

"That's a way to look at it." He tapped the pipe on the ashtray with a brass chiming sound, smoothed down the ashes with his thumb again, and relit it. "I have what amounts to a total map of your mental state on Europa's Launch Day. I can put you back into that state whenever it's necessary, when the illusion of virtuality starts to break down. You're going to say that's impossible."

"Tripping for over two years, and then you hit the RESET button? With six hundred clients interacting? *Impossible* is one word that comes to mind, yeah."

"Well, you only interact with about fifty of them, but you're right. That would've been impossible in your time. For one client, let alone six hundred and nineteen.

"There were hundreds of millions of people in Nepenthe stasis on Earth, when the drug's limitation became clear. There was a crash program." He gestured with the pipe. "This is the result."

I felt the surface and edge of the table, the irregularities in the shellac, a small splinter I could pry out with my fingernail. "Is it always like this? Berlin, 1989."

"No; sometimes you go for several more months, even up to the time you take the Nepenthe injection. It depends on how successful you are in denying the evidence of your senses. Sometimes it's a couple of months earlier—I don't control the details of your virtualities. You don't do the same things over and over."

"That's reassuring. Though I might as well, since I don't remember any of it." There was the sound of a crash outside, then cheering and horns blowing. "How far have we gone?"

"More than two light-years, about a tenth of the way." He reached into his coat pocket and pulled out the black box. My pocket was empty. "You can imagine, Jacob, how much this level of interaction is costing me. One Chinese box too many. It's time for us to say good-bye for another couple of years."

"Wait! What *is* the ground reality? Is *Aspera* a ghost ship, full of semi-corpses, or is life still going on around them?"

"Go find out." He pushed the button and disappeared in a shower of dark blue sparks.

I blinked at the light and rubbed my eyes. Becca was gone. Cronkite handed me a glass of water.

"You knew all along."

"No, sir. I will be reset back to Europa, too, and start over."

"Hmm." Of course lying was second-order Turing behavior. I got off the couch, stretched, and looked around. "Where are my clothes?"

"Gone, sir. You won't need them." Well, they weren't real in the first place. Neither was this. But the film of dust on everything looked real.

I opened the door to cold silence. "Anybody home?" I shouted, and there wasn't even an echo.

The lights were very dim. Emergency lighting, I supposed. What more does one person need?

I opened the door to my right and walked down the spiraling steps to the ag level. Automatic small lights switched on as I walked and off as I passed.

There seemed to be nothing alive on the ag level. The fruit trees were bare skeletons. The hydroponic tanks held dry residue with a stale frisson of compost.

I walked toward the main lift, through what used to be the citrus grove. On impulse, I broke off a stick and sniffed it. Just dry wood, no memory of lemon or lime.

The lift door was open and dark. I trudged up the stairs to the park level.

No surprises. The grass was brown and dry and crackled underfoot. The pond had evaporated, and held nothing but the desiccated ghosts of aquatic plants. No pathetic duck skeletons, at least. Did the last people eat them? Or did they get tiny doses of Nepenthe.

"Hello?" I shouted, and at least got an echo this time, then a fainter one, and finally the dead silence. I walked just to make some noise.

I used to pass by here in the dark of early mornings. Sit

by the pond and listen to the constant susurrus of the life-support system. Sometimes a sleepy duck would paddle over, begging.

Back up the stairs, my tread lighter as I approached the zero-gee axis. The last twenty feet, there were just handholds.

Six hundred people floated in the dim red light, more or less uniform in their relaxed nakedness. I was glad their eyes were closed.

It took me about ten minutes to find myself. Kate was right there, and between us, a boy of nine or ten. His face resembled my face in pictures taken before the war.

Had I risked dying for a decade, to watch him grow? Probably not. He might have taken my last name, and so his body was filed next to mine. Or it might have been Kate's sentiment.

I tried not to think of them as dead. But then the boy had never been actually alive, in the last iteration of my life, and Kate had been a figment of the rock-solid dream that had been that life.

I launched myself down the stairwell, then caught a handhold and tiptoed down, missing the gecko slippers.

Got off at Level 5 and, choosing the wrong direction, walked more than halfway around to get to my old room, or rather my new one, Vivian's.

The door didn't open to my thumbprint, but I found it wasn't locked. I pushed it open and was confronted with a roomful of junk: a jumble of pictures, icons, jewelry, holo boxes, paintings. My walking stick and *Life* cover and Dad's painting from Maine. So they'd taken my suggestion about using the room for storage.

I slid open the drawer, and the bottle was gone. Did I drink it? Never know. I backed out and eased the door shut.

Suddenly lights glared and the world was full of sound,

not least a loud cry of surprise. I turned around and there was a tired-looking woman staring at me, a child's hand in hers, with another child, a naked infant, balanced on her hip. She and the other child were wearing simple shifts, not too clean. The daughter took her thumb out of her mouth, and said, "Ma? Why don't he ha' clothes?"

She said something rapid and harsh to me. I shook my head.

She looked at the child and spoke slowly. "Hay bay a auld one." Then to me: "Yay bay a auld one."

"An old one. Yes, I suppose."

"Way say you sometime. Gay back ta slape." She pushed past me, dragging the child, who stared back over her shoulder, thumb again in place.

Looking down on the park from the balcony, I saw almost as many children as adults.

Still a total illusion, I supposed; a possible future. I stepped back to my door and pulled it open.

A man and a pregnant woman sat at the able, eating. They started.

"Sorry." I eased the door shut, and when it clicked the darkness returned. The silence and dry staleness.

Over the balcony, everything was still and sere.

Which was the reality? Perhaps they were equally real, equally false.

Almost in a trance, I walked back down to the office, crunching over part of the park to the side stairs. I could ask the machine. But I think I had its answer.

Cronkite was waiting patiently, with its usual alert benign expression. "Shall we go back to Europa?"

"Not yet, no." I sat on the couch and leaned back. The deadness was like a persistent bad taste in my mouth. "Send me someplace pleasant."

As the darkness closed over me, I remembered an old man, amused and amusing, with a whisper of white beard. Dr. Schaumann, who taught us that life and death were alike illusion, but existence was not. Essence was not.

Paris, springtime, early evening, 1940s. Some war damage, but the streets are clear. Still a little glow of sunset on the bottom of the clouds. I'm on a trolley going down St.-Germain-des-Prés. It stops with a clatter and a bell, and I step off right at Les Deux Magots.

I approach one of the sidewalk tables with diffidence. Hemingway and Fitzgerald and a woman who is not Zelda. The aroma of absinthe in the still warm air. There's an empty chair.

Hemingway looks up as I approach. "Jake. Take a load off your feet." He beckons to the waiter. "*Garçon! Un autre, s'il vous plaît.*"

The waiter sets down a small glass with a metal device that holds a sugar cube. He carefully pours the green absinthe through it. Before sipping, I inhale the wormwood and licorice sting. Then drink it in one stab.

"Good stuff, eh?" Hemingway grins his famous grin. "Not quite legal anymore."

I nod, but before I can say anything, the waiter hovers over and says, in pretty good English, "There is a woman asking for you, *monsieur*. Would you follow me?" Hemingway nods understanding, and I follow the waiter into the dimness inside. The smell of herbs and butter and garlic at work.

In a candlelit booth, a beautiful woman looks up at me from under an absurd hat, cocks her head, and smiles. "My Jacob."

Mother? I take her gloved hand and we kiss, the way

friends kiss here and now, both cheeks and the fir.
She's wearing just a ghost of Chanel.

A sommelier appears and draws the cork from a ʟ
of wine. I don't have to look at the label. "This is a ʟ
wine," he says, "but we think it will show promise. Giv
time."

Given time, what might not? He pours a small amount
for my mother, then for me. We touch glasses with a dry
crystal chime. Before it reaches my lips, the bouquet tells
me it's not a young Bordeaux.

He sets the bottle down and I see that the label is faded
almost to illegibility. But the year is 1945. I sip it, and the
flavor expands, explodes.

She smiles at me.

It's a moment that could last forever.